RUNNING IN HEELS

The Liberty Lawrence Series: Book Four

Bea Stevens

Table of Contents

Copyright

Dedication

To Tilly – Thank you for all your help and support, as always.

I hope you enjoy it.

Lots of love xxx

I'm so excited to be going back to work—and that's not something I say very often. The girls I work with at the *Daily Chronicle*'s fashion supplement are lovely. I've had several get-well wishes from them, cards and flowers, not to mention numerous chats with Fran, Beulah, Siobhan, and even Brie and Eva. I've been through an awful ordeal—someone actually tried to kill me and my boss, Valerie Fulton-Coombes. Imagine that. I mean, I know Valerie wasn't particularly likeable when I first met her, but to try to kill her was a bit extreme— and what about me? *I* hadn't done anything wrong. Anyway, it's all sorted now. The demented woman is behind bars—Davinia Urquhart that is, not Valerie—and Valerie and I are both okay. In fact, the whole experience seems to have had an amazingly positive effect on Valerie, who turned out to be really nice. Who knew?

The Tube's packed, as always, but it doesn't bother me today. I'm wearing a powder-blue dress and jacket ensemble by Oasis along with my new nude-to-black ombre Louboutins from Suzanne—my boyfriend, James', ex-wife, *long story*—and a black bag. I'm shivering to death but look amazing! It's November, and I've come out without a proper coat. James would go mad if he knew, what with my recent recovery and all, but I didn't want to hide my lovely outfit. Besides, it gets quite stuffy on the Tube at rush-hour, and I certainly didn't want to be all sweaty when I greeted the office girls.

As if to make my point, a big guy lurches forwards with the jolt of the train. He's holding the grab rail above my head and I'm suddenly treated to a waft of stale BO and a glimpse of the sweat patches under his arms. Whether or not BO is contagious is debatable, but I'm not taking any chances. I use my one free hand to whip out my bottle of J'adore and fumigate myself. The big guy coughs and I inwardly dare him to complain. Better his coughing than my puking any day!

It's a relief when the Tube stops and I finally get off. Just for good measure, I smother myself in perfume again and take the short walk to the office, grateful for the fresh—if bloody freezing—air.

As soon as I step out of the lift, Fran comes running down the corridor to meet me. She's beaming, her beautiful, red curls billowing around her flushed face as she calls my name. She's wearing a gorgeous, dark green boho-style dress and brown boots.

'You're here!' she shouts, throwing her arms around me.

I'm a little taken aback but get a lovely warm feeling knowing that I've got such a good friend in her. Practically every day since I went away, she's texted me about the changes that are happening in the office, and I can't wait to see it all for myself. I also feel much closer to her now, as we chatted about other stuff such as her dreadful love life, and how she was thinking of moving now that she's had a pay rise. And that's another thing. Money. Apparently, everyone in the department's had a rise—even me, and I wasn't even there!

There's a big cheer and a round of applause when I go into the office. Everyone looks up and smiles at me, as they move forwards. I didn't realise they were all so huggy, but they all give me a really warm welcome, even Izzy, though her body feels a bit stiff next to mine. It reminds me that I was absolutely right not to wear a coat. I send up a silent thank-you prayer to Mr Dior.

Valerie steps out of her office and gives me a squeeze.

'It's lovely to have you back, Liberty.'

She looks radiant. Younger, too. She's relaxed and smiling. Even her clothes don't look quite as starchy and severe as usual. She's wearing a dress today, Jaeger,

I think. It's not as fitted as she usually wears, and has a cute, sweetheart neckline. It's a sort of teal colour, which really brings out the green in her eyes.

'I'm so happy to be back,' I confess. 'Broadstairs was lovely, but I really missed you guys.'

There are smiles and chatter all around me and a few girls say they actually missed me, too.

'Let me show you around,' Valerie says, graciously, wafting her arm in the air as she leads me away from the crowd.

My heart's racing nineteen-to-the-dozen. 'Ooh, yes please,' I say, beaming, 'I can't wait to see all the changes.'

'Well, there are certainly a few of those,' Siobhan pipes up as the girls all drift back to their workstations.

The large room is still as spacious and airy as I remember, but there are definitive areas now where the girls work in their own sections. There are lovely framed pictures of glamorous models and film stars on the walls. As the girls get back to work, Valerie ushers me over to the corner of the room nearest her office. This whole area seems much larger without the huge table that dominated the room, although a slightly smaller one, which is still quite massive, has been placed farther up the department to one side. The desks that used to line the sides have been replaced with bright white ones that face the middle of the room. Now, matching cupboards and drawers, topped by large work surface line the walls.

The large mirror on the wall and swivel chair in front of it immediately tell me this is Eva's section. She beams up at me from her desk.

'Welcome to my world,' she says, standing.

'Eva, as you can see, is in charge of the hair department,' Valerie says. 'A little bird told me this is her forte.' She winks at me and I giggle, remembering the conversation we had about the girls, while we were at the hospital. We discussed all their various talents, and Valerie realised that they were being vastly underused.

'I'm helping out with make-up and nails, too,' Eva says, but this is my main concern.'

Eva is beautiful, with long, dark, wavy hair and a figure to die for. She has big, expressive eyes and a gorgeous smile. I'd guess she's in her early thirties, and one of the most feminine, classy ladies I've ever met.

'So, you all sort of work together?' I raise my eyebrows, relieved that they're not all segregated and working alone.

'Oh, yes,' Valerie interjects. 'I want to play to the girls' strengths—which often cross over to different departments anyway. But I was concerned not to split everyone up, so they all work as a team, but with their own areas of responsibility as well.'

'We've been promoted to heads of section,' Eva tells me with a wide smile. 'Apparently, Valerie had a brainwave while all that awful stuff was going on and came back and made a load of changes.'

'For the better, I hope?' Valerie queries, a smile teasing her lips.

'Of course. Now we've been assigned defined responsibilities we can plan our own schedules and organise ourselves far better.' Eva winks at me and I get the impression she already guessed who gave Valerie the idea.

'Brie and I are also trying to get a few celebrities in here,' Eva goes on.

'Yes, we're giving the supplement a new look, focussing more on fashion,' Valerie says. 'It will have a glossy cover and better-quality pages as of today, making it more of a magazine than a newspaper supplement.'

'That's brilliant,' I say. 'And you're actually having celebrities come here to the office?' My mind whirls, hoping Eva has links with Jamie Dornan or Brad Pitt. The Hemsworth brothers, maybe? God, I love my job!

'Sometimes,' Valerie says with a shrug. 'We also have a hotline to the photography department, so we can go out and interview the stars on location if we need to.

Mr Peerless has removed the restriction on how often we can call on them, providing they're available, of course.'

Mr Peerless is in overall charge of the *Daily Chronicle* and a hard man to negotiate with. Goodness knows how Valerie managed to persuade him to allow this.

'Everyone's going to get a shot at interviewing celebs,' Eva adds, giving me a knowing look.

My stomach flutters. This is a dream come true.

'And over here we have skincare and make-up,' Valerie continues, gliding over to the section opposite.

I don't hear her at first, as I'm busy interviewing Channing Tatum in my head. It's not until Eva clears her throat that I come back to the present and quickly scoot over to where Valerie's standing, talking to Brie.

'Brianna is in charge of this section,' she says, turning to face me.

No shit!

Brie rolls her eyes and then smiles at me. She is absolutely stunning, with short, wavy hair that frames her face beautifully and she's always immaculately made up. She's very slim and elegant, like Eva, and probably around the same age. Both have worked as models in the past, and I think that's how they first met.

'I'm also helping with hair and nails,' Brie tells me, 'but this is my section.'

'Fantastic,' I say.

I notice the lit-up mirror on the wall and guess it'll be getting a lot more use now we're working for a fashion magazine.

'We *are* still a supplement to the *Daily Chronicle,* aren't we?' I ask Valerie.

'Well... yes. Why do you ask?' She raises her eyebrows curiously.

'Well, I was just thinking that there are already enough glossy magazines out there with fashion, make-up and celebrities,' I say, warily. 'I wondered what made us different?'

'That's a good point.' Valerie frowns.

Brie looks a little uneasy. 'We need a USP,' she says.

'Yes,' Valerie narrows her eyes in thought. 'A unique selling point. But what?'

'Well, if we're still affiliated to the local paper, then shouldn't we keep the content local, too?' I ask, quietly thrilled that I've come up with an idea.

'Local? You mean only interview local celebrities?' Brie says with a pout.

'Not necessarily. I was thinking more of tying in with the *Chronicle*'s stories. I mean, obviously local celebs would be a great idea, but what about other celebrities who are *appearing* locally? Like at the theatres and stuff? It's still local news but it's also big-name celebs. And if they might happen to be wearing something that we're featuring in one of our sections, then so much the better.'

'I think we might have to pay a lot more to get a celebrity to wear one of our featured fashions,' Valerie says, doubtfully.

'But we can offer to do their hair and make-up for a photo shoot, can't we? After all, someone has to get them camera-ready.'

Brie's face brightens. 'Of course. And if we happen to use a product that we're doing a feature on...'

'Yes.' Valerie's eyes sparkle with enthusiasm.

'And we can always offer them a bag or a scarf or whatever as a prop?' I add, thinking on my feet.

'I love it!' Valerie clasps her hands together. 'That's what we'll do.'

'What?' Izzy walks over, frowning. She's the eldest of the girls, probably in her late thirties and I can imagine she won't be pleased at the thought of missing out on something. She's very tall and slender, with prominent cheekbones and a white-blonde urchin crop that just accentuates her beauty. I find her quite austere and am a little wary of her, to be honest.

'Brianna will explain,' Valerie says, flippantly.

Izzy narrows her eyes at the boss.

'We're coming to look at your section now,' Valerie informs her, before she even has time to ask Brie what we were discussing.

Huffing, Izzy goes back to her area and we follow.

'This is the nail bar,' Valerie tells me. 'Isobella will be testing new products and getting them photographed as well as writing articles.'

'Ooh, I love having my nails done,' I say with a smile. I was hoping Izzy might smile back, but she doesn't.

Her workstation is next to Eva's, back on the other side of the room, and a peninsular table stands at ninety degrees to the cupboards, narrow enough to sit either side so Izzy can apply or manicure the nails of the person opposite. Two swivel stools are tucked neatly underneath it, and I can't wait to try them out.

'Isobella also helps with hair and make-up,' Valerie goes on, clearly oblivious to the hostile atmosphere.

'Great.' I try to sound excited, but it's totally wasted on Izzy, who scowls at me. She clearly thinks I'm betraying her by having that conversation and not telling her about it, but I can hardly say anything with Valerie right here, can I?

Opposite Izzy is the fashion section, with rails of clothes lined up in front of the cupboards.

'This looks interesting,' I say, turning to smile at the girls.

Thankfully, Valerie takes the hint and we move over to take a closer look.

'Strictly speaking, Kiera and Francesca oversee the latest fashions, Tamara reports on everyday wear, and Alice and Beulah report on evening wear,' Valerie announces, as the girls come closer.

'But we all work together as well,' Beulah points out.

'You'll be helping in this section, too,' Valerie informs me.

My stomach flutters. I wondered where I would fit in with all this, and I'm glad it's in the department with the most girls. I'd love to work with every one of them.

'Brilliant,' I say, smiling.

'It's going to be great fun with you in our section,' Beulah says, grinning.

'However, you will also have your own area of responsibility,' Valerie goes on.

I gulp.

'This is where you will work,' she says, ushering me to the opposite side of the room again. There's just a desk in front of the cabinets, offering no clue as to what I will be doing there.

My entire body sags for a minute. I'm going to be working alone. It's clearly something clerical as I've only got a computer, no interesting equipment, clothes rails, or anything like everyone else has.

Valerie smiles at me, a twinkle in her eyes.

'Remember we talked about an agony aunt's position? Well, as you know that post has recently become vacant and I want you to fill it.'

'Me?'

'Yes, of course. You said you'd like to help people with their problems You also suggested that, instead of the usual personal woes, it would be more fitting to have a fashion advisor, rather than a traditional agony aunt. That's what I'd like you to do. What do you think?'

My mind whirls. We discussed this when Davinia told Valerie how much she hated her job. I meant it when I said I'd like to be in her shoes—well, maybe not those Santonis with the squared-off toe, exactly—but I would want to do it differently. My way. Valerie obviously remembered it all.

'I'd love to do it,' I tell her, my face flushing with excitement. 'It would be a great job. Thank you.' I want to hug her, but it wouldn't be appropriate here with everyone around, so I clench my hands together and settle for giving her a huge smile instead.

She smiles back.

'I'm glad you like the idea, I haven't a clue how I thought of it.'

We both giggle like a couple of schoolgirls, and I can see that almost getting killed has had a positive effect on the boss. She seems much more human today— I just pray that it lasts.

'Siobhan will be working next to you,' Valerie points out, indicating the stunning girl in the corner with the precise, black bob.

I look over at her. Then a thought crosses my mind. So will Izzy, whose desk is to the side of me with Siobhan's opposite, in a large corner section. I really don't think Izzy likes me very much, but I can hardly tell Valerie that.

'It's so good to have you back,' Siobhan says, dragging my attention to the matter at hand.

'It's great to *be* back, I can't wait to get started,' I reply, as she sits behind her large, L-shaped desk overlooking the whole room.

'Siobhan's the department manager,' Valerie announces, proudly. 'Her job is to oversee the whole office and deal with the magazine's editorial issues. You'll still report to her, as usual.'

'Well, I'm glad that hasn't changed.'

'Something else *has* changed,' Siobhan says coyly.

'Really?'

She holds out her left hand, showing me a gorgeous diamond ring that catches the light and glistens on her long, slender finger.

'I'm getting married.' Her face flushes as she tells me, and I whiz over and give her a big hug. I can't help it. It might not be the most appropriate thing to do, but I don't even think about it and just squeeze her as hard as I can.

'I'm so happy for you!' I say, my voice a little higher pitched than normal.

'Thank you,' she whispers.

'Well, I'll leave you to settle in,' Valerie says before returning to her office.

'I mean it, Libby,' Siobhan murmurs once we're alone at her desk. 'Thank you for everything. Valerie told me you'd had a bit of a heart to heart and she's really taken it all on board. We've all been promoted with huge hikes in our pay—some of us more than others.' She looks cagey—embarrassed, almost.

'You deserve it,' I tell her in a hushed tone. 'And overseeing all of us should make you eligible for a medal, let alone anything else. And there's all the crap you have to put up with from Valerie—although she doesn't seem so bad today.'

'She's been like this ever since she came back,' Siobhan tells me. 'She must have Phil Peerless wrapped around her little finger judging by the amount of money she's been throwing around.'

'The office does look brilliant,' I say.

'It's not just the furniture. We all have new computers, and the girls have the latest equipment for their work—she can't do enough for us.'

'Good.' I don't know what else to say.

'Anyway,' she continues, conspiratorially. 'What about you? Any sign of you having one of these any time soon?' She holds up her finger, her ring glinting in the fluorescent lights. 'I don't mean to pry or anything, but Cassie said James had taken you away. She also alluded that it might be for more than just a bit of R and R.'

Oh, shit! Her face is glowing with expectation, and I know she wants me to give her some good news. But… how can I?

'We had a nice time,' I say, forcing a smile. 'But it was no more than that, really.'

Siobhan looks crestfallen.

The office is deathly quiet. Damn, I didn't realise everyone else was listening.

'We haven't been going out together *that* long,' I say with a nervous laugh. 'But it was really romantic.'

'That's good.' Siobhan smiles.

'Just *how* romantic are we talking here?' Fran comes over, grinning.

I roll my eyes.

'He was very... attentive,' I say, choosing my words carefully. 'And we had a great time.'

Just at that moment, Valerie comes out of her office and Fran quickly returns to her section, throwing me a knowing look.

'Liberty, we must think up a name for your column,' Valerie says, swooping over to where Siobhan and I are standing. 'I don't think we should stick with "Ask Auntie Annie". Have you any ideas?' She smiles at me.

My mind whirls for second. 'How about something like "Problem Solved"?' I suggest. 'It might inspire confidence in the reader, which is what we need, isn't it?'

'After your predecessor, I'd say it's *definitely* what we need.' Valerie gives a little chuckle. 'Yes, I like that. "Problem Solved" it is. We've already run an article announcing the changes in the department, and that you're taking over from Davinia but not in the same role. We've asked readers to write in with their fashion problems instead of their personal ones. I think Siobhan's already received a few queries.' She raises her eyebrows at Siobhan who nods and reaches into her desk drawer.

'Here you go. Good luck with these,' she says, laughing as she hands them to me.

'Thanks.'

'I've sifted through them and they seem genuine enough,' Siobhan assures me. 'Unlike some of the rubbish Davinia was sent. I think the readers just invented worse and worse "problems" just to wind her up.'

'Christ, I hope they don't do that to me.' I grimace.

Valerie shakes her head. 'I'm sure the readers will love you,' she says happily. 'That's why I want you in this role. I'm hoping our audience will be able to relate to you and trust you to help solve their fashion dilemmas.'

I suddenly feel a huge weight on my shoulders. I had never considered that people might actually *rely* on me. What if I get it wrong? They'll hate me.

'If anyone knows about fashion, it's you, Liberty. And I'm sure you'll be able to empathise with the readers.' It's as if Valerie just read my mind. I gasp in amazement. Cassie, my best friend and flatmate, can usually read my thoughts, and I read hers. My boyfriend, James, has started tuning into me, too. I didn't expect my boss to be so perceptive, though. This is a bit spooky.

'I'll do my best,' I tell her, trying to sound far more confident than I feel.

'You'll do a splendid job,' Valerie assures me, as she looks around the room. 'Keira, I'd like a word if you're free?'

Everyone goes silent again. I'm not sure if it's because we all know Kiki doesn't like to use her full name, or because Valerie is actually asking her if it's convenient. The boss really has changed since our ordeal with the crazy Davinia Urquhart.

I go over to my desk, sit down and fire up the computer. I've never been so grateful for an intervention by Valerie and I'm relieved no one's asking any more questions about James and me. In a way, I feel like a fraud, being the magazine's agony aunt, when, in fact, it's me who needs advice—and not the fashion kind.

James and I had a lovely few days in Kent to help me recover from all the horrid goings-on with Davinia. We saw my family in Broadstairs, and while we were on the beach at Viking Bay, James asked me to move in with him. It was very romantic, the sun setting over the horizon and the shush of waves in the background.

He told me he'd already spoken to my parents about what he had in mind, and for a split second, I thought he was about to propose. I quashed that notion straight away though—I'd thought that once before and was horrified when he didn't. Now, I realise it's far too early for anything like that. We haven't even been together a year yet, and although we get on great, I now know I'm not ready for that. However, I wasn't sure I was ready for what he *did* propose, either.

To say I was stunned would be an understatement. I didn't know what to say. I couldn't help feeling thrilled, of course, but then the enormity of the implication hit me. James wants me to leave Cassie in the flat all by herself and move in with him, in Fulham. I love James. I honestly do, and I know he loves me too, but to be honest, I had the impression I irritate him a bit

at times. I never guessed he'd want to live with me—
well, not yet, anyway.

Suzanne, his ex-wife, has just moved out, so it's
the perfect time for me to move in. Perfect time for him,
anyway. I've been looking forward to being able to pop
in and out of his place, instead of having to check first if
Suzanne was there—which she usually was. I want to be
able to spend nights over there—we've hardly had a
chance for much of that, but when we did, I have to admit
it was amazing.

Of course, I said yes when he asked me—
eventually—what else was I supposed to say? But
afterwards I couldn't help wondering if it was all a bit
soon. I mean, you'd think he'd want to enjoy the space
once he'd got his flat to himself again. And I've sort of
got used to having Cassie around all the time—not that
she's actually there *all* the time, now that she spends so
much time over at Rob's. He's her boyfriend and a really
nice guy. He works here at the *Daily Chronicle*, as a
reporter. He and Cassie were made for each other.

I get that familiar feeling as tears start to prick
my eyes and I stare at the screen in front of me, willing
myself not to cry. I've been doing that quite a bit
recently, and the doctor says it's quite normal after
everything I've been through. It's nothing to do with
Davinia this time, though. I just don't know what to do.
I mean, I do *want* to move in with James, but I can't

simply leave Cassie on her own. She's been so good to me—she pays most of the rent, helps me out when I'm broke, lends me her clothes and shoes, and is a great listener as well as the best friend anyone could ask for. I just can't let her down. But then it means letting James down and he looked so excited when he asked me. Oh, God, this is all such a mess!

I haven't told anyone about moving in with James, not even Cassie. As I said, my family know because James spoke to my parents before he even asked me. He wanted their approval, which I thought was very chivalrous of him, if a tad unnecessary. James can be a bit old-fashioned sometimes, though, it's one of the things I love about him.

I try to bury myself in my work to take my mind off everything. One of the letters is from Tara, a young woman from Kensington who wants a stunning outfit to wear to a wedding. Apparently, her husband's ex will be there, so she needs something very super special. Straight away, I start browsing the Harvey Nichols website to see what's out there. She's sent me her size and a photo that shows she's really slim—as well as gorgeous—so she can wear anything and look great in it. *Not that I'm jealous or anything.* She needs to look stunning though, without upstaging the bride.

I find her a beautiful, short, red cocktail dress by Alexander McQueen. It's off-the-shoulder, so it will accentuate her elegant neck, and above the knee to show off her long legs. She'll look classy and at the same time flaunt her lovely figure. What's more, the dress is thirty percent off in the sale, bringing it down to £1,249. Who doesn't love a bargain? I team it with an Alexander McQueen black clutch, with a gorgeous knuckle clasp. When she slips her fingers through the gold circles it will look as if she's wearing four beautiful, sparkly rings, each with different Swarovski stones. Admittedly, it's quite costly at £1,595 but it's well worth it. I'm suggesting really high Jimmy Choos to complete the outfit. Lancer black patent leather shoes with straps going around the ankle. They're absolutely divine, and only £495. She can't fail to look amazing in that outfit.

While I'm on the page, I also notice a pair of gorgeous, black suede Saint Laurent boots. They're knee-high and slightly slouchy. Perfect. They'd go with any of my clothes, and on days like today would be much warmer than shoes. I print off the details and pop them into my bag. I've got a little tin at home that I use for saving up for things like this, so I'll put the picture in there to remind me and keep me motivated. At £1,200 they're a bit expensive and will take a while to save for, but they really are amazing.

I sit back with a satisfied sigh. I've already decided I love my new role.

'Aren't you coming for coffee?' Beulah asks, sauntering over to my desk.

I hadn't noticed the time.

'Of course.' I grab my bag and follow the rest of the girls out of the office.

'We want to know all the gossip,' Fran tells me as we sit down with our skinny lattes.

'Yeah, starting with what on earth went on between you and Valerie to make her change so drastically?' Eva chips in. 'I mean, I've heard of turning over a new leaf, but she's ploughed a whole forest.'

Tammy giggles from her seat opposite me. 'Not that any of us is complaining, of course,' she assures me.

Everyone looks at me expectantly, as we sit at the largest table in the refectory.

'Well, Davinia told Valerie how much she hates her job, and poor Valerie was gobsmacked,' I begin. 'She had no idea that Davinia felt that way. She thought she'd done her a favour giving her that role, even though she was hopeless at it.'

'You can say that again,' Izzy chips in, rolling her eyes.

'Well, later, Valerie mentioned how invaluable Siobhan was, and I told her she should show her more appreciation.' I glance at Siobhan who blushes, staring into her coffee. 'From there, we went on to talk about the rest of you and how I thought your skills were being wasted. She said she was going to do something about it, but to be honest, I didn't expect her to go this far.'

'When Valerie gets an idea into her head, she tends to run with it,' Siobhan agrees, nodding. 'I don't know what she said to Phil Peerless, but it obviously worked. She's managed to get him to unlock the coffers big-time and get things moving.'

'The new magazine's going to be so much better than the old supplement,' Fran chips in, before taking a sip of her drink.

'We've just got to make it work,' Siobhan says. 'The onus is on us to get some really good articles together and make sure the sales of the paper increase to repay the extra costs.'

'Rob and Ben said the reporters have all been told to up their game, too,' Tammy tells us around a mouthful of biscuit. 'They don't want to be outdone by the supplement.'

'It'll help get the sales up as well,' Siobhan says, thoughtfully. 'Though I didn't realise we'd be in competition.'

'No pressure, then,' I joke, shaking my head.

'That's the thing,' Eva replies. 'It doesn't feel pressured in the office anymore. The whole atmosphere's changed.'

'Yeah, it's a lot more fun,' Brie adds.

'And Valerie's so much more chilled,' Fran points out. 'I think nearly getting killed might have made her rethink her whole life.'

'Did it have that effect on you, Libby?' Beulah asks with a frown. 'Did you see your life flash before you, and decide then and there that you'd change it?'

I shrug. It might be a bit shallow of me, but it didn't have much effect on me at all. At the time, I was focusing on getting us out of a burning building, and then, all I wanted was to get better so I could be normal again. The only person who seems to think it should change things is James. He told me how scared he was that he was going to lose me, and he wanted to make sure it never happened again. That's probably why he's so keen for me to move in with him. It's so we can be together all the time. Though, I have to admit, it's a lovely thought.

'Not really. I suppose I was just too busy dealing with the here and now.' I confess with a shudder.

'Don't think about it, hon.' Eva leans over and strokes my arm.

I smile gratefully.

'Come on, I think it's time we got back to the grind,' Izzy declares, standing. It's unusual for her to be the first one on her feet, and I wonder if she's unhappy with me being the centre of attention for a change.

I quickly text James on my way back to office.

He doesn't answer straight away, so he must be busy. He's a police sergeant so he has an important job to do and can't always find time to check his phone. I can't blame him. Well, I suppose I could, but I know I shouldn't.

Valerie's waiting for us when we arrive back at the office. Usually that would be a bad thing—I'd be worried that we were late and going to get into trouble or something—but she's smiling today. I could get used to this!

'Ladies, I've just been speaking to Mr Peerless, and the first edition of the new magazine will be out on Saturday,' she announces with a smile.

There are gasps all round.

'We need to think about the cover,' she adds, nodding at Brie and Eva. 'Would you ladies be able to come up with something eye-catching?'

'Of course.' Eva beams confidently, but I can imagine her mind must be in a whirl. Talk about being put on the spot.

'Everyone else, you'll need to have your content ready for my approval by Thursday at the very latest. Mr Peerless wants to check every detail before we go to print. This has to be good.' Valerie looks slightly nervous.

'We'll blow his socks off,' I tell her, and everyone giggles.

Valerie glows. 'That's the spirit.'

She goes over to talk with Brie and Eva, and the rest of us get back to work.

I stare at my computer screen, suddenly not feeling quite so confident. Impressing Phil Peerless is a challenge at the best of times, but I know he hates my guts. How am I ever going to convince him that I'm not a troublemaker and that I should be given this job permanently? I know Valerie said I was no longer on probation when all that stuff with Davinia was going on, but I'm not convinced Mr Peerless is aware of that— perhaps I should mention it sometime? Maybe not right now, though. I've got a feature to get cracking on with— and it had better be a damn good one, too.

3

My next letter is from an elderly lady, originally from Essex, who wants to smarten up her wardrobe. She says that her granddaughters came to visit her recently and advised her to get some colour into her outfits, as she mostly wears black and grey to hide her curvy figure. The lady, Ms P. Frobisher, says that she is worried about looking like mutton dressed as lamb in the modern, garish colours she's seen on the high street and would value my advice. I feel quite honoured as I start searching through the internet. Unlike Tara from Kensington, Ms P. Frobisher has a modest budget, so I'm searching the more regular high street stores for her clothes.

As she kindly sent me some photos of her garments, I can see why her granddaughters were concerned. The only light-coloured items she has are white. She's a retired lady who does flower arranging as a hobby but judging by her pictures she must do it dressed in smart suits and office outfits. I'm sure she'd be much more comfortable in some nice dresses or slightly flared skirts.

I begin by targeting John Lewis and Marks and Spencer. I'm sure they'll have the sort of thing she needs, and they're classy without being too pricey.

By the time lunchtime rolls round I've picked out four skirts, a jacket, three tops, and two dresses for my client. I've avoided vibrant colours in favour of muted, subtle shades of lilac, green, and burgundy. She should be able to mix them easily with the darker shades in her wardrobe, too. I've also pointed out some pretty scarves and jewellery that might brighten her look a little—it's often cheaper to accessorise than buy a whole outfit, and she does seem to have a lot of clothes already, albeit in dark colours. I'm hoping that by spring she might feel more confident about buying paler hues, but it's best to ease her in gently—and besides, it *is* the middle of winter.

'So, that fit copper was your boyfriend?' Brie asks, as we all sit at the large table in the refectory. It's the only one big enough for all of us to fit around, and Fran or Beulah always pop down just before we break for lunch to save the table for us. It gets really busy down here at peak times.

'Yes.' I feel quite proud to admit it.

'Lucky you,' Eva pipes up.

Kiki whistles. 'He's gorgeous.'

'He seems like a nice guy, too,' Siobhan cuts in. 'Cassie thinks you two were made for each other.'

I swallow hard. *Cassie said that?* I knew she liked James, but I hadn't realised she had such strong views on our relationship. It's good to hear.

'He's very protective of you,' Beulah says smiling. 'I wish I had a man like that.'

'Does he have a friend?' Kiki teases.

My face starts to get hot.

'Did you have a nice time in Kent?' Alice asks, throwing me a sympathetic smile. She's always quite quiet, but I get the impression she absorbs the information and atmosphere around her like a sponge.

I nod, grateful to be asked a sensible question. 'Yes, thanks. We went to see my parents in Broadstairs, and then up to Rochester where one of my brothers and his girlfriend have just opened a boutique.'

'Ooh, I'd love to do that,' Fran says, with a faraway look. 'Own a boutique, I mean, not see your parents—although I'm sure they're very nice.' She's turned redder than I am and is so flustered she knocks over her coffee. 'Damn.'

We all automatically pass her our napkins so she can mop up the spill.

'It's lovely,' I tell her, trying to divert the attention from her accident. 'It's all pink and silver inside with lots of light and mirrors.'

'And does she choose all the fashions herself?' Beulah asks.

'Yes.' I nod smiling. 'Hers is the first shop to stock Crystal fashions, outside of their own chain.'

Crystal is a very high-end designer company with superb outfits. Cassie works for them and actually helped select the colours for the new season's collection. She's a designer with some fantastic ideas, though she's only been there a few months and is still learning the ropes.

The girls gasp.

'I heard they were planning to franchise out,' Kiki says, wide-eyed. 'I hadn't realised they'd started already.'

I nod, proudly. Actually, it was my suggestion that the company use franchisers to get their fashions into more outlets. It's early days, but Natalie, my brother's girlfriend, told me they're selling really well in her shop.

'Do you get staff discount?' Izzy asks. I'm not sure if she's being sarcastic or not—it's always hard to tell with her—so I just smile and shake my head. It's safer that way. *I can't help thinking it would be a nice idea, though, and start figuring out how to ask Natalie*

My phone pings with a message from James.

*Sorry, I didn't get back to you earlier, it's been
hectic. Investigating a robbery at a high street store.
Look forward to hearing your news xx*

My heart races. What high street store? And does
he mean an armed robbery or a shoplifter? I know he's
busy, but I do wish he'd fill me in on these things—
especially when it concerns shops. After all, it's my *job*
to know about stuff like this. Sort of.

I spend the afternoon putting together a capsule
wardrobe for someone called Lisa from West Brompton
and picking out an interview outfit for Sharon from
Battersea. Although it's only a local paper, it does cover
a large area. And I suppose it's the sort of thing people
will pass on to friends and relatives to read, as it's really
quite interesting at times—especially now that the
supplement's getting a re-vamp. Kiki and the fashion
girls are writing an article on jackets for the winter, so I
include one from their featured range for Sharon's
interview. It'll look great with the Oasis skirt I've picked
out for her, as well as a neat blouse and, of course,
stunning shoes.

James is working late, so I won't see him tonight,
which is a shame, but it gives me a chance to spend some
time with Cassie. She's been really good to me while

I've been going through my ordeal, and even took time off work so I wouldn't be on my own while James was on shift.

I haven't told her that James has asked me to move in with him, although she'll have to know sooner or later. I think James expected me to go home and pack straight away when we got back from Kent, but I told him I couldn't leave Cassie in the lurch and had to pay my rent until the end of the month, at least. He was disappointed, but I think he understood. I felt like I'd let him down and I really do want to be with him, but it's all so complicated. I know Cassie will be devastated, too. In our last jobs, we shared a room in the hotel where we both worked, and then Cassie got this flat in Chelsea and asked me to move in with her.

Her family are quite rich, so her parents give her an allowance. Her job's well-paid, too, so she doesn't have any financial worries—unlike me. My credit and store cards are maxed out and even with my recent pay rise I'm still earning less than Cassie does. She doesn't charge me the full rent because she knows I couldn't afford it, and she's usually the one who does the main food shopping. How can I tell someone who's been that good to me that I don't want to live with her anymore?

I sigh as I pop a frozen lasagne in the oven. Cassie's not home yet, but I'm sure she won't be long. I nip into my bedroom and pull on some comfy jogging bottoms and a baggy T-shirt. With my fluffy slippers snuggling my feet, I begin to relax a little more.

I've been dying to read the latest novel by Paige Toon, which I know Cassie bought as soon as it came out. She says it's great and I'm welcome to borrow it any time I want, so this is my perfect opportunity. I go into her bedroom where she keeps all her chick lit novels neatly on a shelf. She's got them all there; Lindsey Kelk, Keris Stainton, Colleen Coleman, Sophie Kinsella—and she always manages to get their latest novels before me, somehow.

I pick out the book I came for but as I turn to leave, something catches my eye and I wander over to the bedside cabinet. It's usually clear apart from a lamp that matches the one on the other side, where Cassie sleeps. There's a small, black comb and a glass of water sitting there. Cassie has a glass of water on the other cabinet, too, and I know she wouldn't need two.

I check the back of the door and notice there's a man's dressing gown hanging there, next to Cassie's pink one. A pair of size ten shoes under the bed also gives me cause for concern. I know Rob stays over occasionally, although they usually prefer to sleep at his place for more privacy, but this looks a little more... permanent. I tentatively poke around in the laundry basket and notice a pair of Rob's socks and one of his T-shirts. *Curiouser and curiouser.*

A pang of guilt zips through me and I quickly leave the room. Rob's clearly been making himself at home here while I was away, and I wonder just how long he's been leaving his stuff here. I knew they were getting closer, but I didn't expect this. I grin. It looks like my bestie is in a full-on relationship, and I couldn't be happier for her. I would have liked her to tell me more about how things were going between them, but have to admit with everything that's been happening at work lately, and with me being in Kent for a while, we've hardly had time for a proper heart to heart.

The lasagne's ready when I get back to the kitchen and I take half of it, leaving the rest for Cassie, who I'm expecting home any minute. I sit at the kitchen counter and eat while reading the book.

When Cassie comes in with Rob a short while later, I'm giggling—the book's brilliant.

'You found it, then?' Cassie asks as she plonks a couple of shopping bags on the floor.

'Yes, thanks. It's great.'

'Rob and I are going to the cinema in a bit,' she says, a little cagily. 'Do you want to come with us?'

I can see from Rob's expression that the correct answer here is 'no, thank you,' but it's really kind of Cassie to offer.

'Erm...'

Rob's face is tense, and I can't resist winding him up a little. He's a good-looking guy who dotes on my bestie, but sometimes these things just *have* to be done.

'What're you going to see? I haven't been to the cinema in ages.' I put on my most thoughtful expression.

Cassie throws Rob a look, and I gather that she was hoping for a romantic evening, too. 'I'm not sure,' she says.

'We thought we'd decide when we get there,' Rob adds. 'But it'll be an action movie of some kind. Something with lots of guts and gore, probably.'

'Yeah, it's Rob's turn to choose,' Cassie says grimacing.

'Oh. Well, in that case, I don't think so, thanks,' I say, pouting. 'I'd rather read this.'

They try to smother their sighs of relief, but I can hear them anyway. I smirk, hiding my face behind the book. Did they really think I'd want to play gooseberry?

***

The next couple of days are really hectic at work, with getting everything ready to go to print on time. The magazine's going to be much thicker than the old supplement, with human interest stories as well as fashion, celebrities, and, of course, my column. I've helped Beulah and the girls with their articles on a new range that a local store is selling, and even had my photo taken for the editorial section. I never had my picture in the *Chronicle* when I worked in the newsroom, so I feel a bit like a celeb. Okay, a very minor one, but everyone has to start somewhere.

James has been really busy with work, though he's not giving much away, which usually means it's something serious. Although he's rung me every night and we've texted throughout the day, we haven't seen each other since the weekend, as he's on the night shift and I, of course, work in the daytime. He's hinted a couple of times that when I move in with him this won't be a problem, as we'll get to see each other whenever he's off work, and I just agreed but said nothing committal. I feel really jittery about the subject with a mixture of excitement and trepidation, but I can't tell him that.

The atmosphere relaxes once the magazine's finished and placed firmly in Phil Peerless' clammy hands.

'This is where the worrying really begins,' Valerie tells us with a frown, but I don't agree.

'It's up to him now,' I tell her, 'there's nothing more we can do, so why worry?'

'She does have a point,' Siobhan says cheerfully. 'Let's not fret until we need to.'

'You're right.' Valerie smiles. 'The best thing is to keep busy and think about something else.'

I watch her return to her office before rolling my eyes. We've worked our fingers to the bone this week trying to get this perfect for the boss, and I think we deserve a bit of a break now it's done.

Fran sags as she sits at her desk, so I go over to her.

'Well that's that for another week,' I say trying to sound jolly as I perch on her desk.

'As long as 'Picky Peerless' doesn't find fault with it, anyhow,' she replies with a pout.

I shrug. 'You don't look very happy,' I tell her, studying her face.

Sitting back in her chair, she shakes her head.

'It's not the magazine.'

She told me on the phone all about her disastrous love life when I was away.

'Things not improved with Jeremy?' I ask sympathetically.

She looks at me wide-eyed. 'It's not Jeremy,' she reveals incredulously. 'I binned him a couple of weeks ago. It's bloody Tyler now.'

'Oh.' I don't know what to say.

She sighs. 'Jeremy got on my nerves, always talking about his ex. I told him to go and get her back if she was that precious to him. Tyler was one of his friends. I fancied him for ages—well, about a week or two, anyway. I sort of told him Jeremy and I had finished, and he took me for a drink to cheer me up.'

'You don't *look* very cheerful.'

She gawps at me. 'We saw each other a few times after that, and then he started talking about getting engaged.'

I gape. 'Oh, no!'

'That's what I said—or, at least, it's what I *would* have said if I hadn't been so drunk.'

My jaw slackens and my gut twists. I immediately check her left hand. There's nothing there. Phew!

'So... what exactly *did* you say?' I hardly dare ask.

Her body sags even more as she looks at me with huge eyes. 'I'm not really sure.'

I frown. 'Well, what does he *think* you said?'

She gives me a vacant look. 'I'm not really sure about that, either.'

'Well, he hasn't given you a ring, so that's a good sign.' I hope I sound reassuring.

If the expression on her face is anything to go by, I've failed. She blushes.

'We had a great night out—lots of booze and laughs. The next day, I realised there was an elastic band wrapped around this finger.' She holds up the third finger of her left hand.

I put my hand over my mouth in horror.

'At first, I thought I must have just been messing with it and took it off and threw it away. My finger was already starting to swell a bit.'

'And?'

'That night, I went out with Tyler again and he was really off with me. Started saying stuff about me lying to him and letting him down. Originally, I'd forgotten about his thing with engagements, but then it hit me—what if he had proposed, and I'd said yes?'

'That swollen finger might be a good clue.'

'Well, that's just it. He never asked about the elastic band. You'd think he'd just come right out and ask what I'd done with it, wouldn't you? Not that I'd want to tell him I threw it in the bin if it was supposed to be some kind of... you know... promissory, engagement ring thingy.'

'Did you ask him outright?' The look on her face tells me the answer and I just shake my head. 'You need to talk to him.'

'And say what? Have I promised to marry you? Did you give me an elastic band as an engagement ring? We haven't known each other five minutes.' She looks mortified. 'Then I'll have to admit I can't remember what happened, and he'll be devastated. He might have done a really long speech or something.'

'Don't you remember *anything*?'

She looks thoughtful for a minute, then shakes her head, her red curls bouncing with it. 'He's a bit of a bore, actually,' she confides. 'Tends to go on and on about stuff. I shut off after a while and just carry on drinking.'

'So, he might have said something really romantic and you wouldn't have listened?' It's rhetorical. I can just imagine it. I wonder sometimes if James doesn't switch off when I'm talking—not that *I'm* boring or anything.

'It's possible,' she admits with another pout.

'Is this about Tyler?' Beulah joins us, grinning as she sits on the desk next to me. 'What a mess.'

'You can say that again,' Fran says.

'You'll have to tell him.' Beulah shakes her head.

'Tell him what? I was too drunk to know whether he proposed or not?' Fran's voice is a bit louder than usual, and the rest of the girls suddenly go quiet, staring our way.

'You *what*?' Kiki gapes, walking towards us.

Fran rolls her eyes, her face turning bright red again.

'So, are you actually engaged?' Izzy smirks, checking out Fran's finger. 'There's a small mark here.

You've had a ring on.' She sounds accusing, and poor Fran looks like she's shrinking with shame.

'It wasn't a ring,' Fran mumbles.

'Well, it was definitely round. And too small.' Izzy announces, still holding Fran's finger.

'It was a misunderstanding that's all,' I say, feeling sorry for Fran, what with everyone staring at her like this.

'How can you have a misunderstanding about a marriage proposal?' Brie comes over, looking bemused.

'She was drunk,' I tell her. 'She can't remember what was said. Now the guy's getting all antsy with her and won't say why.'

Eva and Siobhan join us, giggling.

'You just need to tell him,' Eva says, as if it's the easiest thing in the world.

'That's what I said, but she doesn't know how,' I reply, trying to defend Fran.

'Honesty's always the best policy,' Siobhan adds, and I stare at her.

For a second, it feels like she's talking to me. My insides feel all hot. Is she right? Should I just tell Cassie that James wants me to move in with him? Or do I tell James that Cassie would be too upset, and I can't do that to her? Oh, shit! Here I am worrying about the mess Fran's got herself into when I really should be sorting out my own problems.

4

It's Friday afternoon before Phil Peerless announces that the magazine's a goer. I'm sure he must have decided as soon as he'd seen the articles but just wanted to keep us all on tenterhooks. *Bastard.*

'Let's all go for a drink tonight to celebrate,' Brie suggests, grinning. 'The first round's on me.'

Everyone cheers in agreement. We've never all gone out together and it would be lovely to socialise with the girls.

'We should invite Valerie,' Siobhan says, quietly.

Izzy scowls. 'Who wants the boss there on a girls' night out?'

'She's done us a lot of favours lately,' Siobhan reminds her. 'And it would be nice to include her. After all, it's *her* success as well, isn't it?'

'Absolutely,' Eva says. 'I'll go and ask her.'

She doesn't wait for Izzy's approval before striding straight into the boss' office. The blinds are all up, and I watch her smile as she goes over to the desk and asks Valerie to join us. The boss looks stunned. I get the impression she's never been asked to join the staff on a night out before. That's sad, and I'm a little disappointed when she shakes her head. I spent some time with Valerie at the hospital and she genuinely is a nice person under all that bluster. I'd have liked to get to know her a bit better. It would be good for the other girls to see her the way I do, as they might understand her more if they did. Perhaps she thinks it's inappropriate to socialise with the staff. I can understand it, but it's still a shame.

'She already has plans,' Eva tells us, returning to the office. 'But she was very grateful to be asked.'

Siobhan nods. 'Fair enough.'

Izzy rolls her eyes but says nothing.

'I can only stop for a short while,' Kiki announces. 'I'm going out to dinner tonight.'

'Anyone we know?' Brie teases.

'I hope not.' Kiki giggles.

'Well, I think that says it all.' Brie bursts out laughing, and Kiki goes red in the face.

'I've got an appointment at half five, so I think I'll have to bow out, I'm afraid, guys. Have a great time, though.' Alice looks disappointed.

'Yeah, I need to be somewhere, too,' Tammy pipes up. 'I'll come next time, though, for definite.'

'Well, we'll just go to The Rose and Crown,' Brie says. 'We'll have a couple in there and if anyone wants to go on somewhere else afterwards, we can play it by ear, if that's okay.'

'Good idea,' Beulah says, 'I like it there.'

'It's practically on the doorstep,' I agree.

'Oh, no. Tyler goes there sometimes,' Fran mutters. 'I don't want to risk bumping into him.'

'Well, you've got to face him at some point,' Beulah tells her with a grin. 'Come on. It'll be like ripping off a plaster. Once it's done, you'll feel much better.'

'Can I have that in writing?' Fran grumbles, clearly unconvinced.

'It'll be fine, honestly,' I assure her.

Cassie's going out with Rob straight from work tonight, and James will still be at the station, so I'm looking forward to having the girls for company. I'd only start worrying about my own situation again if I went home.

It's not long before we're all logging off our computers and tidying our desks.

'Have a great weekend, everyone,' Valerie says, poking her head out of her door. 'And very well done.'

'Thanks, you too,' we all chorus, grabbing our jackets and heading for the door.

The pub is literally a two-minute walk from the office building, and we all pile in and start moving the little tables nearer to each other so we can sit together. Brie brings over a tray full of drinks for us and we sit down, some on comfy chairs, a couple perched on stools.

'To the magazine,' Brie says, raising her glass.

We all drink to it, happily, after a chorus of 'cheers' and 'to the magazine'.

'I think it needs a new name,' I say, after swallowing my first sip. 'After all, everything else about it's different.'

'What have you got against it?' Izzy asks, with a half-smile, half-smirk.

'Nothing,' I reply quickly, afraid that I'm sounding like a troublemaker. *Not that I am one, of course.* 'Although... am I the only one that thinks "Woman Matters" sounds a bit… you know.'

Izzy shakes her head while the others start to snigger. I know she's just winding me up, but I could really do without it, thank you very much. 'No, what does it sound like?'

I huff, take another—much larger—sip of my wine, then blurt it out. 'It sounds like something to do with the menopause or something. Women's problems. I can't be the only one who thinks that.' I look around at the other girls for support, but they're all too busy laughing.

'Trust you to think that,' Brie says, shaking her head.

'Oh, come on, you all know it,' I protest.

'Hmm, it has been mentioned a time or two,' Eva admits, wiping her eyes from laughing. 'But who wants to tell Valerie?'

I'm guessing it was her idea in the first place. They all look at me.

'Oh, thanks, guys. You really want me to lose this job, don't you?' I shake my head incredulously.

'Well, you do seem to be the golden girl,' Izzy sneers.

'I'm not that old,' I object straight away, thinking of the old sitcom series on TV.

The other girls laugh again, but Izzy just rolls her eyes.

'You know what I mean,' she says, curtly. 'You can do no wrong in the eyes of Valerie Fulton-Coombes. She couldn't stop singing your praises while you were away.'

My face glows hot. *Really?* Valerie had something good to say about me after everything I'd done. Not that I've done anything wrong, of course. It's just that Valerie and I seem to have totally different ways of looking at things, and unfortunately, it seems to always get me into trouble.

'I don't think there's any point in mentioning it to Valerie unless we can come up with a good alternative,' Siobhan declares.

I sigh with relief.

'That's true,' Brie pipes up. 'We'll have to think of something really good.'

'And something more appropriate for the changing face of the supplement,' Eva agrees. 'It's supposed to be supporting the main paper, remember, not just another women's magazine.'

'It's certainly worth considering,' Siobhan confirms, nodding slowly. 'Why don't we all have a think and see what we come up with? We won't speak to Valerie about it until we've got a good contender.'

'Take her a solution, not a problem,' I add.

'Well, that'll be a change for you,' Izzy mumbles, just loud enough for everyone to hear. *I knew she didn't like me.*

Siobhan gives me a knowing look and shakes her head. I take it as a sign not to retaliate, so I just take another sip of my drink, pretending I didn't hear it. Everyone else does the same. I suppose I'm relieved they don't all agree with her, but it's still not a very nice thing to say.

After a few more drinks most of the girls have gone, and I sit back in my chair with a contented sigh. This is nice, just hanging out with the gang. The atmosphere lifted as soon as Izzy went and I get the impression I'm not the only one who feels a bit intimidated by her.

Eva and Brie left at the same time, and then Siobhan went off to meet her fiancé. It's good to see her so happy.

'Let's get another round,' Beulah says, standing up on wobbly legs. 'Oops.'

Fran and I giggle as she staggers over to the bar.

'She can never hold her drink,' Fran says, grinning. 'It's one of the things I love about her.'

I snigger, not wanting to mention that my head feels a bit fuzzy now, too. I started off with wine but then someone gave me vodka by accident and then with the next round Eva just said, 'same again,' and I didn't think to correct her, so I just carried on with it.

'I think he's here,' Beulah whispers as soon as she returns, and places our drinks on the table.

'Who?' I automatically look around the bar, which is quite crowded by now.

'Him.' She looks pointedly at Fran, who groans.

'Oh, no. Not Tyler?'

Beulah nods. 'I think it's him, I might be wrong. I've only seen him once before, but he had the same shirt on and I'm sure I'd recognise that funny haircut of his anywhere.'

Now I'm intrigued. I start searching for a guy with funny hair and wearing a shirt. There are just too many to choose from.

'Which one is he?' I'm sitting up straight, rather like a meerkat now, my head twitching in all directions as I seek out the guy.

'Stop being so obvious!' Fran yanks my arm, her eyes wide with worry.

'Well, how can I avoid him if I don't know who he is?' I protest.

'He's coming over,' Beulah announces, grinning. 'Look.'

'I'm going to the loo,' Fran says, standing up and swaying a little. Seems like she's not that good at holding her drink either—or maybe we've all had a bit more than we remember.

'Steady.' A guy with a blue striped shirt and a very severe crew cut suddenly appears behind her.

'Oh.' She looks stunned. Obviously, she wasn't quick enough.

'I thought it was you, babe.' He puts his free arm around her and gives her a sloppy kiss. Beulah and I look away. Unfortunately, we can't help hearing it though, even above the hubbub. With all the effort the guy's putting in, I'm amazed he doesn't spill his pint.

Another guy saunters over, a bottle in his hand. He grins at us and we both glance at each other, cringing.

He's wearing scruffy jeans and a blue T-shirt that has beer stains down the front.

'Hey, Ty, aren't you going to introduce us?' he asks.

Tyler finally releases Fran and looks around. He frowns.

'Drew? What the hell are you doing here?'

The tension in the air sobers me up a little.

'Just thought I'd join you,' the guy says, pulling back a chair to sit down.

'Fuck off,' Tyler growls at him.

Drew puts his free hand up in surrender. 'Okay, okay, I get the message. You want all these gorgeous girlies to yourself. I don't blame you.' He throws me a smarmy smile. 'I won't piss on your parade. I just came to offer my services in case you needed to buy the lovely lady a ring or anything.' He nods at Fran.

My stomach lurches and I stare at him.

'Fuck. Off.' Tyler takes a step closer to him and Drew immediately backs away, his hand still palm up.

'Okay, keep your hair on. Oh, I see it's too late for that,' he says, once he's a safe distance from Tyler. 'I was only trying to help.'

'Well, don't.' Tyler's handsome face is stiff with anger as he watches Drew wander off towards the bar.

I can't help noticing the guy's shoes. They're smart, black lace-ups and as he walks away, I notice the big white letters V L T N written across his thick, rubber heels. The guy clearly doesn't worry too much about his clothes, but he's spent a lot on his footwear.

'I've got to go to the loo,' Fran says, scooting off while Tyler's busy watching his nemesis.

'I'll wait here for you, darling,' Tyler replies to her back as he sits down facing Beulah and me.

'So, you're Fran's friends, are you?' he says, smiling.

He certainly seems very sure of himself.

'That's right, we work together. I've seen you in here before, haven't I?' Beulah asks.

He nods. 'It's my local. I'm Tyler, by the way. Call me Ty.'

'Beulah,' she says.

He stares at her. 'As in the whale?' He bursts out laughing.

She immediately shrinks back in her seat, her arm covering her stomach. Not that she's fat by any means, but she's obviously a little self-conscious.

'No,' I point out, angrily. 'You're thinking of *beluga*. I'm Libby.'

'Oh.' He looks disappointed.

I want to throttle him for insulting my friend, but I don't want to upset him for Fran's sake. Instead, I lean forward, sensing my chance for a bit of fishing.

'So, how long have you been going out with Fran?' I ask, as innocently as I can.

'Not long,' he replies, begrudgingly. He sits back in his seat and takes a large glug of his beer. He can't make it any clearer that he doesn't want to talk anymore, but I don't care. Especially not after he's been so rude to Beulah.

'Any long-term plans?' I ask, forcing a smile.

He shrugs.

'That guy mentioned a ring.'

'I wouldn't buy anything from him.' Tyler sneers.

'But are you planning to get her a ring, then?' Beulah's obviously cottoned on to where this is going.

He shrugs again, fidgeting in his seat. 'Dunno.'

'Are you engaged?' I ask bluntly.

He glares at me. 'Don't you *know*?'

'She's been very secretive lately,' I tell him, praying Fran doesn't return at the wrong moment. 'She said something's happened but wouldn't tell us what. Have you proposed or something?'

He takes another gulp of his beer.

'We can keep a secret,' Beulah adds, sitting forwards. 'Perhaps we could help with a surprise or something?'

I love the way this girl thinks.

He scratches his head.

I hold my breath.

'She should tell you herself,' he says at last. 'It's her news, really.'

'So, it's true? You've asked her to marry you?' Beulah smiles as though it's the greatest news in the world.

'Did she say yes? Are you two engaged?' I beam back at him, hoping that he'll see how happy we are about it all and start talking.

He downs the rest of his pint, then smacks his lips together.

Yep,' he says, at last. 'We're getting hitched as soon as possible.'

My stomach lurches. 'Why the hurry?'

He stares at me incredulously. '*Sheesh!* Why do you think?' He rolls his eyes. 'She's pregnant, of course.'

5

Beulah's jaw drops and she gapes back at me. I'm sure Fran would have mentioned something like this. Pregnant? And with *his* child? They've only been out a few times, and she wouldn't have had time to find out she's pregnant this soon. *And* she's been drinking me under the table all night—there's no way she'd do that if she was pregnant. This guy's off his rocker.

'Are you sure?' I ask, scraping my own chin off the floor. 'You haven't been together long.'

'Long enough,' He sniffs, staring into his empty beer glass.

Beulah frowns at him. 'Who says she's pregnant? She hasn't said anything to us and we're her best friends.'

He shrugs. 'That's what she told me.'

'Are you sure she wasn't drunk?' I query. 'Or maybe *you* were? It can't be right.'

He stands up, scraping his chair back, and leans over the table to yell into my face, 'Of course, it's right.

What the hell would you know about it? Some friends you are!'

He stalks back over to the bar.

'Let's find Fran,' I say, and Beulah and I grab our bags and head to the ladies'.

'Fran? Are you in here?' I'm surprised to find that she's locked herself in a cubicle. *Did she expect Romeo to follow her in here or something?*

'Are you on your own?'

Now she thinks we've brought him with us!

'I'm here, too,' Beulah calls out as we determine which stall she's in. 'But it's only us.'

She slowly emerges, looking wide-eyed. A girl in a too-tight mini-dress barges past her and slams the door loudly.

'What did he say?' Fran's voice is almost a whisper.

I bite my lip at first, glancing at Beulah. She nods slightly.

'Maybe you should have another drink before we talk,' I suggest.

'No, I've had plenty. Besides, is he still out there?'

'He went to the bar,' Beulah assures her. 'We can probably make it out the door without him noticing if we're quick.'

I'm not sure whether he clocks us as we make a mad dash for it, out the loo, down the back of the room—trying to look inconspicuous—and finally through the door. We run as fast as we can down the road and dive into a Starbucks.

'I hate running in heels,' I moan, as we grab a table in a dark corner. 'The first day I worked in the newsroom I discovered that my mentor, Dave Chandler, insists on running everywhere whenever we'd get a story, so I had no choice but to follow suit. I started wearing flats after that.'

'I'll get the drinks,' Beulah offers, fishing her purse out of her Marc Jacobs bag. She nods at Fran. 'And you need to rest for a bit. It can't be good for you, all this stress and running around.' She gives me a cheeky wink and strolls over to the counter.

Fran frowns at me. 'What's that supposed to mean?'

'You'll have to ask her,' I say, trying to shrug it off. Trust Beulah to leave me like this.

'I'm asking *you*,' Fran insists. 'That guy's great between the sheets but he can't be right in the head. Who gets engaged after just a few dates?'

'You tell me,' I say, sitting up a little straighter as Beulah returns with our coffees.

'I take it you haven't spilled the beans, then?' Beulah asks, smirking as she sits down.

'Me? Who made it my job?' I stare at her.

'Will someone tell me what's going on?' Fran snaps, a look of desperation in her eyes. 'What did he say?'

I take a small sip of my coffee to compose myself. They both look at me, expectantly.

'He said you're engaged,' I say, studying her reaction.

She gapes at me. 'You're joking! How can I have agreed to that?'

Beulah gives me a knowing look. 'Oh, that's only half of it,' she says with a giggle.

I narrow my eyes at her. She's really not helping. Poor Fran looks horrified. I take a deep breath.

'Well, according to that brain of Britain you've been seeing, you're getting married because you're pregnant.' I couldn't think of any other way of putting it. She had to know the truth. I wish I hadn't been the one to tell her, though. She's almost crying.

'Fran, we know it can't be true,' Beulah assures her, calmly. 'The bloke's a head case.'

'But he said you told him,' I say, apologetically.

'Oh, no! Just how drunk was I?' She's clearly mortified.

'You'll just have to explain that to him,' I point out, knowing full well it's not as easy as it sounds.

Staring at her coffee cup, Fran shifts a little uncomfortably.

'It's not true, is it?' Beulah's obviously picked up on her vibe. 'Tell me you're not pregnant?' Her eyes widen at the thought.

Fran gapes at her, panic-stricken. 'I don't know,' she admits in a whisper. 'What if I am?'

'After a couple of weeks? Would you have even thought to check this early?' I shake my head. 'Fran, I'm sure you'd know if you were, babe.'

'But why else would he say that?'

'Because he's a knob,' Beulah offers, voicing my thoughts exactly.

'What if it's me? What if I got so drunk, I just came out and said it? Have I led him on? Oh, gosh, what if *I'm* the knob!' Tears fill Fran's beautiful green eyes.

'You wouldn't have said something like that unless it was true,' Beulah says, thoughtfully.

Fran's hand immediately goes to her stomach. 'So, I could be?'

'No. I think he's just playing some sort of game. Don't let him mess with your head,' I say, putting a hand on her arm. 'He's just a weirdo.'

'I hope you're right,' Beulah mutters.

'What if you're wrong?' Fran whispers, her arm trembling.

I try not to take it personally. It's true, I have been wrong in the past—*very* wrong on some occasions—but this is different. My every instinct is telling me there's something very off here and I won't let my friend suffer because of some scumbag liar.

'Have you missed a period lately?' I ask, quietly.

Fran shrugs. 'They're always irregular. I don't really know.'

'Okay. There's an all-night chemist just down the road. I'll fetch you a pregnancy test, you can pop into the loo and check. You two stay here and finish your coffees, I won't be long.'

I feel quite adult as I grab my bag and head down the street. It's unusual for me to come up with a solution, but it's the only thing that makes any sense. I'd forgotten how cold it is, though, and I shiver as I hurry to the shop.

I've never had to check out pregnancy tests before, and I'm amazed at the range. I choose one that's supposed to identify the baby from the very early stages and head for the till. There are a couple of people looking at the medicines and a man choosing deodorant, but not many others in the shop. I get to the counter and wait for the guy in front of me to be served. He turns to go, and I recognise his attractive face. It's Ben, one of the reporters from work, and a good friend of Cassie's boyfriend, Rob.

'Hi, Libby. Are you okay?'

He has a large box of condoms in his hand and a huge grin on his face.

'Yes, thanks.' I smile, then notice his face fall as he sees the package in my hand. He gives me a quizzical look.

'Oh... this is just for a friend,' I tell him hurriedly.

'Oh, right. You take care now,' he shouts as he heads for the door.

I pay for the test and slip it into my handbag before returning to the girls.

'Here you go,' I say, surreptitiously sliding the small box to Fran. She furtively puts it straight into her bag, frowning nervously.

'Thanks,' she says.

'Shall we get it over with?' Beulah asks, eyeing Fran's bag. 'The sooner we know what we're dealing with the better, don't you think?'

Fran nods and we follow her to the ladies'. Luckily, there's no one in there, so we both give Fran a reassuring hug and wait while she goes into the cubicle.

I fidget anxiously while Beulah walks up and down the tiny room, setting off the hand drier as she passes it. It bursts into action, making me jump. I frown at Beulah. I'm hoping Fran will shout out as soon as she gets the result, but with that thing blasting out at 1000 decibels I won't hear a thing.

When it finally stops, I notice snivelling coming from the cubicle and rush to the door.

'Fran? Are you okay, babe? What did it say?'

Beulah joins me and we just stare at each other, not daring to breathe.

After what feels like an eternity, Fran opens the door and holds up the little stick.

'I'm not pregnant,' she announces, before bursting into tears again.

We both throw our arms around her and hold her tight.

'Come on, let's get you cleaned up before someone comes in,' Beulah says softly. 'Then we can grab another coffee.'

I must admit, I have to dry my own eyes, and check my make-up before we go back to our table. It's a relief, but for some reason, it also feels a bit sad. I don't know why. The timing's obviously way off, but it would be nice to see Fran with a baby. It would suit her.

'Thanks, so much for all this,' she croaks, as we sit together while Beulah goes to get more drinks for us.

'It's okay. I'm glad we know for sure, anyway.' I smile at her and she wipes her face again.

She nods and manages a weak smile back. 'It's such a relief. I'd hate to think I'd got drunk and...'

'Here you go.' Beulah places our drinks in front of us. 'Well, that was quite emotional, wasn't it?' She smiles.

'I think, maybe the amount of alcohol we had earlier might have added to that,' I admit.

Fran feigns an innocent face. 'I don't know what you mean, Liberty.'

We all chuckle. It's nice to see she's perked up a bit.

'Well that's one worry out of the way,' I say before taking a sip of my latte. 'Now all we have to do is figure out what that arsehole boyfriend of yours is up to.'

***

I'm grateful for a bit of a lie-in the following day, as it's Saturday. My head aches from last night and I'm not sure if it's down to all the wine or the drama that ensued afterwards. It was a good job we switched to coffee when we did, though. The girls were both fine when we parted company, and I'm really looking forward to going back to work on Monday and seeing them again. I think all three of us are on the same wavelength.

I eventually get up and shower. Cassie's still over at Rob's, and I've planned to see James shortly. We've been texting and calling each other all week, but with his shifts we haven't been able to see each other at all. I know it's something he'll bring up while we're having lunch and I also know he's absolutely right. If I moved in with him, I'd get to see him every night, no matter how late he worked. I really love the idea. Being with James makes me feel all warm and gooey. It would be wonderful to have that every night. It's just Cassie. How can I tell her? She's my best friend and a girl really needs her friends. I need James, too, of course, just in a different way.

I'm just getting my things ready to leave when Cassie bursts through the door, followed by Rob.

'Libby, are you okay?' Her eyes are wide and she's panting.

I stop dead in my tracks. 'Of course, why?'

Her body sags a little in relief and she forces a smile. 'Oh, nothing. I just wanted to make sure.' She shrugs rather unconvincingly. 'We need to make more time for each other. I feel that all we do is work. What're you doing this afternoon? Maybe we could go somewhere?'

My stomach lurches. 'I'm actually going out with James,' I tell her and bite my lip. That wasn't the answer she wanted.

Her face falls. 'Will you be home tonight?'

Guilt gnaws at me. 'No, I thought I'd stay over with him. He's been on lates all week, and we haven't seen each other.' My voice sounds weak and feeble.

'Okay.' She puts on that fake smile again, and I feel like I've just kicked a puppy.

'Are you sure you're all right?' I ask, trying to read her face.

'Yes, of course. Rob and I'll find something to do.'

Rob nods.

'I'll see you tomorrow, then,' I say, and go over to give her a hug.

She grips me a little tighter than I expected.

'I'm here for you, you know that, don't you?' she whispers.

I nod, uncertainly.

All the way to Fulham, I can't help thinking I've let Cassie down. I haven't even moved out yet, and it's obvious she's already worried we're not seeing enough of each other. I must admit, it was *her* who went out with Rob last night, and to the cinema the other night. She clearly doesn't see it that way, though, and she's hurt. I could see in her face that she was crushed that I couldn't spend some time with her this afternoon. We're best mates, after all.

As I walk up the street towards James' place, I can't help thinking how lovely it would be to live here.

It's much quieter in this little cul-de-sac, and I think I'd fit in here nicely. James is absolutely right. We'd see much more of each other and we would share a bed—which has been a bit of a problem lately with his ex-wife moving in and all, as James had to sleep on the sofa. But now she's left, so it'll just me the two of us, like it should be.

He opens his door and stands there, perfection personified. His hair's still wet from the shower, his damp stubble catches the light and his smile warms my heart. He's wearing jeans today, with a shirt that's partially undone, showing off his muscular chest every time I look at him from the right angle.

'Come in,' His voice is like dark chocolate and his eyes flash with mischief.

I remove my coat and he hangs it in the hall with my bag before taking me in his arms He smells delicious and his body is all warm and strong. I close my eyes as he takes my lips in a soft, sensual kiss and I melt into him. I want this. I want to be here all the time. With him. I never want to leave. *Oh, shit!*

We finally leave the flat over an hour later, having worked up a huge appetite, if you catch my drift. James takes me to a lovely little bistro that overlooks the river. Fulham sits in a bow of the Thames, so it has some lovely views.

'Well, so much for not letting you out of my sight,' he says, settling down after fetching the drinks and ordering our meals.

Something burns inside me, and I want to tell him that I'm going to move in tonight. I know it's what he wants. But how can I?

'It's just unfortunate you've been on the late shift,' I say before taking a sip of my Cabernet Sauvignon. 'Next week will be different. I can come over any night you like.'

'Or you could just stay over all week?' he suggests, a hopeful expression on his gorgeous face.

My mind wanders back to the last couple of hours and I wrestle with my conscience. I want to be with

James. It's magical when we're together, like earlier, and I can't get enough of him. I know he feels the same about me, and it's madness that I should be the one keeping us apart.

'I think Cassie needs me,' I say quietly, not daring to look at the hurt that I know will be marring his handsome face. 'She was acting a bit odd when she came home today. She wanted to spend the afternoon with me, but I said I was coming here.'

I chance a glimpse of his face as I take another sip of wine. He's frowning.

'You could've cancelled,' he says slowly.

My stomach lurches. I'd be a lunatic to pass up the last couple of hours spent with him.

'I didn't want to.' I stroke his arm across the table. 'I was dying to see you. It's been ages.'

'Is Cassie okay? Do you need to go back early or anything? I can take you now if...'

'No. Rob's with her. She didn't say anything was wrong, it's just... you know that feeling when you sense something's off?'

'Yes, I do,' he says, frowning at me even more.

Thankfully, the waitress arrives with our meals just then and we turn our attention to the food.

'This looks lovely,' I say, trying to lighten the atmosphere.

'So, was Cassie upset or feeling poorly?' James goes on, picking up his knife and fork.

I shake my head, my mouth already full of chicken. It takes a few moments before I can speak. 'No, nothing like that. She just looked worried and said we needed to spend more time together.'

'We do.' He takes a swig of his wine.

'Not you and me, she meant me and *her*.' I tell him.

'Oh.'

'She *is* right, though. We're like ships that pass in the night sometimes.'

'Are we still talking about you and her, or you and me?'

I swallow hard. He's got a point. It's the same situation with us.

Putting down his cutlery, he sighs and wipes his mouth with his napkin. 'Libby, have you actually told Cassie you're moving in with me?' He looks like he's on duty now. Once a copper...

I bite my lip. 'Not exactly.'

'Well, what the hell does that mean? Have you, or haven't you?' His eyes are wide and his expression is a mixture of exasperation and hurt.

'I couldn't,' I say, weakly. 'It's not that easy.'

'Why not? You're moving in with me, not disappearing half-way round the world. You'll still see each other. You know you will.' He makes it all sound so easy.

'I know,' I say, my body sagging at the thought. 'And I fully intended to tell her, but she's been so busy. She stayed at Rob's a few times this week, so we didn't get much chance to talk properly. And then today when she came home, she seemed really worried about something. She had Rob with her, so I suppose she didn't want to tell me there and then, but she gave me the biggest hug ever. She was even disappointed I wasn't going back home tonight. I know she needs to speak to me about something bad, so I can hardly blurt out that I'm leaving her on top of whatever else is going on, can I?'

James purses his lips. 'Do you want to go back home tonight and find out what the problem is?'

I sigh. I'd really like to get it over with as soon as possible, but I promised James I'd stay with him tonight. Besides, I've been really looking forward to seeing him and I don't want to spoil it all.

'I've already told her I'm spending some time with you. She'll have probably gone over to Rob's, or he'll stay at ours. There's no point in changing everything now.' I'm trying to sound cheerful about it, in case James thinks I don't want to stay with him, but he doesn't look convinced. 'It could just be something about work or whatever. I'm sure if it was anything really important, she would have told me on the spot, wouldn't she?' I'm clutching at straws here. The look on Cassie's face told me it definitely wasn't just office gossip—she was really worried about something.

'Well, it's up to you.' He lifts his knife and fork again and gets back to his lunch. 'If you'd rather go home you just have to say the word.'

'I'd rather be with you.' I put my knife down and run my fingers over his hand.

Unfortunately, it's his left hand and he'd already loaded his fork with beef. As I stroke his fingers the food falls off and plops into his gravy, splashing it over the pristine, white tablecloth. He looks down, closes his eyes for a second and shakes his head.

I've annoyed him. I didn't mean to, but I have. I quickly withdraw my hand with a mumbled apology that I can tell he's not listening to. All the lovey-dovey feelings from earlier seem to have vanished into the ether and all that's left is a dirty tablecloth. *Damn!*

'I mean it,' he says, not even looking at me. 'If you'd rather go home and be with Cassie tonight, I understand. She is your best friend, after all.'

I stare at the soggy mess in front of us, wondering if what he really means is that *he'd* rather I went back home. I want to stay with him, though. I want everything to be back to how it was just a short while ago when we were giggling and kissing and... stuff.

'Is it what *you* want?' I ask him, quietly. I watch his expression as he looks up.

'No, of course not.' He doesn't sound as antsy as I expected, which has to be a good thing. 'I told you, I want you to move in with me. Libby. With everything that's happened to you lately, I'm afraid to let you out of my sight, you know that. I want you with me as much as possible, but if it's not what you want...'

'It is,' I interrupt quickly. 'Of course, I want to live with you. I've hated not having you around this week, I really missed you.' I stare into his striking face, hoping he believes me.

'Then, why are you making it so difficult?' he asks, calmly.

'I'm not.' My face heats up. 'I mean—I don't mean to. I want to just go back, pack my things and move in with you. I've already explained, though, that I don't want to hurt Cassie. She's been so good to me and I can't just leave her.'

'Why?'

His bluntness catches me by surprise, and I gape at him.

'She's my friend.'

'And I'm your boyfriend.'

It sounds so lovely when he says it, and I take a second to enjoy it.

'The ball's in your court,' he says, taking advantage of the silence. *I hate it when that happens.*

'I know. And I *will* tell her. And I'll move in with you soon, I promise. I just need to pick my moment that's all.'

'It'll never be the right moment.' He places his cutlery together on his plate, wipes his mouth and places his napkin on the table. He's only eaten half his dinner.

'It will,' I tell him firmly. 'I'll just find out what's happened and once it's all sorted, I'll move out. She'll understand.'

'I'm not sure that *I* do,' he says, rolling his eyes. 'But you do it your way. Just don't take too long about it, okay?' He sighs.

'I promise.' I nod, feeling slightly better about the situation.

I eat a little more of my meal, but it feels awkward with him not eating with me, so I give up, leaving my plate still half-full.

'What do you want to do this afternoon?' I ask him, as he indicates to the waitress to bring the bill over.

'Well, I thought maybe a walk by the river,' he says, looking out the window.

That sounds romantic. I'm pleased he's thought of something like that.

'Great idea,' I tell him, standing up. 'I'll just nip to the loo. Won't be a minute.'

I return a few moments later to see him standing by the doorway. The waitress has already cleared our table and the lunchtime rush is well and truly over.

He opens the door for me, and I exit with him, turning back to take his hand.

'James, I'm really sorry about all this,' I tell him as we walk down the road. 'If everything was okay with Cassie, you know I'd be with you like a shot. I just need to find out what's going on, first.'

He nods. 'I know.'

I snuggle a little closer into him and he puts an arm around me. That's when I know it's going to be okay. He understands.

We spend the afternoon strolling along the side of the Thames, but I don't really take in much of the scenery. My mind's on Cassie and that big hug she gave me. I excuse myself when we find a public loo and quickly send her a text from the privacy of a cubicle.

Hi Cassie, are you okay, hon? You looked quite worried when I left xx

She texts back almost straight away. *I'm fine, thanks. Are you all right? xx*

That surprised me. *Yes, just going for a walk with James. Do you need me to come home or anything?*

The reply is instant. *No, of course not. Just enjoy yourself, take it easy and have a great time. I'm staying at Rob's tonight xx*

I feel better already. She's got company and she wouldn't be at home even if I went back.

Okay, babe. As long as you're okay. Have fun xx I text back quickly, concerned that James will come looking for me any minute.

You too xx

I slip the phone back into my bag and leave, checking my lip gloss on my way out.

'Are you okay?' James is waiting patiently by a railing.

I smile, feeling much happier. 'Fine, thanks. How far do you want to walk?'

A smile twitches his lips. 'Why? Have you got boundless energy and want to walk for miles, or have you had second thoughts and want to turn back?' He eyes me suspiciously. That's the trouble with dating a copper. They're never off duty. *And you can't get away with anything.*

I gesture for him to continue the walk. 'Lead on, MacDu—' I stop myself just in time before I totally misquote the bard. I clear my throat, as James looks back at me expectantly. 'Carry on,' I say, airily.

He chuckles, taking my hand. 'You're learning.'

I smile but say nothing. I'm secretly glad he's noticed. I once used the popular misquote, and James was quick to correct me. I won't give him that satisfaction again.

The walk's really pleasant after that. I cuddle up to James and we enjoy the winter sunshine glinting on the water. I am relieved that Cassie's okay, and no longer feel guilty for being with James tonight. I just have to convince him that I'm not putting my best friend before him. I need him to understand just how important my friends are to me, but that it's him that I love. It's going to be a long night...

***

I awake the next morning with James' arm around me and a huge smile on my face. I won't go into detail, but I think I managed to make it quite clear that *he's* my number one priority.

We get up late and enjoy hot croissants and coffee at the flat. It's really neat now that Suzanne and all her stuff have left. The walls and surfaces are now clear again and the place looks much bigger. I could get used to living here, spending my weekends like this and just enjoying James' company.

'Are you okay?' I ask, gazing at his handsome face across the little table.

He smiles. He's been doing a lot of that since yesterday. 'I'm fine,' he assures me.

'You're not worried about work, are you?' Sometimes, he's so secretive about his job that I wonder what's running through his head.

'Not especially. I told you, Alex is on the case, too. We'll catch the thieves soon enough.'

He told me yesterday about the case he is working on. It seems that an organised gang of thieves has hit the area and they've been systematically robbing the high street stores of shoes and clothing, as well as some electrical items. It sounds like they've got good taste, as they've hit some pretty expensive shops, too. James and Alex think the thieves are stealing to order, judging by what's been taken, and have managed to pick up a couple of shoplifters, but not the ones running the operation.

I shudder. I hate the thought of rubbing shoulders with criminals when I'm out and about, but I know it can't be avoided. They don't exactly wear striped jumpers and carry bags marked 'swag' now, do they?

'Do you think they're dangerous?' I ask, wiping crumbs from my fingers.

He sighs. 'Any crook can be unpredictable,' he says. 'I expect once we get the big boys there'll be some action—they won't go down without a fight. They've got too much to lose. The rest just seem to be petty criminals, nothing much to worry about. We just need to get them to talk, that's all.'

'It must be so exciting,' I gush, imagining myself arresting shoplifters. Maybe I should think about a change of career.

'It's not,' James assures me. 'It's satisfying once we get them, though.'

He gives me a warning look and I guess he's read my mind again. He's been doing a lot of that, lately. I say nothing and tidy the dishes into the sink.

We go to the cinema in the afternoon and then out to dinner at a little restaurant. It's a lovely day and comes to an end far too soon.

'I'd best get back,' I tell him with a sigh. 'I need to get my things sorted out for the morning.'

'I know.' He's well aware of my little routine. I always sort out an outfit ready for the next day, complete with accessories. It takes a while, but it's worth it when I get up the following morning and it's all ready for me.

He walks me to the Tube station and gives me a lingering kiss on the platform, just as the train arrives. My stomach burns and I really wish I didn't have to go. I make a promise to myself that I'll move in with him just as soon as I'm convinced Cassie's okay.

***

Cassie isn't okay. I walk into the flat a short while later to see her drumming her fingers on the kitchen table, a glass of Merlot in her other hand. She looks worried sick.

'Do you want to tell me what's wrong?' I ask, going straight over and plonking myself on the chair opposite her.

She stares at me. 'I was about to ask you the same question.'

'Me?' I frown. 'I'm fine, I told you. But you look like you've got the weight of the world on your shoulders. Is it Rob? Are things not working out with you two? I thought everything was okay, but...'

'It's not him.' Her curt tone takes me by surprise.

'Then it must be work? Is Perdita being horrible to you? Do you want to leave? I hoped once they started franchising the brand it would be easier on you guys, the atmosphere would be better and...'

'Work's fine.' She stares at me incredulously. 'It's *you*. Why don't you talk to me? Properly, I mean. I know we don't get that much time with each other, what with Rob and James, but I'm still your bestie, aren't I? You should be able to talk to me.' Tears well in her eyes and my stomach lurches. I stroke her arm across the table.

'You don't need to worry about me. I'm absolutely fine,' I assure her. 'I've almost forgotten all that shit Davinia put me through and things are really good at work. And James and I are absolutely great. Better than great, actually.' I remember last night with an uncontrollable smile.

She narrows her eyes at me. 'Are you happy? *Really* happy, I mean?'

'Of course. I love him, Cassie. I wouldn't want to be with anyone else. Now, what's this really all about?'

She shrugs. 'I just worry that stuff's going on and you're hiding it from me, that's all. I've told Rob I'm not going to stay over at his so much in future so we can have more girly time together.'

She takes a sip of her wine.

'You don't need to do that. We see each other all the time,' I tell her. 'Besides, I'll be staying with James more now that he's on the early shift. Don't feel that you can't see your boyfriend just because of me.'

'I'm your best friend, Libby,' she says, firmly. 'I have to be here for you whenever you need me, and I don't think I have been just lately. I've been a shit friend, to be honest.'

I go over and give her a big hug, nearly making her spill her drink.

'You could never be shit,' I assure her, squeezing her tightly. 'You're the best friend anyone could have. You took time off when I was recovering, you visited me in hospital and you've really looked after me. I know everything was horrid for a while back then, but it's all okay now. Davinia's behind bars, as is Quinton Bellis.

They can't hurt me now. And Valerie's been a changed woman since it all happened. I love working there now.'

'Good,' she says, muffled by the grip I have on her.

I release her, concerned that she might not be able to breathe.

'You don't need to worry,' I assure her again.

'But if there was anything... anything you needed to tell me... you would speak to me, wouldn't you? I *am* your best friend and I'd understand and support you all the way, you know that, right?'

'Of course.' I go back to my seat, realising that she must have felt left out of things when all that business was going on. 'If I have any suspicions about anything ever again, I'll tell you straight away, okay? I won't let myself get into such a dangerous situation again.' I mean it. Not just to keep her happy, but because it was downright terrifying.

She looks more relaxed and I hope it's not just because of the wine. She's such a good friend to worry about me so much. No wonder I feel so awful at the thought of leaving her. She'd be devastated. I wonder for a second if she's got an inkling that James has asked me to move in with him. What if that's what's worrying her? I haven't told her. She thinks I might just disappear. No, I don't think that's it. She'd just come right out and ask me if it was that... I think.

7

It's great to see the girls again, when I reach work the next day.

'I was nursing a damn hangover all weekend,' Eva admits, looking quite sorry for herself.

'Lightweight,' Brie says with a grin. 'We didn't have *that* much.'

It turns out they'd gone on to a club after leaving us on Friday evening and had a whale of a time. Seems like Eva paid for it afterwards, though. She still looks as beautiful as ever, mind you.

'What happened to you guys?' Eva asks, 'Did you stay long?'

'I left them to it,' Siobhan quips. 'And *my* head's absolutely fine, thank you.'

'We only had a few,' Beulah points out. 'And we went for coffee afterwards.'

Brie stares over at her from her position by the mirror. 'Wow. That was very sensible of you. I'm impressed. I really thought you youngsters would be in a worse state than Eva today.'

'Thanks for that,' Eva says, playfully.

I can't help thinking that if Tyler hadn't shown up, we *would* be in a much worse state than Eva by now.

Beulah, Fran and I have been texting each other over the weekend, whenever there was time. They both seem fine this morning, but I'm dying to know what's going on between Fran and Tyler. She told us he'd texted her, but it was complicated and she'd explain when she saw us. I can't wait for break time.

Valerie comes in with a huge bunch of flowers in her hand.

'Morning, ladies,' she says, cheerfully. 'Mr Peerless has kindly given me these to thank me for all my efforts on the supplement last week. I'm pleased to announce it was a roaring success and the *Chronicle*'s sales are much higher than in recent weeks.'

We all cheer. It's such a relief that all our efforts were worth it.

'I feel that as it's you ladies who did all the hard work, these flowers should be for you. We can put them somewhere prominent so you can all enjoy them. Thank you for your endeavours, now let's do it all again. We want even more sales this week.' She hands the flowers to Siobhan as we all clap and cheer. The atmosphere's electric as we all settle back down to work. Siobhan puts the flowers in a vase on the windowsill.

My letters, which must have arrived over the weekend, all seem to be from professional, affluent women with plenty of money but not enough time to peruse the shops. I love this kind of thing as I get to investigate all the high-end fashions and spend their money for them in my head. I'd love to be in their position. Unfortunately, although my wages have risen quite a bit since I returned to work, my credit card bills have done the same. I'll be glad when I've paid them off. That's a pipedream of mine; to pay off all my creditors and be debt-free. It will happen one day. Not today, though.

I'm glad to be wearing such a nice outfit as I peruse clothes for my readers. I've borrowed Cassie's Malene Birger, black midi-length skirt, with lace-up on one side and gorgeous buttons down the other. It looks great with my Anna Quan, cotton-twill white blouse with satin trim. I bought it on eBay, but it was nearly new. I'm also wearing my nude-to-black ombre Louboutins and I've got Cassie's Marc Jacobs bag to finish it off.

I flick through several websites looking for something suitable for the clients. There are so many lovely clothes out there, I'm spoiled for choice, trying to put together a compact holiday wardrobe for Miss

Jessica Beaman of Hammersmith, and an interview ensemble for Ms Newman of Chelsea.

'I think I'll have to check out the shops for these,' I decide, after spending far too long making notes from the internet pages only to find that items are out of stock or not available in the sizes I need.

'Good idea,' Siobhan agrees, glancing at my copious scribbles.

I can't believe I've got a job where I'm paid good money to go shopping, but that's exactly what I'm doing. Sort of.

My first stop is Harvey Nichols. They have the most stunning suits that would be ideal for Ms Newman'sinterview. I steer away from black, navy, and grey as they're too obvious. This lady's going for an executive position and wants to stand out. She says she wants to wear trousers, but not normal, straight leg ones. Something different. Something vibrant that will suit her vivacious personality as well as the occasion. There are so many to choose from, but I eventually plump for a red trouser suit by Anna October. The jacket is fitted with puff sleeves and the trousers are wide-legged. It's absolutely gorgeous and will certainly get her noticed for all the right reasons. I take a note of the details and photograph the suit on my phone, just for my own reference. I know there will be much better images available, but I like to keep my own record, if I can. I'm already thinking about a pair of Jimmy Choos that I noticed on the web earlier, which would team up nicely with it.

My next stop is a little boutique just down the road. They always have lovely pieces, and I'm sure there will be some holiday clothes for my other client. It's nice to get out of the cold, and I'm hoping that concentrating on a Caribbean cruise might help me warm up a bit. As I pass one of the rails, a white, lacy jumper catches my eye. I stop to take a closer look. It's absolutely beautiful and would go with practically any outfit. I'm suddenly aware of a shuffling sound behind me and turn around to see a girl stuffing a top under her coat.

We catch each other's eye at the same time and my face burns. She's using me to block the view of the security camera.

'What're you doing? You'll end up in prison,' I hiss at her.

She continues to stare at me, petrified, frozen.

'I have to,' she hisses, finally finding her voice and throwing the hanger underneath the rail.

'No, you don't.' I try to assure her.

'Mind your own business.' A male voice takes me by surprise and a man glares at me from the other side of the rail. He's heavily built and has an evil snarl— the kind of bloke you wouldn't want to meet in a dark alley.

The girl barges past me and disappears towards the door.

'You say one word and I'll be after you, bitch.' The guy narrows his eyes at me before following the woman.

My heart's racing. That poor girl looked terrified. It was clear the guy was bullying her into shoplifting, so I daren't report her to security. Which means I can't report the thug, either. My head starts to ache with the enormity of the dilemma, and I decide to treat myself to a coffee while I gather my thoughts.

Starbucks is quite busy, but I don't care. I take deep breaths while queuing up for my drink, trying to calm my nerves. I treat myself to a Caffé Misto with hazelnut syrup and whipped cream and find a seat at a tiny table in the far corner. I know I could have bought a cheaper drink and saved a bit more towards my boots, but now's not the time to worry about that. I've got enough on my mind.

My phone pings, making me jump. I'm so nervy. It's Beulah.

You're missing break x

I'm at Starbucks x I reply straight away.

You'll miss all the gossip. Fran's promised to spill the beans, remember?

Damn! I'd forgotten about all that. I'm dying to know what that boyfriend of hers is playing at—as if I didn't have enough drama in my life right now.

You'll have to tell me when I get back. Sorry x

There's no time to get back to the office before the end of break, unfortunately.

Okay. Have fun x

I'm sure she thinks I'm skiving out here. I'm entitled to a coffee break and besides, I really need this right now. I place my phone on the table and pick up my cup with trembling hands. I really need to get a grip—literally. That guy looked vicious, though. I can't get his ugly face out of my head.

The coffee's delicious, and I put the cup back down after taking a sip. I stare back at my phone. I ought to ring James and warn him that there are thieves in Knightsbridge. It might help with his case. But that woman would be arrested, and it wasn't her fault. Anyone with half an eye could see the bloke had put her up to it but proving it might be a different matter. It's her word against his. And he's got a bigger mouth.

On the other hand, James is my boyfriend and he made me promise to tell him everything after all that business with Davinia. I chew my lip. I made a similar promise to Cassie, too. But she's so worried at the moment, and I really don't want to add to it. Besides, what is there to tell? For all I know, the woman might have dumped the top before leaving the shop. I could end up reporting a theft that never happened. James is a stickler for evidence, and I've got absolutely nothing. My guess is that even the bully might have been hidden from the CCTV, with me standing right there. Oh, no! That means if she *did* steal the top, I'll look like an accessory!

I take a big gulp of my drink. This is all wrong. Imagine me being charged with aiding and abetting a criminal. I'd lose my job. James would lose face at the station. It would be a disaster all round. No. The best thing for all concerned is to keep shtum. What James doesn't know won't hurt him—or lose him his job.

I finish my coffee, get my grown-up head on and go back to work. I've got a holiday wardrobe to put together.

*∗∗

Spending the rest of the morning choosing clothes for Miss Jessica Beaman's Caribbean cruise really soothes my soul. I'm much more cheerful when I return to the office with all the details of some fantastic clothes—including one or two bargains. I must admit I received some funny looks as I splayed a few items over the rail, ensuring that everything co-ordinated well, but it was worth it. I even made friends with Ellie-Blanche, one of the assistants in L.K. Bennett who was very helpful when I asked about some little ballet pumps for Jessica's holiday. She seemed a little disappointed that I didn't actually *buy* them, although I took loads of photos. But when I explained who I was, and what I was doing, she was only too happy to help. She brought out loads of espadrilles, sandals, and some sweet little flip-flops with diamante trim. Jessica will be spoiled for choice. I know *I* was.

The girls are all pleased to see me, and Siobhan looks pleased that I managed to sort out the outfits.

'A lot more came in today's post,' she tells me, plonking a pile of letters on my desk. 'That'll keep you busy for a while.'

I smile, more than up for the challenge. It's a relief that I'm needed in this role, having initially thought up the job on the spur of the moment whilst at the mercy of Davinia Urquhart. Davinia had been the supplement's Agony Aunt, and made a right pig's ear of it. She gave such awful advice that people complained. Some wrote in with such bizarre 'problems' we're all sure they were just winding her up. Valerie felt that we should change the role to something more befitting to the new magazine and liked my suggestion. We're also hoping it'll impress the readers band avoid any further complaints.

Beulah comes over to my desk as I settle down to write up my findings.

'It's worse than we thought,' she mutters. 'About Fran.'

I look over to where Fran's pinning a dress onto a mannequin. She looks a bit pale.

'Has she spoken to him?' I mutter back, aware that Siobhan's watching us.

'Not exactly.' Beulah frowns. 'We'll tell you at lunch.'

She goes back to help Fran with the dress—which is gorgeous, incidentally—and I try to resume my work. It's not easy though. I've got all these thoughts running through my head. Fran, Cassie, James, the shoplifter, the thug, it's no wonder I can't think straight. I'm trying to concentrate on Jessica Beaman's holiday outfits, and all these worries keep whizzing around like a giant whirlpool in my brain.

***

It's a relief when lunchtime comes round, and we all head down to the canteen. Beulah went on ahead to grab us the big table, so I catch up with Fran in the corridor.

'Are you okay, babe?' I ask, linking her arm.

She shakes her head. 'I'm not sure *what* I am, to be honest.'

'Well, at least we're sure what you're *not*,' I mutter, squeezing her arm.

She smiles. 'That's true.'

'You are *glad*, aren't you?' I enquire, watching her expression.

'What? Oh, yes, of course. Much as I'd love to be a mother one day, today is not the day. I'm just worried that Tyler thinks I am. I'd never tell a guy I was pregnant if I wasn't. Maybe, not even if I was. It just depends on the circumstances. But this has got me really worried. I must have been even drunker than I thought.'

'Have you heard from him?' I ask, as we arrive at the refectory.

'Yeah. I'll tell you later,' she says, as Alice joins us.

'Are you okay, girls?' She's really pretty with blonde hair and big, innocent-looking eyes.

'Yeah, of course. How did your appointment go on Friday?' I ask, cheerfully.

She slumps a little. 'Oh, it was fine. Just a check-up at the dentist.'

'Lucky you.' Fran smiles at her as we arrive at the large table where most of the seats have already been taken.

'We'll squeeze in at the end,' I tell Fran, gesturing to the bottom of the table where there's still some space. We pull up a couple of chairs, while Alice goes to sit with Siobhan.

There are a couple of empty seats where Beulah and Kiki have gone to fetch our food. We're now allowed to place our orders early and have the food plated up ready for us when we come down. I don't know if all the departments get this privilege—I think it might be another of Valerie's touches.

It's hard to have a private conversation with all the girls huddled around one large table, so we make general chit-chat until some of the girls finish lunch and wander off. We're just finishing our desserts when Beulah comes over with her coffee and takes the seat next to Fran.

'So, have you told her?' she whispers to Fran.

'Not yet.'

'Told me what?' I ask, guessing what this is about.

Fran sighs. Brie and Eva are talking down the other end of the table, but the rest have gone. She fishes her phone out of her bag and brings up a message.

'Here.'

I take it from her and gape.

Hey gorgeous. I've been thinking about the wedding. How about we go look at some venues this week? Maybe a hotel or something? I'll organise it. You just tell me what you want. Love you, sugar. Can't wait to see you.

The message ends with a gazillion kisses and just about every emoji in the phone.

'He's serious?' I stare at Fran.

She nods. 'Looks like it. He's starting to make plans.'

'You'll just have to tell him,' Beulah says.

'It's not that easy. He's obsessed.' Fran looks ready to cry.

'When's all this supposed to have happened?' I ask. 'You've only been with him five minutes.'

Fran bites her lip. 'Actually, there were a couple of occasions before Jeffery and I broke up. We were on a break.' She adds the last bit quickly. 'Once we got back together again, Tyler and I stopped.'

'Pity you started up again,' Beulah noted, bluntly.

I roll my eyes at her. *Not helpful.*

'And you think he must have proposed that night at the party? The one you can't remember anything about?' I frown.

Fran nods. 'That's when I woke up afterwards wearing the elastic wedding band. All I know is we went to his mate's house and there was loads of booze flowing and loud music. I can't even remember who we met or anything. Just noise and lights and then... nothing.'

'Your drink must have been spiked.' I blurt out my thoughts without thinking.

Poor Fran looks devastated. 'You think?'

Beulah nods. 'It's the only thing that makes sense. It was one of those wild parties with goodness-knows-what flying around, and someone slipped something in your drink.' She sounds very matter of fact about it.

'So, in that case I *might* have said I was pregnant,' Fran looks horrified. 'And I could have accepted his proposal.'

'It still doesn't count,' Beulah assures her. 'You have to be sober and in your right mind for any of it to hold up in court.'

'Court?' Fran blurts out, making Brie and Eva look over.

'No, it won't come to that,' I say, shaking my head and smiling at the other two, who are looking quite concerned.

'Is everything okay, guys?' Eva asks. 'I mean, I don't want to pry or anything...'

'It's fine,' Beulah assures her, nodding. 'Nothing to worry about.'

I wish I had her confidence, but at least Eva doesn't press the issue, as she and Brie get up and leave.

'When are you seeing him?' I ask Fran.

'We're supposed to be going to the pub tomorrow night,' she replies, biting her lip. 'He wanted to see me over the weekend, but I told him I was going away. I had to spend the whole time in the flat with the curtains closed and checked my phone every time it rang in case it was him. Which it was. Several times.'

'That's awful,' I agree. 'You're just going to have to break it off with him, Fran. You shouldn't be doing stuff like that. It's just not right.'

'I want to tell him to bugger off,' she admits. 'I mean, he's really fit, you've got to admit, but he's a total nutcase. I worry what he's going to say next.'

Her phone pings and we all stare at it.

'It's him,' she says, bringing up the text. She shows us.

Hey gorgeous, I've seen the ideal place for our wedding. It's a lovely hotel by the river. And they've had a cancellation. We can go and see it tonight, and if we like it and book it today, we get a discount. Woohoo! I'll pick you up after work.

Again, there are kisses an emojis galore—which he's clearly got group-saved on his phone as they look suspiciously identical to the ones he used last time.

'Shit! How do I say no to that? He's got it all worked out.' Fran throws her hands in the air. 'I already told him I couldn't see him tonight. I only agreed to tomorrow to shut him up until I find an excuse to cancel.'

'We'll think of something,' I say, trying to convince myself as much as her.

'Bugger—the time!' Beulah jumps up. 'We're late, guys.'

'Great! All I need now is to lose my job on top of everything else,' Fran moans as we leave the table.

'At least if you get the sack, you'll be at home tonight when he shows up here,' Beulah says with a snigger.

'That's it!' I stop still in the corridor. 'We'll tell Siobhan you're not feeling well, and you'll have to go home. *We'll* deal with lover-boy when he comes to meet you. That'll get us off the hook for being late back, too.' I can't believe I've come up with such a brilliant plan. Now, all we have to do is execute it...

8

Siobhan looks up when we arrive at the office. Everyone else suddenly stops talking, and stares at us as if we've just landed from Mars.

'Is everything all right?' Siobhan comes over to us, frowning.

We've both linked arms with Fran, who actually looks paler than she did earlier.

'Sorry we're late. Fran's been sick,' I offer. 'We've been looking after her but she's not at all well.' I feel awful fibbing to Siobhan, and secretly cross the fingers of my free hand behind my back.

Siobhan gives Fran a sympathetic look. 'You look almost white. Are you okay to get home?'

Fran nods. 'I'll take a taxi. It's not far.'

'I'll get you some sick bags,' Beulah offers, going over to the First Aid kit. 'For some reason, taxi drivers seem to have a strange aversion to passengers throwing up in the back of their cabs.'

I help Fran get her coat and things together. 'Don't worry,' I whisper, 'It'll be fine. Don't answer your phone if he rings. I'll message you later.'

I have to admit she really does look poorly as she leaves. I think this business with Tyler is really getting to her. I'm not surprised. It's all a bit creepy, if you ask me.

Keeping my mind on the job all afternoon is hard. I'm just writing up a report for Valerie on what clothes I've chosen for the readers and why, giving details about where and how I came across the outfits. I suppose it's to justify my time out of the office. They even want to know which shops I went to and roughly how long I spent in each one. And this is all *before* I write up my column. It sounds more like an instruction from Phil Peerless than Valerie. I know he doesn't like me, but I didn't realise he didn't trust me either.

At five o' clock, we all get up to leave and Beulah comes over to me, grinning.

'This is going to be fun,' she mutters.

I follow her out the door. 'We need to sound believable,' I say quietly, once we get into the lift. 'That means getting our story straight. I thought we'd say we're bridesmaids and she's asked us to go along because she trusts us to make a good decision on her behalf.'

'We can't do any worse than *her* decisions,' she states rolling her eyes. 'Whatever possessed her to get involved with that head case is beyond me.'

'You've got to admit he's quite good-looking.'

'Yeah, if you've got your beer goggles on, I suppose. And you don't look at his hair.'

'Anyway.' I swiftly change the subject. 'We'll say she had to go on a course at short notice and that her phone's broken so she couldn't let him know.'

She nods. 'At least that'll save him going round to her place tonight.'

'Exactly. I think this business is worrying her sick. She genuinely looked ill when she went home earlier.'

We go outside and look down the street for any sign of Tyler.

'Here he is,' Beulah says, walking slowly to her left.

I suddenly feel quite nervous. He doesn't look happy to see us and is peering around, clearly looking for Fran.

'Hi, Tyler,' I greet him cheerfully. 'We met the other night at the pub. I'm Libby and this is Beulah. We're Fran's friends.'

He frowns suspiciously. 'Where is she?'

'She had to go on a course this afternoon. It was short notice, I'm afraid. She'd have called you but her phone's broken.' I'm sticking to the plan, but he doesn't look the slightest bit convinced.

'So, we're going to look at the venue in her place,' Beulah announces. 'Fran's asked us to be bridesmaids. I'm the chief bridesmaid, so I've got to check out the venue and report back to her.'

'What?' He looks incredulous. 'But she needs to see it for herself.'

'She trusts us,' Beulah says, shaking her head.

'Actually, she also likes surprises,' I add quickly. 'So, it would be great if we could arrange it all without her and give her a really special day, wouldn't it?'

Beulah looks at me accusingly, and I know I've gone off piste a bit, but sometimes you have to think on your feet. Ad-libbing is actually one of my fortes, I noticed recently.

'She told me she hates surprises.' He's frowning again.

'Most of the time she does, but she wants us to surprise her this time,' Beulah remarks. 'Come on.'

We head for the Tube, which is packed, as usual at this time of day. Of course, we don't get to sit down and it's really hard to have a conversation with all the noise, so we say nothing until we arrive.

We clamber off at Sloane Square and he leads us in the direction of the Saatchi gallery. It's a lovely area, and I'm sure it would be wonderful to have a wedding near here, but I can't help thinking it all looks very expensive.

'What do you do?' I ask Tyler as we take a small side-street.

I'm in IT,' he says, vaguely.

'Ooh. That's handy,' Beulah replies.

'We're here,' he announces as we arrive at a lovely little hotel with pots of Christmas Roses either side of the door.

'This looks nice,' I say.

He stops suddenly. 'Look, are you sure it wouldn't be better to wait until Fran can come? It's going to look a bit odd without the bride being here.'

'But she's not available,' Beulah says bluntly.

'And you'd miss out on the discount,' I add quickly.

'Okay. You're sure she's happy for you to make the decision for her? I mean, I don't want her to say afterwards that she wants to get married somewhere else after we've paid the deposit?'

'Quite sure,' I tell him, though I'm not at all sure about his use of the word 'we' when referring to the deposit. I'm certainly not forking out for a wedding that's not even going to happen.

The hotel manager is much younger than I expected, and he comes to greet us in the foyer.

'Welcome to The Falcon's Wing Hotel,' he announces, and then does a double take when he sees that there are three of us.

'Thank you.' Tyler shakes his hand.

'And which of you gorgeous ladies is the bride-to-be?' He looks quite smarmy as he glances at Beulah and me, and I can't help feeling a little unnerved by him.

'She couldn't come,' Beulah informs him. 'I'm the chief bridesmaid and this is one of the other bridesmaids.'

I balk at her introduction but say nothing.

'Fran got called away on a course or something,' Tyler explains. 'These two have come in her place. Fran said they can decide on her behalf whether we want to book or not.'

The manager looks a little disgruntled, and I'm not sure if it's the absence of Fran or the possibility of Tyler not booking that's got him so rattled.

'I could see me getting married in a place like this,' Beulah says, as we walk down pristine white corridors and feel the sumptuous carpets beneath our feet.

Everywhere is decorated in white and gold, making the small hotel look quite spacious and airy. It's also much quieter than I expected, given the time. When I worked at The Chalfont Hotel, there was always staff and guests milling around, but this place is more like the

Mary Celeste. And I can't help thinking I'd have been in big trouble leaving the reception desk unattended, but there was definitely no one there when we arrived.

'This is the room we use for the ceremony,' the manager tells us, opening the door to a small room. The huge windows are curtained behind thick, velvet drapes and the furniture is dark oak.

'It looks lovely,' I coo, taking photos on my phone. 'How many can it seat, Mr... er?'

'Just call me Dan. Daniel,' he corrects quickly.

I nod, giving him an expectant look.

He seems to suddenly realise I'm still awaiting an answer.

'Um, about twenty-five.'

'Oh, I'm not sure that'll be enough,' I say, pursing my lips.

'Well, I thought Tyler said it was just a small affair?' Daniel's clearly off-guard.

'It is,' Tyler interjects quickly.

'Really? So, are Fran's family not coming then?' Beulah asks. 'They'll be devastated not to be invited.'

'Oh, yes, especially all her big brothers,' I add, enjoying watching Tyler squirm.

He frowns. 'She didn't mention anything about them.'

'Really? They're very close,' I reply. '*All* of them.'

He looks more than a little irked.

'And then there's their wives and children,' Beulah adds, 'you can't leave them out.'

'Hmm, I think you'll need a bigger room than this,' I say, frowning. 'Especially with all the bridesmaids.'

Tyler stares at me. 'What bloody bridesmaids? I didn't know she was having any until you two showed up.'

'Oh, yes, she's asked all the girls in the office,' Beulah tells him with an innocent expression.

'And there will be her sisters, too,' I add, 'and didn't she say she's got some uni friends she wants to invite?'

Tyler and Daniel exchange worried looks and start to back out of the room.

'Well, this is the ballroom,' Daniel says, leading us down the corridor. I can hear Beulah clicking away with her phone, taking pictures of anything and everything.

Double doors open out into a beautiful room with a huge, gold chandelier hanging in the middle of it. The glass sparkles, casting pretty shadows on the walls and wooden floor.

'Oh, she'll love this,' Beulah says, and I can see she's enjoying getting into character.

'It'll be absolutely perfect for the evening 'do'. I nod.

'How many have you got coming?' Daniel asks, a little tentatively.

'About three hundred,' I reply, without thinking.

Tyler gapes at me. '*What?*'

'Oh, sorry,' I say, enjoying his expression. 'I'm sure she said it was about that.'

'Or was it *four* hundred?' Beulah asks, with a frown. 'You might be thinking of the reception.'

'Oh, right.' I'm a little thrown but play along anyway. This is getting a tad out of hand.

'Yes, where's the room for that?' Beulah asks.

'Well, we usually use this room for the reception and then everyone goes to the bar while we set it up for the evening do. The hotel restaurant only holds about forty people.'

My suspicions rise at his lack of jargon.

'And how many covers do you get in here?' I ask, using the correct term.

He looks a little taken aback. 'Umm, about two hundred and fifty,' he says.

For a hotel manager, he's not very competent. He should know *exactly* how many covers he can get into a conference room like this.

'And how do you set them out?' I enquire, trying to sound casual.

'What do you mean?' He frowns at me. *He does that a lot, I've noticed.*

'Well, to get two hundred and fifty covers in, do you place the tables in a traditional 'U' shape, or use separate ones? And what shaped tables do you use? And where do you usually have the top table?'

He's frowning even harder now.

'Does it matter?' Tyler snaps.

I stare at him. 'Of course, it matters. Fran will need all the details.'

'I thought you were making the decision for her?' Daniel looks from me to Tyler.

'Of course, we are, but she'll still need to know everything,' Beulah chips in.

'Or will it all be in the conference pack?' I ask.

'What?' Daniel looks more than flummoxed.

'The conference pack. Or the wedding pack if you have them separate.' I raise my eyebrows, not really surprised to see that he's fiddling frantically with a key in his hand.

'Yes, of course,' he says. 'I'll just... er... fetch it. If you'd like to follow me—'

'Actually, could we pick it up on the way out?' Beulah asks, wandering around the room.' She points to the drapes. 'Are those French windows? Can we see outside?'

Daniel's clearly fuming. 'I'd have to get the key.' He checks his watch nervously.

'I don't think we need to see out there,' Tyler says, irritably. 'We'll be inside, won't we?'

'Yes, but we want to have a nice view,' Beulah points out.

'And what if we need a marquee? You know, for extra space.' I try not to smirk at the look of horror on Tyler's face.

'Good point,' Beulah agrees. 'That wouldn't be a problem, would it, Daniel?'

By now, he's just staring at us, gaping.

'It would cost extra, of course,' he points out, slowly.

'How much are we talking here?' I ask, giving him a studious look. 'And how much is the discount you're offering?'

Daniel looks over at Tyler. 'Have you decided, then? Are you going to book it?'

'Fran was supposed to be paying half,' he says, looking cagily at me. 'Are you paying her share?'

Beulah snorts. 'We said we could make a decision, not pay for the venue,' she points out. 'And besides, in her condition, shouldn't *you* be paying for her? Alleviate the stress, and all that?'

'Yeah, especially as it was *you who* proposed to *her*?' I add.

'Look, either way, we need to get moving.' Daniel looks around nervously as someone comes up the corridor.

'Hi, Dan,' the woman says as she passes him in the doorway. 'I didn't recognise you for a minute.'

He forces a smile. 'Evening, Julia,' he replies, his jaw tightening.

'Why do you need a decision tonight?' I ask, as we start walking back towards Reception.

'It's company policy,' Daniel informs me.

'And how long is the cooling off period?' I ask.

'Umm, twenty-four hours,' he mumbles.

'What? Are you sure that's legal?' I retort, standing still for a second.

He looks anxiously down the corridor.

'Come, on, we've got to get going,' Tyler says.

'But what about the deposit? We can't lose out on such a lovely venue,' Beulah asks, her eyes wide with surprise.

'Absolutely. We've got to have it,' I say, 'as long as we can agree the cost, of course. And we'd need your confirmation that we can definitely fit all the guests in.'

Daniel huffs, clearly in a hurry to get rid of us. 'Look, I'll tell you what. As Tyler's a friend I'll do you a favour. You can decide tomorrow. I'll give you until tomorrow evening to pay the deposit and still get the discount.'

'Good man, Fran should be back by then. I think I'll need to bring her, after all.' Tyler looks relieved.

'But what about the surprise?' Beulah whines. 'You'll ruin it all if you do that.'

'Hey, I didn't realise you were friends,' I say, trying to look innocent. 'Does that mean you can do the venue at mate's rates, then?'

Tyler and Daniel look at each other awkwardly.

'Well... um... er...' Daniel murmurs.

Two men walk towards us. They're both dressed in black trousers and white shirts with the hotel emblem on their pocket, and one is putting on a black tie. They grin at Daniel.

'Woo. Look at you! What's the occasion?' One of them hoots.

'Not been back in court, have you, Dan?' the other quips.

Daniel looks like he wants the ground to swallow him up. 'Guys, just give me a minute, will you?' he says, putting up a hand in a placating manner.

'Ooh!' They both laugh and walk on.

'They're all very informal,' Beulah notes. 'Do they always treat you with this much disrespect?' She looks shocked.

'Oh, they don't mean anything by it,' he says, forcing another smile. 'They're just in high spirits tonight. That's all. I'm sure they'll apologise later.'

'Well, I would certainly hope so.' Beulah's clearly enjoying this, and I suddenly want to giggle.

'Well, I'll be in touch tomorrow,' Tyler says, shaking Daniel's hand as soon as we reach the foyer.

'Yes, and if we could just get a copy of your wedding details?' I pick up a hotel brochure from the display near the reception desk.

'Oh, yes, I can't wait to see what menus you offer,' Beulah says, smiling.

'And what kind of accommodation discount you offer wedding guests,' I add quickly.

'That's strange, I thought I had one here,' Daniel remarks, searching behind the desk. 'I'll pop one in the post to you.'

'It's okay, I'll pick one up tomorrow when I come with the deposit,' Tyler says, hurriedly, as more staff arrive at the front doors.

'No problem,' Daniel says. 'I'll see you tomorrow.'

We all thank each other and leave the hotel, much to Daniel's obvious relief.

'Well… that went well,' Beulah says as we walk back towards the Tube.

'You think?' Tyler snaps.

'He didn't seem to know much about his own hotel, did he?' I say, trying to ignore his scowls.

'He's only young. He can't have been in the position long,' Beulah says. 'I didn't realise he was a friend of yours, Tyler. How long have you known him?'

'He's not a friend exactly,' Tyler replies, sulkily. 'And we only met a short while ago.'

'As long as it's enough time to give you a good rate on your wedding that's all that counts,' I say, trying to sound cheerful.

'What did you think of the place?' Beulah asks him, airily. 'Is it what you wanted?'

'Well, I don't know, now that it seems our little wedding isn't as little as I'd planned.' He speaks through gritted teeth.

'*You'd* planned? Surely it's for you and Fran to plan *together*?' I query.

Even in the light of the streetlamp I can see his face turn red. 'Yes... well... that's what I meant,' he says quickly.

'So, how come you didn't know about her big family?' Beulah asks. 'Hadn't you discussed it?'

'Not really. Look, it's really none of your business, is it?' He sounds vicious.

'Yes, it is, when you're expecting us to pay half your deposit,' I point out.

'Yeah, about that,' Beulah says, suddenly standing in front of him. 'I mean—what the fuck?'

I roll my eyes. Beulah has such a lovely turn of phrase!

'Well, you don't expect *me* to pay for it all, do you?' He looks astonished. 'If you're taking Fran's place at the meeting, the least you could do is pay her share of the deposit.'

'Ha! You're actually serious, aren't you?' Beulah raises her voice in surprise.

'Fuck you!' He barges past her and struts off down the road.

'What now?' Beulah asks, as we watch him go.

'Now, we have a bit more fun,' I say with a giggle. 'Come on.'

We go back in the direction we've just walked.

The hotel seems much busier when we return, and a woman's sitting behind the reception desk. She stands up when we walk up to her, and smiles.

'Good evening, ladies,' she says politely. 'How can I help you?'

'Is it possible to speak to the manager, please?' I ask, smiling back.

'Of course. Is he expecting you?' she enquires, reaching for the phone.

'No, it's about a wedding,' I tell her.

'Oh.' She looks surprised. 'Well, congratulations.' She looks from me to Beulah, and I can't help wondering if she thinks it's *our* wedding I'm talking about.

There isn't time to put her straight, as a middle-aged man in a smart suit pops his head out from an office behind her.

'Oh, there you are, Mr Thompson. I was just about to call you,' the receptionist tells him.

'How can I help?' he asks, smiling as he comes around our side of the desk.

'Oh, no, I'm sorry, it was the other manager I meant,' I say. 'Daniel.'

Mr Thompson looks back at the receptionist with a frown.

'Daniel?' he asks curiously.

'That's right.' Beulah says, as I rummage in my handbag.

'I'm afraid we only have one manager here and that's Mr Thompson,' the receptionist explains.

'Well, who's Daniel, then?' Beulah asks.

'We don't have a Daniel here,' the manager replies, taken aback. 'Unless you mean Dan?'

'Well, he said to call him Daniel, but I noticed some of the other staff called him Dan,' I chip in. 'This is him.' I show him my phone. 'He was just helping us with our wedding enquiry. Said we had to decide straight away in order to get the discount.'

'And pay the deposit tonight,' Beulah adds.

Mr Thompson's eyes grow until they look like saucers as he stares at the photo. 'Would you mind coming into my office, ladies?' he requests, hurriedly.

For the first time in my life, I don't get that awful feeling of dread when I'm asked into the manager's office. In fact, I find it hard not to smile just a little...

9

Mr Thompson's office is much smaller than I imagined, but very plush and neat. He offers us each a comfy chair in front of his desk and asks for all the details of our visit.

'I see,' he says, gravely, when we've finished. 'And did you give him any money?'

'No,' I tell him. 'He wasn't able to confirm all the details and couldn't find a conference pack, so he said we had until tomorrow evening to pay instead.'

'I see.' Mr Thompson nods.

'Well, I'm sorry to inform you, ladies, that Dan Renfrew isn't the hotel manager, as I'm sure you've already guessed. He's actually one of the porters here, who was being trained to help work on Reception during our busier times. Tonight, we have a special event, so all the catering staff were asked to come in a little later, and as we had no residents to check in, I thought it was an ideal opportunity to give him a little practice on the front desk while it was quiet.'

'A porter?' I say with a nod. I knew he wasn't the manager as he didn't know enough about the hotel. 'So, was he trying to con us out of the deposit?'

'I think we'll let the police decide on that one,' Mr Thompson suggests, reaching for the phone. 'Would you mind waiting just a little longer while they take statements from you?'

Beulah and I glance across at each other. I suppose it hadn't occurred to me that it was a criminal matter, but if he'd taken our money it would have been theft.

'Of course.' Beulah answers for both of us.

While we wait in his office, Mr Thompson organises coffee and biscuits for us.

Fortunately, the police don't take long to arrive. I don't recognise either of the officers who come to take our statements, so at least James won't have to hear about it. Not that I've done anything wrong, of course. *I don't think I have, anyway.*

We reiterate our story and give them our details, while Mr Thompson explains who Dan is and why he was there.

'Tyler was a friend of his,' I tell them. 'He was going to be given mate's rates, I think.'

Mr Thompson snorts while the police write it down. I call Fran to get Tyler's phone number and address, and leave the details with the police.

'Will he be arrested?' I ask.

'We'll certainly go and pick him up for questioning,' the policewoman says, 'along with Daniel Renfrew, of course.'

'Will you have to tell them it was us who told you?' I enquire, suddenly fearing repercussions. 'I mean, we only came back to ask a question about the menus, not get anyone into trouble.' *Okay, I might have been fibbing just a little bit—it's not as if the thought hadn't crossed my mind—but these guys don't need to know that.*

'We don't have to tell them anything,' she assures me. 'As far as anyone knows, Mr Thompson could have picked up the hotel's CCTV footage and reviewed it.' She smiles. 'You don't have to worry.'

We leave a short while later, relieved that it's all over but thankful that the guys will get their comeuppance. Mr Thompson even handed me a copy of their wedding brochure, in case Fran decided to book here, after all—at a discount, of course. *I know Fran was naïve to believe Tyler, but she's not completely mad!*

'If they were in this together, and insisting on an immediate down payment, they must have been planning to con Fran out of her money,' I say, as we walk back to Sloane Square.

'And if we'd been stupid enough to pay her half tonight, we'd have been the ones to lose out,' Beulah replies, wide-eyed. 'The cunning bastard!'

'That's why Tyler was so insistent about it all, and so pissed off that we didn't cough up,' I say, shaking my head.

'So, how far do you think it would've gone?' Beulah asks as we arrive at the Tube station. 'Would he have tried to get *all* the money out of Fran, d'you think?'

'I wouldn't put it past him,' I reply, as we step onto the train. It's nearly eight o'clock so it's fairly quiet and we manage to get a couple of seats, for a change.

'We'll have to Facetime her when we get back,' Beulah, says, 'Tell her everything.'

'That Tyler's a plausible rogue,' I muse. 'You can't blame her for being taken in by him.'

'Yeah, and she's way too nice for her own good,' Beulah says with a sigh. 'She didn't want to hurt his feeling by calling it off, and because of that, she could've fallen for his tricks hook, line, and sinker.' She shakes her head.

'Well, at least we know now why he got her drunk and then made up that rubbish about her being pregnant,' I say, trying to look on the bright side. 'She doesn't have anything to feel guilty about.'

I pick up the evening newspaper on my way home and arrive to an empty flat. Cassie was going to stay in with me tonight, but when I was delayed, she decided to go out for a drink with Perdita and some of the other girls from work. I can't blame her. I certainly expected to be back earlier, but now it's getting late and I haven't had dinner.

I plonk my things on the kitchen counter and flick on the kettle before scooting into the bedroom. I quickly undress and put on my funky pj's with the slogan 'Llamas in Pyjamas' and—you've guessed it—little llamas all over them. James bought them for me while I was in hospital and they're so comfy.

I haven't texted James for a while, so I send him a quick message.

Hi J, just got home. Went out with Beulah after work and we were a bit longer than I expected. Hope you're having a nice evening xx

I'm really missing him at the moment, but he had to see Alex, another detective sergeant, tonight about the thefts they're looking into, so I'd declined an invitation. I'd have been bored stiff with them talking about work all night, although Alex can be good fun. They're a pair of workaholics, though, which is probably why they team up so well.

I return to the kitchen and whip up a quick ham sandwich to go with my tea, and head back into the bedroom to Skype the girls.

Poor Fran looks utterly shocked when Beulah blurts out the evening's events.

'I don't know what to say,' she confesses, almost in a whisper.

'I can think of a few words,' Beulah retorts, bluntly.

'She means to us, not to that scumbag,' I cut in quickly.

'So, he's been arrested?' Fran queries with a frown.

'Well, taken in for questioning, anyway,' I explain, calmly. 'The police have to ascertain what his involvement was before they can decide what to do with him.'

'I know what I'd like to do with him,' Beulah pipes up.

'Hopefully, you won't have to worry about him anymore,' I tell Fran. 'He'll know his plan hasn't worked and probably leave you alone now.'

'Yeah, he'll go and look for another mug to con out of her hard-earned cash,' Beulah grumbles. She must have noticed Fran's hurt expression as she quickly adds, 'Not that *you're* a mug, or anything.'

I roll my eyes and take another bite of my sandwich. Beulah's a lovely girl, but tact isn't exactly her strong point. *And I thought I was bad!*

'You should've seen his face when we told him you had four hundred people coming to the evening do,' I tell Fran, hoping to lighten the mood a little.

'And you said she had all those big brothers,' Beulah adds. 'We had him quaking in his shoes, Fran.'

Fran opens her eyes wide, shaking her head. 'And he *believed* all that?'

'That, and the fact that all the girls in the office were your bridesmaids,' I tell her with a giggle.

'As well as your uni chums,' Beulah chimes in.

'You must have really scared him off,' Fran says laughing. It's the most relaxed she's looked for ages.

'That was the idea,' I admit. 'The rest was just a bonus.'

'You guys are the absolute best,' Fran says with a smile. 'I had no idea how I was going to get out of it. Thanks so much.'

'Totally our pleasure,' I assure her.

'Yeah, I haven't had so much fun in ages.' Beulah giggles. 'It's never a dull moment with you, Libby.

'Not intentionally,' I assure her. 'These things just sort of... happen.'

'Well, I can't thank you enough,' Fran says. 'Honestly, I was losing sleep over the whole thing. I knew he was up to something, but I couldn't for the life of me fathom what.'

'Well, I think we'll all sleep easier tonight,' I tell her with a smile.

***

I was absolutely right. I must have been exhausted after all the excitement because I slept like a log, not stirring until the alarm yelled at me the following morning. *Well, it's a ring, actually, but when you're fast asleep it sounds like a yell. To me, anyway.*

Cassie's already in the kitchen when I go in for breakfast.

'Did you have a good time last night?' I ask, smiling. 'How's Perdita?'

She grins back, handing me a cup of coffee. 'Yeah, it was really good. Everyone's so much happier now that things have settled down at work. Perdita's actually great fun when you get to know her.'

'That's a relief,' I say, burning my fingers on the toaster. 'Ouch!'

Cassie rolls her eyes and comes over to inspect the damage as I wave my hand in the air, trying to cool the offending digit.

'Stick it under the tap,' she says, turning it on.

It feels much better after a minute or two and I resume my toast making.

'You don't need the Marc Jacobs today, do you?' she asks, emptying the Gucci clutch she must have used last night.

'No, I'm using the navy Radley,' I tell her, with a mouth half-full of toast.

She goes over to where I left the handbag on the counter last night.

'May I?' She asks, picking it up.

I nod, my mouth full of tea, this time.

She pulls out my purse and keys and replaces them with her own.

'Thanks,' she says.

'It's yours, anyway,' I remind her.

'Ours.' she winks. 'I've got to get out of here,' she says, slinging the Marc Jacobs over her shoulder.

'Will you be home tonight? Only, I'm not sure if James has planned anything.'

'Yeah. I was hoping we could have a takeaway and a catch-up,' she replies. 'Providing James hasn't got any other ideas, of course.'

My eyes narrow slightly as I try to detect a hint of sarcasm in this, but Cassie's giving nothing away. I give her the benefit of the doubt.

'Well, he could always join us,' I suggest. 'Rob, too. We haven't played Monopoly in ages—how about it?' The idea came to me in a flash, after seeing her look of disappointment at the thought of James taking me out.

She beams 'Great idea. We used to have a great time playing it at the hotel, remember when...' she glances at the kitchen clock. 'I've got to go,' she says hurriedly. 'But tonight—definitely.' She grins before rushing out the door.

It's time I was going, too, so I quickly wash my dishes and leave them to drain. After another swish of lippy, I throw my things into the Radley, grab my coat and head off.

My phone buzzes as I jump on the Tube.

Hey, Libby, you'll never guess what's happened☺

It's from Fran.

I'm standing, as usual, with one hand on the grab rail, the other holding my phone—the same as every other commuter on here.

*What????*I quickly text back, praying the miraculous signal lasts long enough for me to find out.

I get jostled by a well-dressed lady, whose massive handbag is digging into my side. She huffs, as though it's my fault. *Typical!*

When Fran doesn't answer right away, I get frustrated. Well, who wouldn't?

I'm desperate to know if she suffered any repercussions after last night. Would Tyler have contacted her? My stomach lurches. I hope he didn't twig it was Beulah and me who dobbed in his friend. No,

Fran put a smiley face at the end of her text. This was something good, so I quickly text Beulah.

Hey, babe, any idea what's happened with Fran? She's got news, apparently.

My signal drops off and I stand there, gripping the rail for dear life, impatiently willing the little bars at the top of the screen to appear again. After what feels like forever, my phone buzzes.

She's just texted me. Said she'll tell us at work. What do you reckon it is?

Hmm. Beulah's as much in the dark as I am.

She put a smiley on my text. Maybe they've slung them both in jail? ☺ I reply. We can but hope.

Ha! Let's hold that thought! Beulah adds a whole stream of laughing and funny-faced emojis, and I can't help but giggle.

The woman with the large bag gives me a strange look but I don't care.

I get off the Tube as quickly as I can and rush to the office. I'm disappointed to find that Fran hasn't arrived yet, but Beulah's waiting impatiently outside the lift.

'Have you heard anything else?' she asks as soon as I step out.

I shake my head. 'At least we know it's something good,' I tell her, sensing her frustration, which is much the same as mine.

'Yeah, but what? D'you think the cops've been in touch?

'I've no idea. I hoped she'd be here by now.' My stomach's got the jitters and I fiddle nervously with the strap of my Radley.

Kiki and Alice arrive and make straight for the office, but Beulah and I just hang around in the corridor. Eventually, there's another ping from the lift and Fran rushes out.

'I thought I was going to be late,' she gabbles. 'Is Valerie in yet?'

'Never mind that—spill!' Beulah rolls her eyes in frustration.

'Yes, well you'll never guess—'

'We've been guessing for the last half hour but we're still none the wiser,' I point out as we walk towards the office. 'What happened?'

'He's dumped me,' Fran announces.

We're just in the doorway of the office and the girls all stare as we walk in.

'You're kidding!' Kiki says, astonished.

'What a toad!' Alice looks sympathetic and walks over to us.

'You're well rid of him.' Brie points out.

'I know.' Fran beams, 'I couldn't believe my luck.'

I follow her and Beulah over to their workstation and the other girls gather round.

'What did he say?' My heart's pumping like a traction engine.

'He rang me late last night. He said he thinks we might have been rushing into everything and that it's clear from my friends that he and I want different things.' Fran looks up at me. 'He said he hadn't realised what my expectations would be, and he's afraid he can't live up to them. So, he can't see me again.' She giggles.

'What expectations?' Eva asks, frowning at me.

'But what about...' Beulah nods at Fran's stomach.

'Oh, he thinks he might have got the wrong end of the stick.'

We all burst out laughing.

'He can say that again,' Beulah blurts out.

'So, he hasn't admitted that he's been lying all along,' I point out scornfully.

'It doesn't matter,' Fran says, beaming. She looks much more relaxed and happier than she did yesterday, I'm pleased to notice. 'The fact is I don't have to worry about him anymore.'

'But if you didn't want to be with him why didn't you just say?' Izzy wrinkles her nose.

'It's not that easy.' Fran sighs. 'Not for me, anyway.'

'She's too nice,' Beulah explains. 'She didn't want to hurt his feelings.'

'But you didn't mind being dumped?' Izzy looks incredulous, not to mention entirely unimpressed.

'No, as long as it means the whole business is over and I don't have to see him again he can say what he wants,' Fran tells her.

'I don't get it.' Izzy shakes her head and struts back to her desk.

I give Fran a quick hug and she whispers 'thank you' in my ear.

As I get on with my next batch of letters, I feel as light as a feather. I'm so glad Fran's okay; and she can now put all that rubbish behind her. I'm still a little concerned about what happened when the police were called in to speak to Dan and Tyler, but I'm hoping that the fact that Tyler didn't mention any of it to Fran means that he hasn't made the connection with me and Beulah.

I'm surprised that Izzy's obviously perturbed about the whole thing, as she keeps huffing and slamming things down on her workstation. I'm trying to concentrate on Ms B. Masterton from Battersea, who is trying to put together an outfit for her grandson's christening on a small budget. She's sent me her measurements and it seems she's a plus-size lady who finds it hard to find clothes that flatter her shape. Being quite short, she has difficulty sourcing outfits that don't—in her words—drown her. I know that with the right colours and a few key accessories I can find her something that will make her look—and feel—a million dollars. She's sent me some photos of herself and her clothes, and I think I've got an idea of the sort of styles she favours. She already has some lovely nude-coloured court shoes that will go with anything, so she's definitely on the right track.

I flick through a few websites to get a feel for what's out there, but I can't see exactly what I'm looking for. I'm distracted when Izzy drops a bottle of blue nail varnish on the floor and swears like a sailor.

'That's all I need,' she grumbles, reaching for the acetone to clean it up.

I look over at Siobhan who rolls her eyes. Maybe I'm not the only one who's noticed Izzy's bad mood this morning.

'Let's take an early coffee break,' Siobhan suggests, getting up. 'I know I could do with one.'

There are mutters of agreement throughout the office, and we grab our bags.

'Ladies, can we just open the windows on our way out, please?' Siobhan calls out. 'Hopefully, the fumes will have dissipated by the time we get back.'

Izzy snorts, and I look over to see her scowling at Siobhan.

'Do you need any help?' I offer.

'Nope.' Her voice is curt, and I don't need telling twice.

I follow the others down the corridor, catching up with Fran and Beulah on the way.

'You're looking a lot better today,' I tell Fran. 'He really got to you, didn't he?'

She nods. 'I know I'm a bit stupid, but I didn't know what to say to him. I was afraid that if I came out and told him I wasn't interested it would hurt his feelings, and sometimes guys can get a bit funny when they feel rejected.'

It sounds like the voice of experience talking, so I just nod. 'You never know what people are capable of,' I agree.

'Yeah, look at Davinia Urquhart,' Beulah cuts in. 'Who'd have thought she really was insane?'

I swallow hard. It's something I try not to dwell on.

'Well, it's all okay now,' Fran says, cheerfully, giving my arm a squeeze. 'Honestly, thanks, girls. I don't know what I'd have done without you.'

'It's okay. It was actually quite fun,' Beulah admits.

'What was?' Alice asks, joining us as we sit down.

We spend our break explaining to the girls everything that happened, and they laugh at last night's antics.

'I might have known you'd be in the middle of it all, Libby,' Siobhan says, smiling as she shakes her head.

'It wasn't my fault,' I protest. 'I was just helping Fran out of a horrid situation.'

By the time we all return to the office, the air smells much more pleasant and we're all in high spirits having had such a good giggle. Izzy is the only exception. She didn't join us at the big table that we always commandeer, so she missed out on all the fun—though I've got the feeling she wouldn't have found it as funny as the rest of us, anyway.

'I'm going to head out,' I tell Siobhan. 'I need to look at some of the high street stores for this lady.' I hold up a photo of Ms B. Masterton.
'Okay.' She nods with a smile. 'Just don't get into any trouble while you're away.' She chuckles, and I smile back. *I don't know where she gets her ideas, but I'm certainly not one for getting into scrapes, am I?*

It's really busy in town and I have to fight my way through the pre-Christmas crowds to get to where I'm going. There are loads of lovely clothes out there for larger ladies, and I'm determined to find something just perfect for Ms B. Masterton. I want a dress that will skim her figure, as she sounds quite self-conscious about it. I'm looking for a colour that will bring out the blue of her eyes, too. They're one of her best features, though she doesn't seem to realise it, judging by her letter. She really is a beautiful woman, and with the right outfit she could look absolutely stunning.

I pop into a few shops and peruse their ranges. There are some gorgeous dresses, but not quite what I've got in mind for MsMasterton. As I'm wandering down the street, I become aware of a kerfuffle outside one of the shops.

A policeman rushes past me to help a security guard who is having trouble restraining a woman who is carrying a large shopping bag.

'Leave her alone,' a younger guy is yelling at them. 'She hasn't done anything.'

My face starts to burn as I recognise his snarly voice. Then I get a better view of the woman and realise she's familiar, too.

'You, bitch!' Oh, no, the guy's just clocked me and is coming over.

I quickly try to change direction but it's impossible on such a crowded pavement. As I turn, I bump into an old lady.

'I'm sorry.' I can't get past her and I'm jostled by the crowd.

'It was you, you little snitch!' The guy catches up with me and pulls at my arm.

'Who—who are you?' I try to act dumb. For once it doesn't work.

'You know full well who I am—I'm your worst nightmare,' he hisses at me.

It's the thug who tried to threaten me when I saw his girlfriend shoplifting the other day.

'I didn't do anything,' I protest, wishing someone would stop and help me. The London crowds just tut as they walk around us and carry on with their business. Even the copper's too busy arresting that woman to notice what's going on with me. The guy's grip is strong, and I can't get away from him.

'You dobbed her in, didn't you? Got an innocent woman arrested. You spiteful cow!' He snarls at me, his face contorting to an ugly sneer—not that it was handsome to start with, mind you.

'No. I wasn't even there.' My stomach churns with panic.

A police car whizzes down the road and the policeman helps the woman into the back seat.

'Great. They've arrested her.' The guy sounds vicious. 'I hope you're happy now. Are you some kind of undercover store detective?'

His fingers dig into my arm.

'No. I'm just an agony aunt for the *Chronicle*. I write articles about fashion.' My voice is trembling. I added the last bit quickly, in case he thought I was a reporter or something.

His eyes narrow. 'I know you,' he says, accusingly.

I always wanted to be famous, but I've just gone off the idea, if this is what it's like to be recognised in the street.

'I doubt it. I've only just started in the job.' I hope he doesn't think I'm Davinia Urquhart. *Heaven forbid.*

'You advise women to go out and buy designer clothes and stuff. *You're* the reason people like my girlfriend have to steal to try to keep up with everyone else. You make women think they have to own expensive clothes to look good. I wonder how many other girls have resorted to crime because of you.' His crooked teeth are gritted as he spits the words out.

I feel sick. I've only answered a couple of letters so far, and while I did pick out designer outfits for the women, it was only because it's what they wanted. Could I possibly be making people feel inadequate and that they need to steal to look good? Oh, God, I hate myself.

'Well, you'll pay for what you've put my girlfriend and me through, bitch. I don't know what the price of freedom is, but as you've had her arrested and probably slung in prison, I think we'll start at... say... £10,000. I want it by Friday.' He sneers at me.

'I haven't got it,' I tell him, my voice more high-pitched than normal.' He can't be serious! 'I don't have that sort of money.' I shake my head, trembling.

'Well then *find* it!' he barks. 'I want ten grand from you by nine o'clock on Friday night. We'll meet back here. And don't try anything. I know where you work, and I can easily find out where you live. You just come back here with the cash, got it?'

He shoves me and I hurtle into the crowd. Then he runs off, leaving me trembling and on the verge of tears.

'Are you okay?' A young woman asks.

I nod. Luckily the crowd was too dense to let me fall over, so I just bashed into several people, eliciting a few expletives and tuts from them but no actual harm done.

I make my way to Starbucks again—my go-to place after encounters with that thug, it seems—hoping a skinny hazelnut latte might calm my nerves. Luckily, I manage to get the little table in the far corner that I had last time. I plonk myself down and put my head in my hands. I want to cry. To just bawl my eyes out. But I can't. Not here. Instead, I close my eyes and take deep breaths.

My mind's whirling. How can I get hold of ten thousand quid in less than a week? I've got no savings and my credit cards are maxed out. I can't possibly ask Cassie to lend it to me—besides, then I'd have to tell her what it's for. And why should I give him ten grand anyway? The more I think about it, the more annoyed I'm getting about the whole thing. I do feel kind of bad about the woman being arrested, but I don't see how it's *my* fault that she's got herself into this situation. I'm only doing my job, but…oh, God, what if it really does make people feel inadequate if they can't afford expensive clothes? Am I making women become that desperate? But MsB.Masterton is on a limited budget, so my next article will be about looking good without breaking the bank. Perhaps I should see if the *Chronicle* could run a feature on the subject—sort of shopping on a budget kind of thing? I'm not sure if Valerie would go for it, but it's worth a try.

I take a sip of my latte, starting to feel a little better. That thug's face is still haunting me, though, and a thought strikes me—haven't I seen him somewhere before? Not the last time he threatened me, but somewhere else? I trawl the cobwebbed corners of my memory, but I can't place him for love nor money. I'm *sure* I've seen him before,though.

My phone pings and I almost leap out of my skin. I fish it out of my bag. It's James.

Hey, sweetheart, how about coming over tonight?xx

Now there's an offer I can't refuse!

I'd love to xx

A night with my gorgeous boyfriend might be just what I need to get my mind off all this. James always has a good way of distracting me, if you know what I mean.

Great. Come whenever you're ready. I'll be home about 4 xx

Can't wait!xx

It's great to have something to look forward to, and I do love spending time with James. I really want to move in with him, but I just can't leave Cassie in the lurch. It wouldn't be fair on her. I just hope he doesn't bring the subject up again, as I feel so guilty about the whole thing.

I finish my coffee and offer up a quick prayer to the Goddess of Sales and Reductions before leaving the coffee shop and resuming my shopping trip. The goddess is clearly smiling on me today, as the very next shop I enter has just what I'm looking for.

I pick out a gorgeous, royal blue dress with a fitted bodice, which flows gently over the waist and hips. There's also a little nude-coloured bag with a chain strap that can be worn over the shoulder or just as a clutch, which will go beautifully with Ms B.Masterton's shoes while giving a soft contrast to the dress. And just to add icing to the cake, both items have thirty percent off. I take photos on my phone and jot down the details before heading back towards the office.

I check the time. Lunchtime will be half over by the time I get there. My stomach heaves. More expense. I pull out my phone and send a quick text.

Hi, Fran. I'm going to be tied up in town for a while so won't make it back in time for lunch. I'll grab something here. See you later. Lx

I nip into a small supermarket and buy a pre-prepared sandwich and a bottle of water, which I'll have on a park bench on my way back. I know I'll never be able to save £10,000, but if I can just scrape a little bit of money together it might help. I dread to think what that thug's got in mind for me when I don't come up with the full amount. I shudder, trying to shake the thought from my brain.

I walk back to the office to save money on the taxi fare. I really wish I hadn't bothered, though, when I arrive sticky with sweat and my feet aching like mad. As soon as I get back, I dive into the ladies', kick off my Louboutins, have a quick wash and touch up my make-up. My face is really flushed, and I'm not sure if it's the exercise that's caused it or worrying about the guy's threat.

I momentarily consider telling James about what's happened—he's a copper, after all. I mean, what's the worst that could happen? I'd have to explain the whole thing, though. About seeing the woman in the first place. No doubt, James will say I should've reported her for shoplifting. But she looked so desperate. I couldn't make things even worse for her, could I? Mind you, now she's been arrested anyway, so maybe I was just delaying the inevitable.

She shouldn't have been placed in that position in the first place, though. A vision of the thug's vicious face pops into my mind. He's the one to blame in all this, and instead he's the one walking free, making threats to *me*. He deserves to be locked up—and then I wouldn't have to worry about him, and that poor woman would be free of him, too.

I could just imagine James' face if I told him what I've got myself involved in. He'd be so disappointed. He trusts me to keep my nose clean. Oh, gosh, what if he broke up with me? He might think I don't care about him enough to stop getting mixed up in this kind of thing—not that it's my fault, or anything. I can't believe how these things just keep happening to me. I mean, it's not like I go out of my way to find trouble, is it? It just sort of... finds me.

I quickly rethink. James is obviously already miffed that I didn't move in with him as soon as we got back from Broadstairs, I don't want to give him any more reason to dump me. I'll just have to sort this out myself, without worrying him.

That thug's a piece of work, though. If he's desperate there's no telling what he might be capable of. Trouble is, what's going to happen when I turn up without the money? It's Tuesday today—I haven't got long. Dread grips my stomach.

My phone pings, scaring me half to death. It's Cassie.

Still on for tonight? Rob and Ben are coming over; it should be fun! xx

Damn—I'd forgotten all about our plans for tonight.I'm not sure how James will take it if I turn him down now. But what about Cassie? How can I let her down? She was really looking forward to this.

James has asked me to go to his. Shall I put him off? xx

I know it's the coward's way out, putting the ball in her court, but I don't know what to say. How could I have been so distracted that I forgot about Cassie when James asked me? I'm such a rotten friend.

Another ping on my phone, and I hold my breath while I force myself to look at the screen.

No, it's fine. We can do it another time. Have a great night with James xx

I should relax but I feel horrible. What happened to 'mates before dates'? Actually, if I didn't go to James' tonight it would save me the fare, so maybe I should cancel him instead? I feel a twinge inside me. I really do want to see him, though. Why is life so complicated?

***

By the time I get to James' flat that evening I'm feeling a lot more relaxed. Cassie was absolutely fine about me putting her and the boys off and said they were going to go for a drink instead. She really is the best.

James is waiting for me with a glass of wine and a broad smile that makes me melt as soon as I walk in through his front door. He's got that white Ralph Lauren shirt on that I love, and his little chest hairs are just poking through the opened buttons, daring me to reach out and stroke them. I refrain—for now.

'Dinner's almost ready,' he says, leading me into the living room. Well, it's a living room/diner, actually. There's a small table and two chairs by the window. 'Take a seat, I won't be a minute.'

I smile at him, taking a sip of wine before sitting at the table. James is a brilliant cook.

'How's work?' I ask a few moments later, while we tuck into filet steak with all the trimmings.

'The usual,' he says with a grimace. 'We've got the seasonal shoplifters on every street at the moment, keeping us busy.'

My stomach sinks at the word 'shoplifter'.

'Do you arrest many?' I ask, a little warily.

'Yeah. They don't seem to realise we've got cameras everywhere.' He looks as delicious as the meal.

'What happens then? Do they go to jail?' I ask, taking a large gulp of my wine.

'Sometimes,' he says, matter-of-factly. 'It just depends on the severity of the crime and their past form.'

'So, if someone gets caught for their first time, do they go free?' My heart's in my mouth as a vision of that poor, desperate woman flits into my mind.

'If they are arrested and placed in custody it's a case of whether we or the store want to prosecute,' he says. 'Sometimes, if the goods aren't worth much and the store doesn't want the additional hassle, we can just give them a caution, and probably a fine. Of course, it still goes on their criminal record, and they'll probably be banned from the shop and possibly several more once word gets around.'

'Oh.'

'If either we or the store *do* prosecute, they go to court and if found guilty, can get a jail sentence as well as a hefty fine.'

'For just doing it once?' I gasp.

He raises his eyebrows. 'It depends on the circumstances, and more importantly, how much the goods are worth. Anything under two hundred quid can get you up to six months—more than that and you're talking up to seven years. It's something we take very seriously.'

I nod, my mind whirling. I can't exactly ask about what happened to that woman, or James will want to know of my involvement, and I can't tell him. If I admitted that I'd seen her taking something a day or two before she got arrested it might make things ten times worse for her, especially if she's claiming that today was her first time. I could get her sent to jail!

James narrows his eyes as he peers at me. Then he leans forwards. 'You're not contemplating a life of crime, are you?'

I gasp, then realise he's joking.

'Of course, not. I was just interested in your work that's all.' I shrug and smile at him, but I can't hide the way my face suddenly heats up. I look away and take a large swig of my wine to try to cool myself down a little.

I'm not sure if I've convinced him, as he's still watching me closely.

'So, how's your job going?' he asks after a few agonising moments.

'Great. I'm advising people on what to buy for different occasions,' I say, glad of the change of subject.

'So, I'm guessing this takes lots of research then, to see what's in fashion?' He gives a knowing smile.

'Of course.'

'And do you always recommend the most expensive, designer outfits?' He smirks.

'No!' It comes out a bit louder and more defensively than I intended.

He raises his eyebrows in surprise.

'In fact, the last outfit I recommended was from a high street shop, *and* in the sale, for a lady on a limited budget,' I point out.

'Really?' He sounds impressed but still looks bemused.

'Yes. Not everyone who reads the *Chronicle* can afford designer clothes, you know. Some wouldn't want them, anyway.'

'You must find it hard to identify with those people.' He chuckles. 'I mean, it's not as if you can just think about what *you'd* wear for an occasion, is it? And I'll bet it's not half as much fun finding lower-priced items for them.'

I gasp. 'I'm not that shallow, thank you.' I say, pointedly. 'I can do fashion on a budget if I want to. In fact, I'm thinking of asking Siobhan if we can do a feature on it for the supplement. I think it would be very useful for a lot of our readers, especially with Christmas coming up.'

His face straightens and he nods. 'Well, I think that's a very good idea,' he says, standing to stack the plates. 'Well done for coming up with it.'

He actually looks impressed and has stopped smirking at me now. I don't know why he thinks all I care about is designer clothes and spending lots of money. Actually, I'm quite offended by his attitude. I can be thrifty if I want to be. In fact, I'll show him...

11

James gives me a lift to work the following day, as we both got up a little later than we should have.

'I could get used to this,' I say with a smile as I sit in his nice, warm car, listening to the radio.

'Once you move in, I can take you to work more often, depending on my shifts,' he says, giving me a sideways glance. 'That should make life a little easier for you, won't it?'

'Yes. I'll look forward to that.' I try to sound airy, but I know what he's alluding to. We managed to make it through all last night without the subject coming up, and I certainly don't want to get into it right now.

'Have you spoken to Cassie about moving out, yet?' *And there it is.*

'Not exactly. She's been a bit... sort of... clingy lately. I think it's because of what happened with Davinia and all that. She feels a bit protective of me, likes having me around. You do understand, don't you, James?'

'No,' he says bluntly. 'I'd have thought she'd be pleased to have the opportunity to move her own boyfriend in, to be honest. They seemed very close when we were in Broadstairs. And you're not moving a million miles away, are you? You'll still see each other whenever you want.'

I sigh. That wasn't the answer I was hoping for, but I suppose I can see his point.

'I'll talk to her about it soon,' I promise. 'By the way, do you like Monopoly?'

He frowns. I'm used to that. I see a lot of frowning, though I don't really know why.

'I haven't played it in years,' he admits, 'but I used to be quite good at it. Why do you ask?'

'Cassie was thinking we could all have a game sometime,' I say.

'Okay.'

He looks bemused. *I see that a lot, too.*

Luckily, we arrive outside the office building, so I grab my bag. It's a red Louis Vuitton with a cute little padlock on the front. One that Cassie got tired of, but I love it. It matches my lipstick, too. The bag's the only designer item I'm wearing today, believe it or not. I'm in a smart, black suit with a red and white merino jumper, all from Next. My shoes are plain black courts from New Look, but they look as good as a designer pair from a distance. It's all part of my plan.

'Will I see you tonight?' James leans over for a kiss.

His lips are so soft and warm, I could snog him all day. And night. Especially night. In fact that's why we were late getting up today, but we won't go into that.

'Yes.' My voice is breathless. 'I'll ring you later, see what's happening.'

'I'll look forward to it,' he says with a grin, watching me climb out of his car. It's an old Ford Focus, but James likes it.

'Me too.' I'm not sure if he's referring to the phone call or tonight, but whatever it is, I'm right there with him.

I arrive at the office with a huge grin on my face.

'You lucky girl!' Brie walks over from the window and I realise they've all been watching me say goodbye to James. *Damn!*

I can't stop smiling though. Even Izzy's rolling eyes don't get to me today.

'We're only jealous, of course,' Beulah assures me, giggling.

'Well, what can I say?' I giggle too, making my way over to my desk.

'Doesn't he have a brother or anything?' Eva asks, returning to her workstation. 'Preferably an identical twin?'

Everyone chuckles.

It occurs to me that James hasn't told me a lot about his family. He's an only child, I know that much, and he only speaks to his parents occasionally. I really need to get to know them—after all, he's met my folks as well as my brothers.

'How are you getting on with those letters?' Siobhan asks me, gesturing to the pile on my desk.

'Great. In fact, I wanted to ask you about something.'

'Of course.'

'Well, I've just been working on an outfit for this lady, Ms B Masterton,' I explain, showing her the letter and photo of the woman. 'She's on a strict budget, so I've chosen her a really nice dress that she can wear with the shoes she already has in her wardrobe. Anyway, I was thinking—with Christmas just around the corner and everything—there must be other people in her position who can't afford to spend too much on themselves. So, I wondered if we could do a feature for the supplement about it? You know, fashion on a shoestring, sort of thing? We could promote some of the high street fashions for people who don't have the money for designer outfits. Maybe, do an article on party wear too, to tie it in with the season. What do you think?'

'You know what. I think that's a great idea, Libby.' She looks thoughtful. 'We'll have to run it by Valerie, of course, but I think it would be brilliant. We could source affordable make-up, hair, and nail products, and the girls could feature one of our less expensive clothing lines. I'm sure Valerie won't mind if we change things round a bit.' She beams at me. 'Well done, I think that's awesome.'

'It might show our readers that we don't just cater for people who can afford high-end fashions, too,' I say. 'Make us appear more empathic with the whole community.'

'I just love how your mind works,' she says, with a chuckle. 'It's fantastic.'

No one's ever said that to me before. In fact, most people think my brain works in a really strange way— but they should try living with it!

'Come on, I think Valerie's free now,' she goes on, and I notice the blinds being rolled up in the corner office.

I follow her, still carrying the letter, and soon we're all sitting around Valerie's large desk, drinking coffee.

'I'm not sure,' Valerie says frowning. *I must mention Botox to her some time.* 'You see, my idea was that the supplement would be more upmarket now that we've got a glossy new cover and everything. I don't want to confuse the brand.'

'But, as part of the *Chronicle,* shouldn't it be for everyone?' I suggest. 'I mean, we won't cheapen it just by featuring a few high street brands. Some of them are just as lovely as the expensive, designer clothes we put out, and it shows we're in tune with our readership.'

'Libby's right, Valerie,' Siobhan says with a nod. 'We live in a very diverse area and our magazine should reflect that.'

'And the thing is this letter's from one of our readers,' I point out, holding it up to show her. 'This proves that we're writing for a whole range of people in different circumstances. We need to listen to them to find out what they want from us. If we concentrated solely on designer wear, then it's only going to alienate a good number of our readers. We need to relate to everyone if we want them to keep buying the paper, surely?'

Siobhan nods.

'You're right,' Valerie concedes with a smile. 'We have to listen to people.'

'We'll still do it with class though,' I add quickly. 'No one wants to undermine the magazine's brand in any way.'

'Thank you, Liberty.' I get the impression her gratitude is for more than just a good idea. I've probably reminded her of a conversation we had in hospital about paying more attention to the people around us. I'm glad she hasn't forgotten.

'So, is it a goer?' Siobhan asks with a smile.

'I'll just need to make a few calls, but I don't see why not,' Valerie says, reaching for her phone.

'Great. We'll leave it with you then. Thanks, Valerie.' Siobhan gets up.

I want to hug Valerie right now, but I daren't. Especially as all the blinds are up. I just thank her and follow Siobhan out of the room.

***

To be honest, I thought the rest of the team would be just as excited as me about the new feature. Clearly not.

'You're joking. What was the point of revamping the whole magazine just to go down the cheaper route?' I knew Izzy would be the first to find fault.

'We're trying to give the readers what they want,' Siobhan explains. 'Libby's had some letters asking for more affordable outfits, so we thought it prudent to listen to what the customers want.'

'And we're not talking cheap,' I point out. 'Just not mega-expensive designer gear, that's all.'

'I might have known *you'd* be behind the whole thing.' Izzy sneers.

I flinch at her attack. 'What's *that* supposed to mean?' I didn't mean to sound so demanding, but I really do feel indignant about her remark.

161

'You just always change everything.' Izzy shakes her head dismissively. 'Or get Valerie to.'

I really don't like her tone and I'm about to tell her so when Siobhan interrupts.

'Okay, ladies, this is getting us nowhere. The fact is, Valerie wants it done, so let's do as we're asked, shall we? You'll all need to research high street brands for your particular section and check your upcoming features so you can tie them in where you can.'

'Oddly enough, I don't have any upcoming features for cheap nail products,' Izzy grumbles. 'So, it looks like I'll be spending all day looking for some. Thanks for nothing.'

'It's what we're getting paid for, isn't it?' I point out, a little louder than I intended.

'I was doing the job I'm paid for right up until we were told to change everything,' Izzy tells me coldly. 'Now, I've just got additional work to do, which I won't be getting extra pay for, will I?'

'Isobella, could I have a word, please?'

We all jerk around to see Valerie standing in the doorway to her office. Her face is tight, and her lips reduced to a thin line. I know that look. Thank goodness I'm not the one being summoned for a change.

Izzy stands up with a huff and follows her into the office where the blinds are immediately drawn down.

'Any other questions?' Siobhan asks.

Everyone shakes their head and gets back to their work.

Siobhan gives me a tiny wink as we return to our end of the room.

I sort through my letters and pick another couple who want less expensive items and concentrate on those for the rest of the day. I'm really pleased about the feature and think it will show the readers just how much we listen to them. I only wish I could listen in on the conversation in Valerie's office right now. Valerie didn't look at all happy, and Izzy was clearly not used to being pulled up on her attitude. I knew she didn't like me much, but now I think she'll hate me. Oh well, I've dealt with worse...

***

Izzy doesn't speak to anyone for the rest of the day, and doesn't join us for lunch, either.

My phone pings as I'm part-way through my vegetable soup—the cheapest item on the menu and not completely terrible, I'm relieved to discover.

Hey Libby, how about that game of Monopoly tonight? The boys are coming over xx

It's Cassie.

Great. Can I invite James? xx

'Of course. It'll be nice to see him. Is everything okay with you two? Is he looking after you all right? Xx

I roll my eyes. Bless Cassie. She does worry about me still, even though I've tried to convince her that I'm fine now.

Yes, everything's great with James. I'll tell him about 7pm if that's okay? xx

Fab. I'll pick up some snacks on my way home xx

I'm really looking forward to it. It'll be good to see James let his hair down a little with some trivial fun. Not that I'm complaining about the kind of fun we had last night, mind you.

'Everything okay?' Fran asks.

'Yeah. Just Cassie asking about tonight. How are things with you now?'

'I haven't heard from Tyler,' she tells me with a grin. 'You certainly managed to scare him off, all right.'

'Yeah, I have that effect on people,' I say with giggle.

'True. She's terrifying,' Beulah concurs.

'I can't believe I was taken in by him.' Fran shakes her head, making her lovely red curls dance around her shoulders.

'You're just too nice,' Beulah says.

'You don't have that problem, do you, Beulah?' I tease, and we all laugh.

'I just say it how it is,' she says, shrugging.

'I still can't get over the fact that I might have lost all my money just by not wanting to hurt his feelings,' Fran says, incredulously. 'How stupid does that make me?'

'*You're* not the stupid one,' I tell her. '*He's* the one who thought he'd get away with it. Fancy thinking he could scam you out of your hard-earned cash to pay for your own wedding. He's the one who needs his head looking at.'

'Yeah, but I was just too weak to stick up for myself,' Fran says, frowning.

'You're not weak, you're just too nice, like I said,' Beulah points out. 'You need to toughen up a bit and think about number one for a change. Go for what you want, not what makes everyone else happy.'

I nod in agreement, letting her words sink in. I hate to say it, but Beulah's got a good point there. Maybe it's time I took a leaf out of her book...

12

I've been really looking forward to playing Monopoly with James and the boys this evening. I know it's not very cool, but I love a good board game, especially with Cassie—she has this knack where she can make just about anything fun. She's got more than enough nibbles for us, including crisps and dip, nuts, all manner of titbits in plastic bowls, as well as what looks like half of Iceland's finger-food aisle. Luckily, there's some salad too, so I shouldn't be tempted to eat too much junk food. I've lost over a stone in the last few months and have no intention of putting it back on now.

She pulls out the game as soon as everyone arrives, and we all dive in. It's the original game with metal tokens, and has been in her family for years, apparently.

'Bagsy the boot,' I say, snatching out the little silver token. My mind immediately flits back to the black suede Saint Laurent's I'm saving up for.

'No surprise there, then,' Ben says, rolling his eyes. 'I'm having the car.'

'Can I have the dog?' Cassie pipes up, unfolding the board onto the dining table.

'What would you like, James?' Rob asks.

'Any.' He doesn't look half as excited as the rest of us as we choose our playing pieces.

'You can have the top hat then. I'll have the ship.' Rob takes them out and places them all on the 'Go' square.

'I'm being banker,' Ben insists.

'You usually are,' Rob says with a snigger.

Ben throws him a harsh look.

Rob feigns surprise. 'Oh, *banker*,' he says, as Ben starts sorting the money. 'Sorry, I thought you said something else.'

'Yeah, I'll bet you did,' Ben says with a scowl.

The rest of us burst out laughing, including James.

The game's great fun, with everyone getting more competitive as we go along. Rob insists on consulting the rules every time something is queried, and I realise I've been playing it wrongly for years.

James manages to get hotels on Mayfair and Park Lane—he's not so frugal when he's playing—and I somehow manage to get lots of different coloured streets but nothing in a line. Why I buy the Electric Company

I'll never know, as it's so hard to figure out what everyone owes me, especially after a few drinks.

'Are you sure you should be having that?' Ben asks when I reach for the wine for another top up.

'I haven't had *that* much,' I tell him, indignantly.

'I know but...'

'Oh, gosh. I hadn't thought.' Cassie looks panic-stricken. 'I'll get you some water, Libby. See if it will dilute it a bit in your stomach.' She whizzes off and returns with a pint glass full of tap water.

I frown at it. 'I *can* hold my drink, you know, guys?' I wonder just what they're trying to insinuate about me.

James frowns. 'Have you got a problem I don't know about?' he asks, with a bemused expression.

'No.' I say it more forcefully than I intended, which makes me wonder if maybe I have had a bit too much to drink, after all.

Ben and Rob exchange a glance that I don't like the look of, and Cassie bites her lip. I take the glass and glug down some cold water, just to keep them happy. It's not half as nice as the wine, and I wish Ben had kept his mouth shut. I'm sure I don't have a drinking problem—besides, he and Rob are always downing pints of beer and no one says anything to them. I wonder if he's just trying to embarrass me in front of James, yet I can't think why he would. I thought Ben and I were friends.

We resume the game a little quieter than we were. It's not that I'm boisterous when I've been drinking, or anything, it's just that now I don't feel quite so cheerful. Maybe, if I'd been allowed more wine it would have been different.

I get up for the loo after a while—I blame all the water—and Ben pulls his seat back to help me out. He's sitting next to me, with James on my other side, so I find it odd that it's him and not my boyfriend who makes a fuss—although I didn't really expect anyone to.

'Can you manage?' Ben asks, concern etched in his face.

'Yes, thanks.' I realise then that he must still think I'm fragile after all that business with Davinia and the burning building. It's been weeks since I got out of hospital, and I've even been on holiday since then, but he still clearly worries about me. I feel mean now for being so annoyed at him over the drink business. He's only looking out for me. And he must think I'm still on medication and unable to drink much. It's kind of sweet but completely unnecessary.

I return to the table feeling much happier and sit back down. Everyone's tucking into pizza, so I have a small slice.

'I'm winning,' Ben announces, looking at the stack of notes in front of him.

'Funny how you're also the banker,' Rob quips.

'*What* did you call me?' Ben snaps.

We all laugh again, except Ben, who I think might have actually thought Rob had insulted him.

'Anyone want another piece?' Cassie asks, changing the subject as she holds up the pizza plate.

'I will,' Ben says, suddenly cheering up again. It's odd how food has that effect on him.

We resume the game, which looks like it's going to last all night.

'I need to go soon,' James says, glancing at his watch.

Instinctively, I put an arm around him. 'Do you have to?' I whine. 'Why don't you stay tonight? You can get the Tube from here in the morning.'

He cuddles me with a chuckle. 'I'm afraid I can't. I'm on the early shift tomorrow and I haven't got anything with me. Maybe another time.'

Cassie yawns, and I suddenly realise how selfish I'm being.

'What shall we do with the game?' I ask, looking around the table. 'Count up and finish or keep it going?' There were times when Cassie and I worked at the hotel that the staff would stay up until the early hours playing the game, and some games lasted for days.

'Well, I think it's obvious who the winner is,' Ben says, grinning.

'Okay, clever clogs. But let's see who came next, shall we?' Rob suggests, starting to count his money.

James came a close second, followed by Rob, Cassie, and then me. I'm sure I only lost because there were so many of us playing that I couldn't get all the good properties, after all, it's not like I'm useless with money or anything, is it? Still, it was great fun.

The guys all get up to go, and they each hug Cassie and me.

'You're looking good,' Ben murmurs in my ear. 'Just make sure you take care, okay?'

I pat his back. 'You don't have to worry about me, Ben. I'm fine, honestly.'

'You might be now, but it's only going to get harder,' he whispers. 'Just take it easy.'

I smile at him even though I'm unsure what he means. Maybe he had more to drink than I realised. I reach out to hug Rob next.

'Don't go overdoing it,' Rob mutters.

'I won't,' I promise.

James gives me the best hug of all, of course. And his kisses make me go weak at the knees.

'See you tomorrow,' he says, with a smile.

'Can't wait,' I assure him.

Cassie and I look at the mess after the boys have gone.

'Can it wait until the morning?' I ask, with a yawn.

'It's okay. I'll do it now,' she says. 'You get off to bed, you look shattered.'

'I can't leave you to do all the work,' I tell her, going to the kitchen for a couple of bin bags.

'Libby, honestly, I don't mind,' she says, gathering up the pieces of the game and putting them back in the box. 'You need your rest.'

I return and begin throwing the remains of the food into one of the bags and the beer cans in the other. We always use paper plates for this sort of thing so there's not much washing up to do at the end, as we invariably finish late.

'You lot are lovely, but I really am okay now,' I tell her, shaking my head. 'It's been ages since it all happened and I'm absolutely fine.'

'It's not just that…' she stops abruptly.

I frown at her, momentarily stopping my clearing up.

'What do you mean?'

'Everything *is* okay with you and James, isn't it?' she asks, cagily.

'Yes, of course. Why?'

She shrugs. 'Nothing.'

'Do you know something I don't?' I query. 'Has he said something?' My mind whirls. Have we been a bit distant lately? We only couldn't see each other last week while he was working on the late shift. It's always difficult with his hours, but we make up for it when he's on earlies, like tonight. Despite him having to get up at the crack of dawn the next morning.

'No.' She quickly puts everything away, and I resume my tidying. 'I just want to make sure you're happy, that's all.'

'Of course, I'm happy,' I tell her. 'Why wouldn't I be?'

'It's just that things change, don't they?' she says, straightening the chairs.

I wonder for one awful moment if she's got an inkling about me moving out. She doesn't look happy. Oh, no. I was afraid of this. She doesn't want me to leave and can see it's on the cards. What do I do? I can hardly tell her that her fears are well-founded and that's exactly what I'm planning. She'll be gutted. I can't do this to her. I go over and give her a hug.

'Nothing's going to change,' I assure her.

She gives me a half-smile.

'I'll just take the rubbish out,' I say, lifting the bags. 'We don't want the place reeking of pizza in the morning, do we?'

'No, I'll do it.' She grabs the bin bags from my hands. 'I told you. You need to get some rest. Besides, it's dark outside. You could trip or something.'

She's half-way to the door already and I don't have time to object.

'Thanks, Cass,' I say, smiling. I do wish she wouldn't worry so much about me.

I go to bed even more concerned about James. I miss him. I really wish he'd been able to stay over tonight but can see why he couldn't. Besides, he doesn't feel too comfy sleeping with me here. It's much more private at his place and I know he's always far more relaxed over there. I prefer it, too. Not that I've got anything against Cassie's, of course, it's just not the same. But how will I ever be able to move in with him with Cassie feeling like this? I just can't upset her—she's my best mate and she's been so good to me. It would be heartless and cruel to up sticks and leave her. Oh, God, why is life never easy?

***

I get up the following morning feeling confused. It was good of everyone to be so concerned about me last night, I suppose, although, in the cold light of day I find that it's annoyed me more than anything. Fancy stopping me from drinking! I am an adult, don't they get it? I know they're concerned about me after what happened with that evil woman, but I really am fine now. I don't know how I'll ever convince them. Hopefully, in time, they'll realise they don't need to fret anymore, and we can all get back to normal. Not that I don't like them showing concern, it's just not... natural.

I put on a navy trouser suit from Next with a white top I got in the Miss Selfridge sale. My hair looks quite good in a messy bun and I wear my nude-to-black Louboutin courts from Suzanne. I have a nude handbag that goes well with it all—I can't remember where I got it, but it looks designer even though it isn't.

I open the drawer for my lip gloss and notice the box with my boots savings. That familiar feeling of dread engulfs me for a minute, and I hadn't forgotten that tomorrow is D-Day. That thug wants his money and there's no way I can get it. I quickly tot up the notes. There's sixty-five pounds. The change amounts to the princely sum of thirty-seven pence. Not nearly enough for the boots, let alone that thieving scumbag.

'Libby, I'm off.' Cassie shouts, cutting into my thoughts.

I quickly pull out my gloss and close the drawer before she opens my door.

'Are you okay, hun?'

'Yeah, of course. I'm just leaving too, actually.' I force a smile and follow her out the room.

After picking up her Gucci bag, she turns and frowns at me. 'Are you sure you're all right?' she asks, peering closer.

'Yeah, of course. Just a bit tired after last night, I think.' I smile again.

'Well, just take it easy today. Only do as much as you can,' she says.

'I will,' I promise, trying not to roll my eyes at her mollycoddling. Bless her, I know she means well.

After she's left, I sag onto a dining chair. The Monopoly game was so much fun last night. I just wish all the money was real so I could pay that bastard and get rid of him. A thought strikes me. Even if I *could* pay him what he's asked for, it wouldn't end there. It never does with thugs like him. He'll only want more and more. That's how his sort operate. God, this is all so hopeless.

I make my way to the Tube in a cloud of despair. Maybe I should tell James, after all? He could get a squad of police to do a stake out and jump the guy when he comes to collect the cash. If he were locked up, he wouldn't be able to demand any more money, would he?

The more I think about it, the more sense it makes. I should have just come clean with James in the first place. He'd be furious to think I'd kept something like this from him. I'll tell him tonight. We promised no more secrets and I need to stick to it—even if it might backfire. *Things have a habit of doing that when I'm around.*

I feel far more confident by the time I arrive at the office, and even Izzy doesn't seem to be in as much of a bad mood as usual. That's not to say she's in a *good* mood, of course, but we must be thankful for small mercies.

'Valerie's really impressed with you coming up with this idea,' Siobhan tells me in a hushed tone. 'Especially at this time of year. It's just what we need.'

'Sorry if it's given everyone more work to do, though,' I say, giving Izzy a sideways glance.

'Oh, don't worry about her. I think you'll find she's had a change of heart about the whole project now.' Siobhan winks at me before returning to her desk.

I stare over at Izzy, who's tapping away on her computer and making notes on her pad. She must be doing the research Valerie asked for. I wonder what made her change her mind about it overnight.

My letters have amassed to a humungous pile, and I wade through them, picking out the ones that ask for an outfit on a budget. It's amazing how many people are in this position, and I'm really glad we're doing the feature. I hope that woman who was shoplifting for the thug reads it and realises she doesn't have to steal to look good. Mind you, I'm pretty sure she's not doing it for herself—that thug will be forcing her to do it, somehow. I just hope she wasn't kept in custody all night.

'We have some lovely clothes to showcase from high street stores,' Fran tells me over coffee. 'I'd wear them myself.'

'Oh, good.' That says a lot. Fran's into the boho style so she's very choosy about her outfits. 'We need to emphasise the quality as well as affordability,' I remind her. 'It's false economy to buy something that's going to fall to pieces after the first wash.'

'Don't worry, we've got it covered,' Beulah adds with a smile.

'Sorry,' I reply. 'I didn't mean to tell you what to do.'

'You didn't,' Fran says, raising her eyebrows in surprise. 'You're absolutely right. And to be honest, it's your idea, so you've every right to throw in suggestions.'

I reach over and squeeze her arm, thankful for her understanding. I feel quite passionate about this project, but it's no excuse to give orders.

'Thanks, Fran,' I say.

When we get back to the office Valerie's waiting by her door.

'Siobhan, Liberty, can you come here, please? I need a word.' She doesn't look happy.

Siobhan and I exchange a look and follow her into her office, where she immediately lowers the blinds then hands us each a piece of paper as soon as we sit down.

'This is an email I received this morning,' she announces, gravely.

I stare at it, my heart thumping and my whole body heating up.

Dear Editor

I hope you realise the detrimental effects of your new 'Problem Solved' column. The writer obviously has tons of money—I suppose that's thanks to you—and expects everyone else to have, too. All the outfits she suggests are mega-expensive, from big-name designers. Do you really think everyone can afford this sort of thing? Are you aware how many women are now having to steal in order to keep up with your writer's idea of fashion? My girlfriend was slung in jail yesterday for shoplifting. All she was trying to do was keep up with what she thought everyone else was wearing.

I think it only fair and right that you sack your writer straight away before anyone else is harmed. Apart from being pregnant, my girlfriend now has a criminal record, thanks to her.

I don't expect you to print this letter in your rag, but I know plenty of other papers that will—particularly the nationals. I'm sure they'll be very interested in hearing how you intend to resolve this issue.

Yours sincerely

A Very Concerned Reader

'You will see that it was also copied to Mr Peerless,' Valerie says slowly. 'I have a meeting with him in ten minutes to discuss the issue.'

My mind whirls as I read the letter over and over. There are no prizes for guessing who sent it, but why? He's already trying to blackmail me, and now he also wants me to lose my job. It doesn't make sense.

'But we're already redressing the balance,' I point out. 'That's what this feature's all about. And I've already written a couple of replies to women who asked for outfits on a tight budget, they just haven't been printed yet.'

'Yes, but the public don't know that,' Valerie acknowledges sadly. 'Anything we print now will look like a response to his claims. We're too late.'

'Do you really think he'll send this to other newspapers?' Siobhan asks frowning. 'Would they be interested? We're only the weekly supplement to a local paper—will they even care?'

Valerie sighs, sitting back in her chair. 'It's a good story for them. And it might win them some of our readers.'

'But what about the feature we're doing?' I say, exasperated. 'Everyone's working so hard on it, and we started it way before he sent the email. Can't we just push it out there so his letter will be irrelevant?'

'He might have already contacted other papers,' Valerie points out. 'They could be writing up their derogatory articles about us as we speak.'

'Then we need to get our feature out there tonight,' I say, firmly. 'Then, even if they do print anything, it'll look like they've jumped the gun. They'll be the ones with egg on their faces.' It all makes sense in my mind.

Valerie doesn't look so sure. 'But the supplement doesn't go to print yet,' she says. Even if we could alter this week's issue to include the feature—which I very much doubt—it won't be out until Saturday. They could have already discredited us by then.'

'Why did he have to do this now?' I wail, thinking aloud.

'If it is a *he*,' Siobhan says, glumly. 'Just because there's a reference to a girlfriend doesn't mean it has to be a man, does it?'

I bite my lip. I can't tell them I know exactly who's written the stupid email.

'We have to beat them at their own game,' I say, my mind whirring like a machine.

'How can we?' Valerie looks up at her wall clock. 'I'll just have to explain to Mr Peerless that we are already putting a feature together that will negate his claims, but it won't be printed until it's too late.'

'It doesn't have to be,' I add, as she stands up. 'I get that we can't put it in the supplement in time, but what about the actual paper? They don't go to print until this afternoon.'

Valerie stares at me, open-mouthed. 'Liberty, are you suggesting that we produce and edit an entire feature in the next…' she glances at her Cartier watch, '…four hours?'

'It's not impossible,' I say nervously, glancing at Siobhan for moral support.

'But there's not enough *time*,' Valerie states, as though talking to a five-year-old. I remember that tone of hers, and I've liked not hearing it recently.

'We're a great team, everyone has their strengths. If we all knuckle down and take a section each, then help each other out as and when… I think it can be done,' I say with a lot more confidence that I feel. Oh, this *has* to work, it's the only way we can respond to this pillock without making ourselves look stupid. And me not getting the sack would be great, too.

Siobhan shifts awkwardly in her seat then clears her throat.

'Valerie, I know this turnaround is far from ideal, and this is far more challenging that anything we've done before, in terms of content as well as timescale…' she trails off and glances at me. I don't know why, so I try to look capable, confident, and encouraging all at once. I'm not sure if it worked, but she turns back to Valerie and resumes talking, so I guess my look must have helped in some way.

'…I do believe the team and I can pull this off,' she continues. 'It won't be easy, but I think we should give it a shot.'

Valerie surveys her for a moment then reluctantly smiles.

'Ladies, I'm not going to say I have *full* faith in you…' Oh, maybe Siobhan wasn't as convincing as I thought. '…In all honesty, it's complete madness, but I think if anyone can pull this out of the bag it's you. You say you can get this done in time for this afternoon's edition? Let's get started then!' Valerie is all broad smiles and clapping hands.

I breathe a sigh of relief and feel Siobhan do the same next to me.

'Fantastic!' Siobhan says. 'I'm sure if we get a wriggle on, we can get it finished by lunchtime.'

'I'll explain it to Mr Peerless now,' Valerie says, hurriedly. 'Can you round up the girls and get the wheels in motion, Siobhan? There isn't a moment to spare.'

'Yes, of course.' Siobhan and I jump to our feet.

'Let's do this.' Valerie sounds very resolute as we all pile out of her office.

'Listen up, ladies,' Siobhan says, while Valerie heads for the lift. 'This is urgent.'

They all stop talking and look over.

'This feature needs to be finished and edited by lunchtime,' she explains.

'Tomorrow?' Izzy looks horrified. 'That doesn't give us long. I thought it was going in *next* weekend's issue?'

'No, today,' Siobhan says firmly. 'It's going in the paper tonight. Anyone have any problems with that?'

All eyes are on Izzy, who just pouts but says nothing.

'Good,' Siobhan declares. 'Then let's put our heads down and get it done.'

I return to my desk. Apart from replying to a couple of letters, which I've already done, and sourced all the photos I need to accompany them, I need to write a piece extolling the virtues of high street fashion. It's just a general piece so it won't take long. Fran and Beulah look a little rattled, though, so I'm hoping I'll get to help them out once I'm finished here.

Izzy keeps huffing but doesn't say anything— which can only be a good thing.

The air is thick with concentration as we all get our work done. I pass my report over to Siobhan to edit as soon as it's finished. It's not hard for me to come up with a bucket-load of reasons to buy from the high street, especially here in London. Some of the non-designer brands are incredible.

'Shall I help the girls with the clothing section?' I offer. 'I think they've got a lot on their plate.'

'Yes, please.' Siobhan smiles.

'We're trying to come up with a nice outfit we could make from these,' Tammy tells me as I follow her to a rail. 'We've got the rest, but we need to incorporate these somehow.'

She shows me a navy-blue skirt, a couple of plain blouses, and three pairs of shoes of differing heights.

'Whatever we do, it looks frumpy,' Fran moans.

'Well, we have to go for the high courts, don't we?' I suggest. 'They're the nicest of the bunch.'

'Yeah, but look how plain they are,' Tammy points out. 'A plain navy skirt, plain white blouse, and then nude courts is going to look so boring.'

I look over to the large table where Alice and Beulah have laid out some evening outfits.

'Can't we accessorise from these?' I ask, going over to the table. 'Look, this powder-blue scarf will tone beautifully with the navy and white, whilst adding a bit of texture as well as pattern.' I drape the scarf around the collar of the blouse and hold the skirt up to show the whole look.

'But that's evening wear,' Tammy moans. 'We're supposed to be doing daywear.'

'We're using that scarf to go with this dress,' Alice points out. 'It's perfect.' She holds up a beautiful evening dress that accentuates the blue of the scarf.

I frown. It's the perfect accessory for both outfits, and I don't want to start an argument over who should use it.

'But isn't that the whole point?' I say, as inspiration hits me. 'We'll use it in *both* articles to show how versatile it is. After all, it's the key to saving money, isn't it? Being able to ring the changes with different accessories. Look, we could add this, too.' I pick up a black clutch with pretty diamante studs on the front. As I open it up, I find exactly what I was hoping would be included. 'It's got a strap we could use for the daywear,' I suggest.

'Great idea. We're using it as a clutch with one of our suits, so that'll show it from both angles,' Beulah agrees with a smile.

'And it'll certainly brighten up the look of our outfit,' I say to Tammy.

'I didn't think we were allowed to mix the two styles,' Alice says, 'but it makes perfect sense for a budget-friendly wardrobe.'

'Exactly,' I say. 'It's a good way to reduce the cost per wear and gives the consumer more looks with fewer clothes. Like a capsule wardrobe.'

Tom from the newsroom comes up to take photos of the outfits as well as the individual items. It's great to see him again, as we used to work near each other in the newsroom and always got along.

'The place just isn't the same without you,' he tells me, grinning. I'm not quite sure how to take his comment, so I just smile.

'We'll include in our write-up how the accessories can swap over from evening to daywear, too,' Beulah pipes up. 'It'll drive the message home and validate some of the prices, in case people still think they're too expensive.'

'Good idea,' I agree with a smile.

***

It takes longer than we'd hoped to finish the feature, and we end up working into our lunchtime, but no one minds as it's all for a good cause. Well, I can't vouch for Izzy, but she doesn't voice any objection, put it that way. It's also fun. I love that I can work with the girls as well as 'do my own thing', as Fran calls it, with the agony aunt column.

Valerie's really pleased with the result and beams at us once it's ready to be put to bed. 'Go and take a well-earned break,' she says. We can tidy this mess up later. You've all done a sterling job today and thank you for working past your break time. I've instructed the canteen to ensure there's some food left for you. Though, I'm not sure if there will be anything hot by now.'

We don't need telling twice as we all pile out of the office and head down the corridor.

'That was great fun,' I tell Siobhan, who's walking alongside me.

'It was hard work,' she says, incredulously. 'My head's aching now.'

'Sorry.' I suddenly realise that it wouldn't have been so easy for Siobhan to edit the whole thing in such a short space of time.

'No, I wasn't complaining,' she assures me. 'It was the right thing to do. If it doesn't go out tonight, goodness knows what will happen.'

'In what way?' Izzy suddenly appears on her other side. Damn!

'Well, um...' Siobhan looks panicked.

'Mr Peerless would've gone mad,' I cut in. 'It's just that he was really eager to get the feature in today's paper. Valerie would never have heard the last of it if we'd let him down, would she?'

'That's right,' Siobhan concurs. 'You know what he's like.'

Mercifully, we've just arrived at the refectory. It's empty for a change, but we all take our usual seats at the big table.

To our surprise, Valerie suddenly appears as we're all deciding what to have. There's not much choice; ploughman's, sandwiches, salad, and a selection of different cakes for pudding.

'Lunch is on me today,' she announces. 'Being as how you missed out on a proper meal. And thank you again for your commitment to the job.'

'You don't have to do that,' Siobhan tells her, but Valerie puts her hand up to stop her.

'I want to,' she says. With a smile, she swoops out of the canteen leaving us all flabbergasted.

I can't help feeling a little relieved. I've been having the cheapest thing on the menu all week—usually soup—in an attempt to save some cash. Now, I can save even more. It's a nice feeling that I'm putting my earning by for the Saint Laurent boots again, instead of trying to appease that thug of a thief. I still don't know how I'm going to explain it all to James, but I somehow feel better just for having made the decision to come clean. I wish I'd decided to days ago and ping a text over to James.

Shall I come to yours tonight? xx

I'm delighted when I get a reply straight away.

Yes, that would be lovely xx

I really need to start leaving some spare clothes at his for occasions like this. It might make him feel that I'm getting closer to moving in with him, too. I really wish I could. I send him a message back.

I'll pop home first, so see you about 7? Xx
Can't wait xx

I tuck into my salad feeling all warm and lovely. James always has that effect on me. I just hope he's in a good mood after I've told him about the whole shoplifting/being blackmailed by a lowlife thug mess. I'm still trying to place that guy's ugly face—I know I've seen it before somewhere, but where?

'Well that was a fun morning—oh, and afternoon.' Izzy's sarcastic comment invades my thoughts.

'At least that feature's all done and dusted,' Kiki pipes up. 'We can move onto the expensive Christmas outfits next. I love doing those.'

'Humph. I still don't see what the hurry was. Why on earth did they decide to run it in the paper instead of the magazine? The fashions won't look half as nice without the glossy paper and bright colours. It just doesn't make sense to me.' Izzy eyes me suspiciously.

'Mr Peerless is a law unto himself,' I say, feeling my cheeks heat up.

'Perhaps, I'll have a word with him. Find out just what's going on,' she says, narrowing her eyes at me.

'Don't you think that might undermine Valerie?' Siobhan cuts in just before I start to really panic.

'I wonder if that woman's going through some kind of old-age crisis,' Izzy retorts. 'She's been making some very odd decisions lately. And she's not acting like herself at all. Makes me wonder if she's ill or something.'

'I'm sure she's fine,' Siobhan replies curtly. 'And 'that woman' has just given you a huge pay rise and now she's paid for the meal you're eating, so you might like to think twice before being rude about her again.' I've never seen Siobhan look so cross, but she manages to keep her cool. I really wish I was more like her.

Izzy gives her a look of disdain and leaves the table.

'Do you think she really will speak to Mr Peerless?' I whisper to Siobhan. I can just imagine her response when she discovers that it's all my fault.

Siobhan shakes her head, her lips still tight. 'I don't think so,' she says, watching Izzy strut over to the door. 'It doesn't really have anything to do with her.'

I say nothing, seeing that Siobhan's clearly still wound up at Izzy's attitude. I hope she's right, though.

***

By the time we return to the office, everyone is chatting happily. No one seems to mind having the day disrupted like that—except Izzy, of course.

'Right, ladies, let's get this place cleaned up please,' Siobhan says, looking at all the clothes and accessories scattered on the large table, and the hair and make-up stations looking like a bomb's hit them.

Everyone really did pull out all the stops, and I'm eternally grateful to them, although I can't say anything. I go over to the table and start putting the clothes back on hangers.

'That was fun,' Beulah says. 'You'll have to come over and join us more often, Libby.'

There's a chorus of agreement from Alice, Kiki, Tammy, and Fran, and I feel myself glow inwardly. It's so nice that they like me here—such a change from the newsroom.

'Anytime,' I reply with a grin, quickly taking a couple of items over to the rail so they can't see my face, which I'm sure looks like a beetroot by now.

We finish tidying the clothes away and I leave Beulah and Kiki to put the cover back on the rail. Last time I helped with a rail cover it was a disaster, and I shudder at the memory.

'Well… that didn't take as long as I thought it would,' Kiki says happily, once we've finished.

I look around the room, noticing that the hair and make-up stations are all back to normal now, too.

'Where's Izzy?' I ask, looking at her messy table.

'I don't think she came back after lunch,' Beulah says, toying with her thick, brown hair.

'Good job,' Fran mutters, 'Seeing the mood she was in.'

'Izzy went home with a bad headache,' Siobhan tells us, obviously noticing us all look her way. 'Would you girls mind tidying her station for her?'

'No problem,' I go over and start clearing things away and immediately regret being so eager. Of course, I don't mind helping Siobhan, and it wouldn't have been fair to leave it for her to do, but Izzy's a totally different story. If I do something wrong or put something in the wrong place, she'll throw a fit at me. It'll just give her a good excuse to berate me for something else. I know she doesn't like me, but I still don't know why.

Fran comes over to help, and we soon have her station looking ship-shape again. I'm very careful to leave her paperwork in a pile on her desk, instead of putting it away neatly in her drawer, so she can't blame me for hiding it.

Valerie comes in when we've finished, looking quite relaxed for a change.

'Thank you, ladies,' she says. 'I knew I could rely on you to rise to the occasion and you've made me proud. Mr Peerless is happy with the feature, which is going in tonight's edition of the *Chronicle*.

I heave a sigh of relief. I wouldn't put it past Phil bloody Peerless to purposely find fault in our work, but I can see it's in his best interests for the feature to be printed tonight. I just hope he doesn't involve Kevin Stratton, the newspaper's owner.

'As you know, Isobella's gone home with a headache,' Valerie continues. 'I think it's only fair that you ladies get to go home early, too, especially after all your hard work. You may all take the rest of the afternoon off. We will start work on something new for the supplement tomorrow.

We all hurry to collect our things. This is a first. I don't think I've ever been allowed to finish early with any of my jobs before—it's usually been the opposite. It'll be nice to surprise James by getting to his place a bit earlier, and we'll have more time together. Everyone's smiling as we walk towards the lift.

Most of the girls are going to spend the extra time shopping, but I head straight for the Tube. I still need to save up for the Saint Laurent boots, and besides, there's nothing I really need to buy right now.

Proud of my own resolve, I turn the corner, not noticing the guy coming the opposite way. I'm sure he purposely bumps into me.

'Sorry,' I say, automatically.

'You will be.'

I recognise his voice and look up in horror. It's the thug who's trying to blackmail me!

'What do you mean by that?' I'm trying to stop the tremble in my voice as I look around in the hope of seeing other people.

The street's bare. It's only a little alley that makes a great short cut to the Tube station, so I assume not many people know about it. Unfortunately. James would go mad if he knew I was coming this way. He's warned me plenty of times not to use back alleys in London, as there are all sorts of undesirables hanging out in them, but I've never seen anyone around here who caused concern—until now.

'Where's my money?' he asks, putting an arm on my shoulder.

'What?' I stutter. 'It's only Th-Thursday.'

'So? I've lost my patience,' he sneers. 'I want it now.'

'I haven't got it.' My mind's in a whirl. He's gripping me tightly, so there's no way I can just run away, and we're out of sight of the main road.

'Well, then, I wonder what a gorgeous girlie like you can give me instead?'

I flinch, not just at him but his turn of phrase. 'Gorgeous girlie' is a term that makes my skin crawl—almost as much as he does. I've heard it recently, but where? His other arm comes around me, pulling me close against him. He smells of BO and cheap beer. His lips get dangerously close to mine before we both jump at the sound of footsteps. He quickly puts one arm tightly around my waist and leads me deeper into the alleyway. I pray the footsteps follow us, but they don't.

I try to hang back, not wanting to go any farther with the vile letch. He takes a step in front of me and I gape at his shoes. Smart, black lace-ups with the letters VLTN written across the backs of the heels. They're leather Derbys by Valentino Garavani. I'd recognise them anywhere. And I know exactly where I've seen them before.

'Come on,' he urges, impatiently, trying to drag me towards him.

Yep, I knew I recognised him from somewhere. It's the guy from the pub. Tyler's friend—or rather, his enemy. The guy who offered to get hold of an engagement ring for him. Dave, was it? Or Drake? No, something like that, anyway. My heart thumps heavily as realisation hits me. He's obviously got some sort of racket going on, stealing to order—or, at least, getting someone else to.

'What happened to your girlfriend?' I spit the words out as he pulls me closer to him. 'I thought you said she was pregnant in that letter that could've lost me my job. What're you doing with *me*?'

'Never mind her,' he growls. 'She's off the scene.'

'You—you mean she's in prison? They locked her up for shoplifting?' My heart thumps even harder and I feel myself go hot. This was my fault.

'No, I mean she's gone. Vamoosed. Disappeared. I'll find her, though. No one gets away from me.' He shrugs. 'Not that she was much use anyway.'

'But she was pregnant with your baby?' My voice is a little harder than I intended, as anger wells inside me. What has he done with her?

'Is that what's bothering you? Well, don't worry, she's not pregnant and she's not my girlfriend.' He gives me a lecherous stare. 'But you could be.'

'I'm—I'm engaged,' I say quickly, as his mouth comes perilously close to mine. '

'So?' He frowns incredulously.

'So, I'm not available.' I spit the words out, trying to shove him off me. 'Nor am I interested.'

He slams me against the wall at the side of the alley.

'You owe me!' He snarls like a rabid beast. *He smells like one, too.*

'Why? You've already tried to ruin my career.' I spit the words at him angrily. 'You contacted the paper and complained about me and my column. That's exactly what you were blackmailing me with. You've got no ammunition left, remember? Now get off me or I'll scream!' My voice gets louder as I try to push his hefty frame away. He's pressed up tight against me and his breath makes me heave.

'I'll do a lot worse than lose you that poxy job,' he scoffs. 'You get me that money tomorrow night or else. Bring it here—got it?'

'We agreed to meet at—'

'I've changed my bloody mind!' He yells at me, making me jump. He looks really fierce, and my anger gives way to fear again.

'Right.' I see this as a means of escape. I had thought for a second he was going to try to kidnap me. 'I'll bring it here tomorrow night.'

'*All* of it,' he demands. 'And I might also have a new job for you. You seem to know your way around designer labels, which should save some time.'

I want to swear at him but instead I bite my lip. This guy's scarier than I thought. He's planning to make me shoplift for him!

I nod. 'Right. Tomorrow night, then.'

Mercifully, he releases me, and I quickly rub my arms where he's been gripping them too tight.

'And don't forget, I know exactly where to find you if you don't show up,' he growls as he takes a step back from me.

I run. Suddenly, I'm thankful to Dave Chandler for making me race all over London for those news stories. I got the hang of running in heels—though, I still wouldn't recommend it.

I reach the Tube station shaking, my mind full of mush. What the heck just happened? And what on earth am I going to do about tomorrow?

***

By the time I get home, I'm an absolute wreck. Tears stream down my face as a mixture of fear and relief swamp my emotions. I'm not as early as I'd hoped, and Cassie's already there when I open the door.

'Oh, no! What's happened?' She immediately comes and gives me a big hug. 'Are you hurt?'

I shake my head. Apart from a few stinging nettles attacking my legs and that thug squeezing the life out of my arms, I'm okay.

'Come and sit down,' she urges, pointing me towards the couch.

She passes me a handful of tissues. 'Do you want to go to A&E? Or I can ring the doctors', try to get you an emergency appointment?' She looks worried sick.

'No, I'm fine, honestly.' I tell her. 'He didn't really hurt me.'

'Who?' she asks.

I wipe my face and blow my nose, stalling for time. I've no idea where to start with this. After a deep breath, I blurt out the whole story. Cassie's a brilliant listener and just sits quietly, taking it all in. That's one of the things I love about her. She's such a good friend.

'You need to tell James,' she says when I've finished.

'He'll go mad,' I mumble.

'Probably, but he'll be able to sort it out,' she says, nodding. 'You certainly can't meet that guy tomorrow night.'

'I know.' I sigh. 'I haven't got his money for a start—'

'That's the least of your problems,' she says softly.

I stare at her.

'That guy sounds dangerous, Libby. There's no telling what he'll do.'

My stomach flips. I know she's right. It's the thought that kept whirling around my head when I was pinned up against that wall. He was drunk and possibly stoned. He might have done anything. I was lucky to escape.

The doorbell buzzes, making us both jump. Cassie goes to answer it. My mouth goes dry as I hear James' voice asking to come in.

'Of course. Come on up,' she tells him.

I whizz into the bathroom to wipe the smudged make-up from my face. I should have worn waterproof mascara today. I look awful. I quickly wipe it all away, miffed that James will have to see me without make-up on tonight. I hope it doesn't put him off me. I mean, he's seen me make-up-less before, but not in broad daylight or with bloodshot, puffy eyes. I must look a right sight. I don't even know what he's doing here. We weren't supposed to be meeting until later, and at his place, not here.

I frown into the mirror, hearing two male voices speaking with Cassie. They don't sound happy. I quickly finish washing my face and head out to see what's going on.

'James, I thought I was coming to your place?' I say, going over to him.

'Actually, we're here on official business.' He bites the words out.

I stop walking. 'But I thought…?'

'Why don't we all sit down?' Cassie offers. 'I've put the kettle on.'

'I think you've met Alex before, haven't you?' James asks politely, turning to me as Cassie heads for the kitchen. Alex is another detective sergeant who often works with James. I've seen him a few times, he seems really nice.

I nod. 'Yes. Hello.' I swallow hard, trying to smile at him.

Both men look extremely serious, and my stomach lurches. This is not how I was hoping tonight would go at all.

'Can you tell us what you've been doing for the past two hours?' Alex asks, pulling his notebook out of his pocket.

The men sit on the sofa opposite me and my heart aches. I had hoped James would sit with me. I could really use a manly hug right now. I stare at Alex.

'Um... well... I was at work and then I came home.' I can see by their faces that they're not buying it. I can't help wondering what they know—and how?

'What time did you finish work?' Alex enquires.

'Well, it was a bit early. We'd finished this project we were working on, so Valerie, my boss, said we could take the rest of the afternoon off.'

The men exchange glances that do nothing to settle my nerves. I'm glad of the distraction when Cassie comes in with the coffees, to be honest. The air is thick with tension and I'm starting to get a headache. She sits on the sofa next to me.

'What exactly is this all about?' I ask, feeling a little braver after a sip of coffee. 'You've obviously got something to say, James, so why not just spit it out?'

James sits forward, his jaw tense. 'Why don't you want to move in with me, Libby?'

I stare at him, my face heating up. Everyone's looking at me and I feel sick. Then I feel annoyed. How dare he come round here and make me feel bad? And is he even allowed to be here on 'official business' given our relationship? Couldn't he have sent one of his minions round to do this with Alex instead? Not that I'd want anyone else to be interviewing me…but then again, I don't particularly want James to be doing it either!

'This is *police* business, is it?' I ask calmly, looking from James to Alex.

James has the grace to study the carpet for a few minutes, while Alex sighs.

'Okay… that bit wasn't,' James admits, fidgeting uncomfortably. 'But I thought what happened today might explain your reluctance to move into my place.'

I can feel Cassie staring at me. I haven't actually told her that James asked me to move in with him. Not yet. But I can't deal with that right now.

I frown. '*What* happened?'

James pulls his phone from his pocket and presses a few buttons. 'Can you explain this?' he asks, passing it to me.

Cassie leans over to watch the video that's just started rolling. It shows me walking up the high street and then turning into the alley. Then the thug appears and lays his hands on my shoulders. I shudder as I remember the feeling. Next, he looks like he's about to kiss me, as his face is so close to mine. We can only see the back of his head, but it looks a lot like he's leaning in for a snog. Then he puts his arm around my waist and leads me farther into the alley. I recall the sound of someone coming—someone I was hoping might rescue me. We walk out of sight then, and the camera picks me up later when I emerge from the alley near the Tube station, straightening my clothes and smoothing my hair. I was thinking at the time how much of a mess I must have looked and was eager to keep up appearances in case anyone recognised me. I look slightly dazed on the film, and with good reason.

The video finishes with me boarding the Tube to Chelsea. My heart's hammering like the devil and I feel sick. I don't want to face James, but I know I have to. I also know exactly how it looks.

'If you wanted to cheat on me, did you have to do it with a known criminal?' James' words cut me like a knife.

My face heats up and I force myself to look at him.

'I didn't.' My voice is small but it's all I can manage right now. I can't *believe* he'd think that, or accuse me of it in front of his colleague and my best friend. Official business indeed!

'The camera never lies,' James says, staring into my face. 'Unlike *people*.'

'I don't lie,' I whisper, as tears roll down my hot cheeks. I suddenly remember telling the thug that I was engaged. It was only a white lie, but I still said it. Suddenly, I can't maintain eye contact with James and I gaze down at my cup.

'What do you know about this man?' Alex asks calmly.

I bite my quivering lip.

Alex throws James a withering look. 'He's not exactly a known criminal,' he clarifies, 'but he's someone we've had our eye on for a while. Anything you can tell us about him would help. Can you give us his name?'

I shake my head. 'He's a shoplifter. I think he makes other people steal for him,' I say, with a big sniff.

'You *know* about him?' James explodes. 'You know what sort of lowlife you're dealing with and yet you *still* want to be with him?' He stands up.

'No, I don't. It's not like that,' I protest, more tears flooding my vision.

'No, of course not. It never is!' James snaps.

'Why don't *I* continue the questioning, mate?' Alex jumps to his feet, too. 'You don't need to hear all this. Go and get some air. I'll call you later, okay?'

James gives me a look I've never seen before. He looks furious, but also terribly hurt. I want to reach up and touch him but I daren't. I've also got such a huge lump in my throat and can't speak. Cassie passes me a handful of tissues from the box on the coffee table while James and Alex have a muffled conversation on the way to the front door.

As soon as they're out of sight, I bawl my eyes out in Cassie's arms. I can't believe James would think I'd been unfaithful to him, but I can't deny that's exactly how it looks on that film.

My mind spins. The front door closes and Alex returns to the room a few minutes later.

'Was he spying on me?' I ask, before he even sits down.

Alex shakes his head. 'No, of course not. We've been tracing a bunch of shoplifters in the area and we were studying the CCTV footage. We recognised you on the tape.'

I sniff. Alex is very calm and non-judgemental, and I understand completely how it's happened, although I'm not exactly thrilled to be accused of God knows what with God knows who.

'That guy you were with is sort of known to us,' he continues. 'We've been trying to track him down but whenever we get close enough to a good arrest, we lose him.'

'A *good* arrest?' Cassie queries, her eyebrows raised.

'I mean, one where we can actually catch him in the act. You'd be amazed how hard it is to get the courts to convict a known criminal just because of a lack of substantial evidence. This guy's quite slippery. We've had our eye on him for some time, on and off. We think he's at the centre of something big, but we've got no proof.'

'He gets people to shoplift for him,' I say, with a nod.

Alex jots something in his notebook. 'And exactly how do you know that?'

Cassie gives me an encouraging smile, and I go on to explain to Alex all the ins and outs of what's been going on.

He listens intently, making notes.

'She got home in a right state,' Cassie tells him.

He shakes his head, incredulously. 'I'm not surprised. He's a nasty piece of rubbish. Takes drugs, too, which makes him totally unpredictable.'

'He said he'd tell my boss that I was encouraging women to shoplift in order to keep up with the current fashion trends I was promoting in my column. He said it would cost me ten thousand quid for him not to,' I explain. 'Then he wrote to my boss anyway, the day before I was supposed to give him the money.'

'Sounds about right,' Alex says. 'So, what about the money?'

'Oh, he still wants it. I have to pay up tomorrow night or else.'

Alex raises his eyebrows at me. 'Or else *what*?'

I shrug. 'He didn't say. Just that it would be far worse than me losing my job.' I sniff again before adding, 'And he wants me to shoplift for him.'

'Sounds like his style,' Alex says, writing it down.

'It was the only way I could escape, by agreeing to meet him tomorrow,' I say, as fresh tears roll down my face. 'I don't know what to do now.'

Cassie takes me in her arms again as I wail a little more, despair taking over me. How can this all have happened to me?

'Don't worry, Libby,' Alex says, putting his notebook away when I've finally recovered. 'We'll sort something out.' He stands up, then looks back at me, chewing his lip. 'Are you sure you don't know what his name is? We think we've got his first name, but he seems to have several different pseudonyms for his surname, so we're trying to ascertain which one's real. It would certainly help the case if we could identify him properly.'

I wipe my nose for the umpteenth time. 'He's never told me,' I say, shaking my head. Then a thought strikes me. 'Hang on. I might be able to find out, though.'

Alex's eyes light up. 'That would be great.'

'I just need my phone.' I look around for my bag, which Cassie quickly finds and hands to me.

I scroll through my messages, find Fran, and send a quick text.

Hi Fran. Do you know the name of that guy at the pub the other night who offered to get Tyler a ring for you? He was the scruffy one with the expensive shoes. Was it Drake or Dave, or something like that?'

My phone pings almost straight away.

He's a nasty scumbag and you need to avoid him at all costs, Libby. His name's Drew Fisher and he's a total nutcase. Dangerous, too. Why do you want to know?

Drew! I knew it was something like that. Of course, I had no idea about his surname but if that's the name Tyler knows him by, it's likely to be right. I pass the information to Alex who writes it down with a smile on his face.

'Great job,' he says. 'Leave it with me. I'll make a few enquiries and get back to you. We'll have something sorted by the time you're due to see him tomorrow, I promise.'

I sigh. 'That would be good.'

'And don't worry about James. It was a knee-jerk reaction that's all. He's been working really hard lately and wasn't thinking straight. I'll show him the report. I'm sure it'll be okay.'

'I hope so.' Even more tears threaten to blind me as I show him out.

'You've done great, Libby,' Alex assures me before he leaves.

Cassie's already running me a hot bath by the time I close the front door. A pang in my heart reminds me I don't know what I'd do without her. An even more painful pang tells me I might not have to find out...

15

I feel better after a relaxing bath and a glass of wine. Cassie had even lit a few scented candles in the bathroom for me. I change into my pyjamas and dry my hair, taking my time. Stalling. I know I need to tell her about James asking me to move in with him, but I've no idea how. I'm mulling it over when she comes to join me in my bedroom.

'Any good?' she asks, smiling kindly.

I nod, putting the hairdryer on the dressing table. 'Yes, thanks.'

She immediately comes over, picks up the comb and begins to run it through my hair. I close my eyes. It's been years since anyone combed my hair for me—apart from the hairdresser, of course, which isn't the same—and it feels so relaxing.

'So, James asked you to move in with him?' she asks, addressing the elephant in the room.

'Yes. While we were in Broadstairs.' I check her face in the mirror, trying to interpret her reaction.

'That was weeks ago,' she says, slowly.

'I know.'

'So, why didn't you mention it? Don't you want to move in with him?'

I sigh. 'That's what he keeps asking. I don't know what to do, Cass. I mean, I love living here with you. And I love being at his place. I don't see why we can't just stay as we are.'

She smiles. 'But things don't stay the same, do they? Change is inevitable. Especially now.'

She gives me a knowing look that just confuses me. *It doesn't take much, to be honest.* 'Do you love him?'

'Yes. Of course, I do. Though I don't think he's that keen on me right now.' I bite my lip as a vision of the look he gave me whizzes through my mind.

'He shouldn't have jumped to conclusions,' Cassie says, continuing to comb my hair.

'It's not like him,' I say, thoughtfully. 'James is the one who looks at everything methodically. He weighs up a situation and makes sure of his facts before he says anything. *I'm* the one who normally jumps the gun.'

She nods. 'Yes, but if he's already concerned that you don't want to move in with him, then maybe he thinks he was seeing his worse fears materialise.'

I stare at her in the mirror. 'He was worried I'd found someone else? Why would he think that? I've never cheated on him, or on anyone for that matter.'

'I think it's everyone's worst nightmare when they're in a relationship,' she says. 'Even if you don't think it'll really happen, there's always the chance that your partner will find someone else.'

I huff. 'I thought at one time that he might get back with Suzanne,' I admit.

She nods. 'It's perfectly natural.'

'The only reason I didn't want to move in with him was because I was afraid of telling you,' I say, slowly.

'Afraid? What of?' She stops combing and stares back at me in the mirror.

'I thought you'd be upset. It doesn't seem fair to leave you on your own.' I feel my eyes burning as I fight back more tears.

To my amazement, she throws her arms around my shoulders.

'Oh, you daft thing,' she says. 'I understand. I knew we couldn't go on like this forever. Things change.' That knowing look again.

'*I* haven't changed,' I protest.

'Libby, you know you can tell me anything, don't you?' she says, a little warily.

'I only didn't tell you because you seemed so worried about me after what happened with Davinia. I know you care about me, Cass, and I didn't want to worry you any more by suddenly moving out.'

She bites her lip, staring at me in the mirror. 'I understand you wanting to move in with James. It's only natural.'

'But you don't want to move in with Rob, do you?' I ask, amazed. 'Why is it natural for me and not you?'

The look in her eyes tells me the answer and I put my hand to my mouth. 'You *do* want to move in with him, don't you?' Suddenly, a vision of Rob's things in her bedroom flashes in front of my eyes. His robe hanging on the back of her door, his comb on the bedside table. *She wants him to move in here.*

'No, but he'll be moving in with me one day, I hope,' she says, pursing her lips.

'*One* day?' I query, my heart pounding.

'Yep.' Her eyes don't meet mine in the mirror anymore.

'But it's *your* place, Cassie. You can move your boyfriend in anytime you want.' I frown, knowing immediately that just wouldn't work.

'I know,' she says, with a sigh. 'It's just...'

I suddenly feel sick. 'It's just that *I'm* here,' I finish for her. 'I'm in the way, aren't I? You've been waiting for me to move out so you and Rob could have the place to yourselves. Like a *normal* couple.' Anger and hurt well inside me. *She doesn't want me here.*

I stand up, suddenly feeling the urge to leave. I don't want to see her face right now. Not because I don't like her, but because I'm embarrassed. Why hadn't it occurred to me before? Of course, they want to live together. They're in love. Just like...

'It's not like that, Libby, and you know it.' I'm surprised at how angry she sounds.

She throws the comb back onto my dressing table and folds her arms, turning to face me. I gawp at her. I've never known her to look so confrontational before.

'Really?' I snap.

'Look, you and I live here together. That's how it's always been since I took on the place. And how we like it. But it's inevitable that someday one or both of us is going to want to live with our partner. It's only natural.'

That word again. Everything's so 'natural' to her.

'You mean you want to live with Rob? Why don't you just say it, Cassie?'

'Because I don't want to hurt your feelings.' She sounds firm.

'Well, it's a bit late for that now, isn't it?' I yell at her. 'Because I *am* hurt, Cassie. I've been through all that shit with Davinia trying to kill me, then that bastard

217

trying to blackmail me, and now you want to get rid of me. Hell, you've practically moved Rob in already!'

'I have not!' Her eyes are wide with indignation and she puts her hands on her hips.

'Well, it's your place anyway. You can do what you like,' I tell her, picking up my vanity case and scooping the contents of my dressing table into it. Go and ring your precious boyfriend and tell him he's welcome to bring the rest of his stuff over—if there's anything left to bring.'

'He's only got a few bits and pieces here,' she shouts at me. 'It's not like he's started moving in already!'

'*Really*?' I stop what I'm doing to turn and sneer at her. 'His dirty washing's in your laundry basket. I'd say that speaks volumes, don't you?'

She raises her perfectly shaped eyebrows in shock. 'You've been snooping in my room!'

'I have not.' I protest loudly.

'You have.'

My mind goes back to the day I went in there to find a book. I suppose I did have a *bit* of a nosey round.

'Well, if you've got such a low opinion of me, then it's best I go and let you and Rob live together in peace,' I snap, my face flaming. I grab my overnight bag and start throwing clothes into it.

'That's right. Be the drama queen you always are.' She waves a hand in the air.

I suddenly stop to stare at her. She's never called me that before.

'Oh, is that what you think? I've actually been through hell and back, but to you I'm just being a drama queen, am I?'

'We've all been through the wringer with everything that's been going on with you,' she yells at me. 'Don't you think the rest of us have been worried sick? It's not just you who's affected by everything, you know. People who care about you have been sick with concern, too.'

'Well, you don't have to be anymore,' I snap back. 'The drama queen will soon be out of your life so you won't have to think about me, will you?'

'So, you're just going to waltz out of here are you? Not even try to put this right?'

'Some things can't be put right, Cass,' I tell her, my tone a little softer. 'Once the damage is done it can't be undone.' I zip my case, then pull on my Ugg boots and my big coat.

'Where are you going?' she demands as I flounce out of the room.

'That's not your problem anymore, is it?' I say, sticking my nose in the air.

I grab my handbag on my way through the hallway and slam the door on my way out. Adrenaline keeps me moving until I'm down the stairs and out of the flat. I'm surprised she's even bothered about where I'm going. A thought strikes me. Where exactly *am* I going?

***

I end up at the Tube station. My first thought is to go to Fulham, but I can't face James right now. Besides, he's made it perfectly clear he doesn't trust me. How could he possibly think I'd be kissing that scumbag? That expression on his face haunts me, though, and I know he's hurt and worried. I'm worried too. Terrified he doesn't want me anymore.

I wonder if any of the girls from work would put me up. Fran and Beulah are probably my closest friends apart from Cassie, but I'm still not sure. How would I explain what's happened? I couldn't possibly tell them about getting mixed up with that Drew-guy, or that James thinks I've been unfaithful. Everyone at the office thinks my love life's perfect. I only wish it was.

Sloane Square's a hive of activity at night—well, all the time, really—and I watch couples snuggling up together on the benches waiting for the next train. I suddenly feel very lonely. And cold.

There's a load of kerfuffle as the next train whizzes into the station. It's on the District Line, so I hop on and go as far as the first stop, which is Victoria. Being such a popular area, it'll be easy to find a bed and breakfast in Westminster for the night. More expense, I know, but I'm hoping Alex will stay true to his word and I won't have to worry about Drew bloody Fisher now. And the Saint Laurent boots will just have to wait.

I'm glad I grabbed my big coat, not only because it's freezing on the Tube, but also because it covers up my pyjamas. I find a seat, though it's hardly worth it for the five-minute journey.

Victoria's a really busy station and I'm glad when I finally get back onto the surface and up the street. It's bitterly cold, but I'm not sure how much of that is because I've only got my pyjamas on, and how much is because I feel so darned miserable. My whole life seems to have fallen apart over the past few hours. I've spent all this time toying with who I should live with, and now it looks like I've lost my chance with both of them. I've got nowhere to go. It's a very lonely feeling, especially when you're in the middle of London at night.

I sigh, promising myself everything will look much brighter in the morning. Alex seemed confident that James would realise his mistake, and I'm sure Cassie will see things from my point of view after a good night's sleep. A nagging doubt at the back of my mind tells me that maybe it's *me* who should be thinking about apologising—after all, I'm the common denominator here, aren't I? Maybe if I'd just told Cassie about James asking me to move in as soon as we got back from Broadstairs things would've been different now. And James wouldn't have even considered anything could happen with Drew flaming Fisher because we'd be so wrapped up in each other it would never cross his mind that I'd cheat on him. I can't help wondering if all these awful things would have happened to me if I'd been living with James in the first place. Not that I need him to protect me or anything, of course.

There's a sign for a guest house just up the road, so I make my way towards it, wishing my holdall wasn't so heavy. I can just imagine the comments when I turn up for work with it in the morning. Everyone will know I've had a row with *someone*. It's a pretty obvious indicator and those women aren't stupid by any means.

I'm about to climb the steps of the Victorian town house when raised voices ahead of me grab my attention.

'Get off me,' a woman yells at someone in a black hoodie and dark jeans. The street lighting isn't great up this end of the road, but it's clear she's trying to push him off her.

I whip out my mobile and take a couple of snaps. James has drummed into me the need for evidence in even the slightest incident, and my phone's come in handy on several occasions for that. I venture a little nearer to get a better picture and I'm shocked when the guy turns to snarl at me. I take a good shot of his face, my blood running cold as I recognise that ugly sneer and those wonky teeth.

'What the fuck d'you think you're doing?' he yells at me as I quickly put the phone in my coat pocket.

'N-nothing.' I quickly turn away from him but it's too late.

'You!' He grabs my arm, swinging me back around to face him as my holdall flies from my hand. 'You just can't keep away, can you?'

'What?' I stare into the eyes of a madman.

'Let her go, Drew. She's done nothing to you,' the woman urges him.

I glance over and realise she's the woman who was shoplifting for him that time. She's the one I watched being arrested, the one he claimed was his pregnant girlfriend. He'd told me she'd disappeared, and I can only hope it was while she was helping the police with their enquiries. Pity he found her again, though.

'Mind your own fucking business!' He grips me tighter as he barks back at her.

'She's nothing to do with us,' the woman continues. 'Just leave her be.'

'She's the bitch that dobbed you into the fucking police, you stupid cow!' Drew's words are a little slurred and he smells really odd. A mixture of stale beer and something else.

'Well, it didn't do her much good, did it? I got away, didn't I?' She's clearly trying to cajole him, and I'm truly grateful for her efforts. It's just a shame it's not working, though, as he grips me even tighter.

People are walking towards us and I pray they intervene, but instead they just cross over the road to avoid a fuss. *Typical!*

In one swift move, Drew spins me around, lays a heavy arm over my chest and digs something sharp into my throat. I gasp. It's a knife.

'Call the police,' I urge the woman, who takes a step back in horror. My voice is very strange all of a sudden and I just hope she understands me.

'I—I haven't got a phone,' she stammers, clearly unaware that he was armed. I can't help wondering if he'd been planning to use the weapon on *her*.

I cock my head, eyeing my pocket and luckily, she gets the hint. She must be telepathic, like Cassie. She quickly reaches over and pulls my mobile from my pocket, much to the anger of Drew, who seemed a little slow on the uptake for some fortunate reason. Probably all the booze, and God knows what else in his system, I'd imagine.

'Call James,' I tell her in a strangled voice as the knife digs a little deeper into my skin. I'm sure I'm bleeding now, but I'm too scared to feel any pain. Adrenaline's pumping through me and I can't help feeling grateful this woman didn't take the opportunity to run when she could have.

There's a flash as she takes a photo of me and Drew and she presses a few buttons, hopefully sending it to James. Goodness knows what he'll make of it, but I know he'll get the message.

A moment later, the phone rings and she presses a button straight away.

'Answer that and she gets it,' Drew hisses, jabbing the tip of the blade into my throat.

I can hardly breathe, let alone speak.

'Drop it!' he demands.

With a sigh, she throws my phone down. I can't hear it hit concrete, so I hope it's landed on the flowerbed of the nearby house. The contract's costing me an arm and a leg and the last thing I need is to pay for a replacement handset on top of everything else.

'Let her go, Drew. She's no use to you.' This woman's got more guts than I imagined.

'Shut up!' he snaps.

'You can't just kill her out here in the street,' she continues. 'You know how nosey these neighbours'll be. They've probably got CCTV cameras on you right now. You know what it's like in a stuck-up area like this.'

I hadn't thought of that, but it gives me hope. Unfortunately, it seems to make Drew even tetchier and his grip on me tightens even more.

'Then I've got nothing to lose, have I?'

That wasn't the reaction I was hoping for.

'That's crap. You can just let her go and leg it. You know how easily you can go to ground,' she says, with much more confidence than I can muster right now. 'Go on, just run. You know you can make it.' She takes a step closer to us as she's talking.

His body sags slightly next to mine and I guess he's considering it. I immediately grab his hand that's holding the knife and yank it away from my throat, twisting around and shoving my weight against him to knock him to the ground. He tenses again, but it's too late—he's lying on his back with my knee in his groin and I've got his arms pinned above his head.

'Get the knife!' I yell, feeling his strength as he struggles against me.

With one large stride, she reaches us and digs the stiletto heel of her Jimmy Choo into his wrist, eliciting a tremendous howl from him as he stops trying to fight me and starts to shiver.

I decide in that moment that I like this woman—a lot!

16

A deafening screech of sirens tells me in no uncertain terms that help is on its way, but I daren't let go of the bastard beneath me. He's twitching like a rabbit's whiskers, and I hope I'm not going to be held for responsible for him having some kind of seizure.

'He's taken coke again,' the woman informs me, as though reading my thoughts. She's still standing on his wrist, despite all his shouting.

I don't know if I'm relieved that he's not having a fit, or even more scared about what he might have done to me, as her words sink into my befuddled brain.

I'm shocked to see an ambulance arrive along with several police cars, and people hurry out of the nearby houses to survey the action. *Pity they weren't so keen on coming out earlier!*

'Get back inside!' a familiar voice yells, much to the clear disappointment of the neighbours. Alex starts ushering people out of the way.

Police cars pull up at the kerbside and even more police come running towards us.

'Careful, she could be pregnant,' I hear James yell as he and Alex reach us.

I gape at the woman who's still got her heel dug into Drew's arm. He told me all that was a lie—though, why I should believe a word he says is beyond me. Has she really put her baby's life at risk just to help me?

A couple of armed police aim their guns at Drew while Alex removes the knife from his bloody hand.

A second later, James' arms envelope me as he lifts me up and even more cops swoop in and haul Drew to his feet, amid a host of expletives and threats that I don't even listen to.

'Libby, are you okay?' James' face is white as he stares into mine.

I'm trembling, unable to speak, but I manage to nod and that seems to suffice for now. With a warm arm firmly around me, he leads me away from the action and I'm surprised to see Cassie waiting by one of the police cars. She rushes towards me, throwing her arms around me.

'Oh, babe, I'm so sorry,' she says, tears streaming down her cheeks. 'I didn't mean any of it, I promise.'

I don't know what to say, so I just enjoy being sandwiched between the two people who mean the world to me.

'Let's get her checked out.'

I turn to see a couple of paramedics behind me.

'I'm fine, really,' I mutter, looking around for the woman who helped me.

'I think we'll be the judges of that,' one of the men tells me.

'You need to go with them, Libby,' James says, softly. 'If not for your sake then...'

I stare at him blankly.

'Then what?'

'We know there's a chance you might be pregnant,' Cassie says, rubbing my arm.

I stare from her to James, speechless.

'Come on.' The paramedics lead me to the ambulance, my mind whirling.

'When was your last period?' a ginger-haired guy asks as soon as we're inside with the doors closed.

That's a bit personal, especially as we've only just met!

'Hang on. I'm not pregnant,' I say, frowning.

'When did you have the test?' He asks, clearly unconvinced.

'What test?'

'I think maybe we'll go straight to the hospital,' the other paramedic says, pursing his lips.

'Okay.' The ginger guy immediately leaves the ambulance and I hear him speaking to James before he slams the door shut behind him.

'Let's get you strapped in,' the other guy says.

'Hang on, I don't understand,' I protest.

'Don't worry. We'll get you up to the hospital and checked over just to make sure you're okay. Do you feel light-headed or anything?'

I suddenly remember I haven't eaten yet, so actually I do feel a bit weak, but I daren't give them anything else to worry about. They've already got the wrong end of the stick for some reason, and I'm not about to make things any worse.

'I'm fine,' I say, resignedly. 'But you're making a mistake. It's the other girl who might be pregnant, not me.'

It's no good. His mind's clearly made up. I'm not even sure if he's listening to me as he pops a thermometer into my mouth.

'Don't talk,' he says as I moan in protest.

Those are my two least favourite words in the English dictionary.

I have to lie down on a hard stretcher and be strapped in like a sack of potatoes so the ambulance can whizz up the road. I really wish James or Cassie had been allowed to ride in here with me, but these guys seemed in too much of a hurry to get going. Luckily, it only takes a few minutes to reach the hospital, and I'm suddenly blinded by bright lights as soon as the back door opens. Immediately, I'm whisked into a side room where a nurse insists I give her a urine sample straight away. I can't usually do them to order, but for a change, with everything that's gone on today, I actually have no trouble.

'You're not pregnant,' she informs me a short while later and stares at me accusingly.

I roll my eyes. 'That's what I've been trying to tell everyone.'

She looks surprised. 'So, why did they all think you were?'

I shrug. 'I've no idea. I never said I was pregnant. The other lady might be, though. The one who was at the scene with me.' That bastard, Drew Fisher, said she was and then that she wasn't, so I'm not really sure.

'Another crew will be looking after her. You don't need to worry.'

I feel a little annoyed with her attitude, but I say nothing. I really don't want to antagonise her in case she's the one in charge of getting me something to eat later. I've noticed how medical staff never seem to want to discharge you until you've eaten, so I'm hoping we get to that bit soon. I'm starving.

She insists on hooking me up to a blood-pressure and heart monitor machine, and I'm glad I'm in my comfy pyjamas—despite the odd looks I get from the nurses who help me out of my big coat.

I can hear my heart rapidly beeping on the machine beside the bed.

'Your blood pressure's quite high,' the nurse says, removing the horrid nylon cuff from my arm. 'You need to rest quietly for a while.'

'Is my boyfriend here—or Cassie, my best mate?' I ask hopefully.

'I don't know,' she says, writing something on my notes. 'But they won't be able to see you for a while even if they are. We need to get you stabilised.'

'But—'

'You won't help yourself by fretting,' she says, looking back at the monitor. 'I told you. Just get some rest. You've been through a lot and your body needs time to recover.'

She puts a dressing on my neck, and I wonder just how deeply that thug had stuck the knife into my throat. It certainly stings a lot more now than it did at the time, and I assume adrenaline must have shielded me from much of the pain.

Once she's dimmed the lights in the little room and stopped fussing over me, I start to relax a little. I close my eyes for a minute and mad scenes rush through my mind. Drew with the knife to my throat, the woman throwing my phone down, then the shriek of sirens as the police arrive.

Sheer relief makes my whole body feel heavy and I can't remember when I stopped hearing the incessant beeping of the monitor by my side.

***

When I open my eyes in the morning, the room looks much brighter, and someone I presume is a nurse is putting a tray on the little over-bed table for me. She looks much friendlier than the nurse who was here before and smiles when she sees me watching her.

'Morning, sleepyhead,' she says, cheerfully. 'I've brought you some cereal. You must be starving.'

I stare at her at first while I get my bearings.

'Have I been here all night?' I ask, slowly sitting up.

'Yes, it's nearly seven thirty,' she says, straightening the pillows behind me. 'I think they gave you something to calm you down when you came in. Your blood pressure was slightly elevated for a while but it's almost normal now.'

The heart monitor's still beeping but it doesn't sound as loud as it did last night.

'That's good. So, can I go home now?'

She chuckles, which shows the dimples on her rosy cheeks. She's quite young and very pretty with a short, unnaturally blonde bob and big green eyes. 'We'll leave that for the doctor to decide, shall we? Why don't you get on with your breakfast before the cereal goes soggy? I've made you a cup of tea as well.'

'Thanks.' Looking at the food suddenly reminds me that I'm actually ravenous, and I tuck in straight away.

'Is my boyfriend here?' I ask the nurse, between mouthfuls of cornflakes. 'Or my best friend, Cassie?'

She frowns in confusion. 'Visiting hours aren't until later,' she tells me. 'There's no one here yet.'

'Oh.' I feel a little deflated and sit back with a sigh. I had hoped after all the drama last night that they'd both be here waiting for me to wake up. They seemed so concerned about me, and Cassie even apologised. Or did I dream it?

'I'm sure they'll be coming,' the nurse says, obviously seeing my disappointment. 'You wouldn't have wanted them to spend all night sitting on those lumpy chairs in the waiting room, would you?'

'I suppose not,' I concede.

'They probably came last night and were told you'd been transferred up here. Then they would have been advised to go home to get some rest. I heard it was quite a to-do.' She reaches over to write something on the little whiteboard above my bed, and I notice her name badge says, Trudy Jacobson, Student Nurse.

'It was,' I say, visions of the incident flashing through my mind.

'Try not to think about it,' she suggests , patting my arm. 'You don't want your blood pressure shooting up again, do you? They'll never send you home then.'

I take a sip of my lukewarm tea and reach for the slightly browning apple in the corner of my tray. I'm just grateful to get anything inside my hollow stomach right now—I didn't eat last night at all.

'When you've finished, I'll help you to the bathroom where you can freshen up,' she tells me. 'That'll make you feel a lot better.'

'What day is it?' I ask, thinking hard.

'Friday, why?'

I suddenly envision the girls at work, wondering where I am.

'I should be at the office.'

'I'm sure they won't mind you taking a day off. You deserve it after what you've been through.'

For someone who's telling me not to think about it, I notice she has a nasty habit of bringing the subject up.

'How long have you worked here?' I ask, trying to change the subject.

'I'm in my second year of my degree, I've been at this hospital for the past few months,' she says, smiling.

'Do you enjoy it?'

'Yes. I love helping people. It makes me feel as if I'm doing something worthwhile. What do you do?'

'I help people, too,' I tell her, thinking how similar our jobs are—in away. I go on to tell her about my position at the *Chronicle,* and she's very impressed to hear I write my own column.

Awhile later, she helps me to the bathroom, and I'm relieved to hear that someone brought my overnight bag here last night. It makes such a difference having my own toothbrush and shower gel to use, and I feel much more human after a good wash. Trudy leaves me to it, after ascertaining that I wasn't about to keel over or anything, and I take my time.

When I return to my bed it's been made, and all the dishes have been taken away. I check my bag, hoping that someone picked up my phone last night at the scene and popped it in, but it's not there. I sigh, thinking how boring it's going to be if I've got to just sit here all day waiting for a doctor or a visitor to come and see me.

The nurses are all busy with their daily routines, so I decide to have a little nosey around. There are groups of staff in little huddles, having meetings, and cleaners are scrubbing walls and sinks. I poke my head into a side-room just down the corridor and am surprised to see a familiar face.

'Hello,' the woman says, smiling. 'It's Libby, isn't it? How are you feeling?'

It's her. The shoplifter who helped me last night. The one with the Jimmy Choos. She's dressed and packing her things into a small bag.

'I'm fine,' I tell her, nodding. 'Thanks to you.'

'Oh, it was my pleasure,' she says, smiling. 'Believe me, I've wanted to do that for a long time. I'm Sam, by the way.'

'So, he wasn't your boyfriend?' I ask, already guessing the answer.

'God, no! Drew's nothing but scum. He uses people for his own means and doesn't give a shit about them. He's dangerous, too.'

'So, how did you end up with him?' I ask, perching on the end of her bed.

'He blackmailed me into shoplifting for him, same as a load of other girls,' she says, ruefully. 'He threatened to hurt my family if I didn't do as he said.'

'Oh, no, that's awful!' A sinking feeling hits my stomach as I realise just what a lowlife he is.

'Yeah, but I had the last laugh,' she says with a sigh. 'I don't know why I hadn't thought of it before. Actually, it was you who gave me the idea.' She smiles.

'Me?'

'Yep. You said I could be arrested. I thought that would be better than what I was doing, so I made sure the next time I was right under the camera when I stuffed a designer blouse up my jumper.' She giggles. 'As soon as Drew saw the police arrive, he scarpered. Once at the station, I told them everything I knew. Who he was working with, which girls he had stealing for him, the lot. The only thing I couldn't help with was his last name—no one seemed to know that.'

I smile, glad that I was able to give the police a significant piece of the puzzle—thanks to Fran.

'I thought I'd go to jail for a while but at least it would be better than the alternative. I was wrong. The police were more than happy to let me off once I'd grassed him up.' She pulls the zip around her bag and places it on the floor.

'So, how come you didn't get away? Why did you go back to him yesterday?' I ask, frowning.

'I was in the wrong place at the wrong time,' she says with a grimace. 'I thought I was safe in Westminster—it's not his usual haunt. I don't know if someone tipped him off that I was there or not, but he suddenly turned up when I was on my way to the Tube. He grabbed me. That's when you showed up.' She shakes her head. 'He's got spies everywhere. Hopefully, the cops'll pick a few of them up now they've caught the main culprit.'

I shudder.

'Don't worry,' she says with a smile. 'Now that he's off the scene they're all likely to stay off the radar. He's the one they all relied on. Without that bastard they've got nothing.'

'Are you going to be all right?' I ask her, as she pulls on her jacket.

'I'll be just fine now.' She grins. 'More than fine, actually. I can get back to my own life and stop looking over my shoulder all the time. You've done me a favour—in fact you've done a lot of women a favour, though they won't know it. They can all get their lives back now.'

'It wasn't just me,' I tell her, my face heating up at the compliment. 'You're the one who stopped him using the knife.'

She giggles. 'Yeah, with a pair of shoes he forced me to steal in the first place,' she confides. 'That little deed certainly came back to bite him in the arse.'

I laugh. 'Oh, the irony.'

'You can say that again,' she says, still chuckling.

'Thanks for calling the police, too. You could easily have just run off without helping me.'

'After all the help you'd given me?' She raises her eyebrows. 'No way, girl! We've got to stick together in these situations. I took a chance that the James Harper in your phone was the same James Harper who'd been helping me at the station. I thought it quicker to send him a picture than try explaining with a message. He obviously thinks a lot of you—he got straight back to me.'

I feel myself blush. I know how much James cares for me and I'm truly grateful for it.

'I don't know what happened to my phone,' I tell her.

'I answered it before throwing it onto the grass,' she says with a grin. 'I'm pretty sure James got the gist even if he couldn't hear the complete conversation.'

Judging by the speed at which they arrived, I'm inclined to agree with her.

'Samantha, your taxi's here now,' Trudy announces as she comes in with some papers for Sam. She looks surprised to see me. 'Libby, the police are waiting to speak to you. We didn't know where you were.'

I flush with embarrassment. 'Sorry,' I say, jumping off the bed.

'Good luck, Libby,' Sam says, waving a hand to me.

'You too, and thanks again.' I quickly scoot out of her room and back to my own.

'Well, we thought we were going to have to file a missing person's report for a minute there,' Alex quips as soon as I walk in the room.

'I was only down the hall, chatting to Sam.'

'I might have known,' James says, following me into the room. 'Gossiping, I imagine?'

'No, actually we weren't. She was telling me what happened and how she got involved with it all,' I protest. I'm glad to see him in a relaxed mood but still feel a bit indignant to his 'gossiping' remark. I want to give him a massive hug, but I don't think it's appropriate while he's here on business—and with Alex here.

I climb back into bed, suddenly feeling a little self-conscious in just my pyjamas.

'You'll be pleased to know we've got Drew Fisher behind bars, where he belongs,' Alex tells me. 'And he's blabbed about quite a few others who were involved in his dirty little ring, too.'

'It's amazing how they never go down quietly,' James says with a grin. 'If they're going to prison, they'll make damn sure they're not the only ones.'

'Good. We need that sort of scum off the streets,' I say, thinking about poor Sam worrying over her family like that.

James raises his eyebrows in surprise. 'Well, you've certainly toughened up,' he says. 'The other night you seemed to think a custodial sentence was a bit much for a shoplifting crime.'

'Only when the thief's being blackmailed into doing it,' I point out. 'The ringleaders deserve everything they get.'

'Well, Fisher will certainly get what's coming to him,' Alex assures me. 'He'll be going down for a long time, believe me. The photo on here helped, too.' He passes me back my phone.

'Thanks.'

I'm surprised how relieved I feel. Today, I was going to have to face that bastard and tell him I didn't have his money. The odd thing was, although I was worried, I wasn't as terrified as I should've been. Had I known before what I know about him now, I'd have been having a complete panic attack over the whole thing. My dad always used to say that ignorance is bliss and I now know exactly what he meant. *Not that I'm ignorant, exactly!*

'The doctor's here now,' Trudy tells me, poking her head around the door.

'We'll be waiting outside,' James says, smiling at me as the men leave the room.

I can still feel some tension between us, and I know we really need to talk. I don't know what he'll make of all that's been going on, but I know he won't be happy that I've kept so much from him.

The doctor comes in and peers at me in that odd way that doctors do. He checks my notes, tells me how lucky I am and signs the discharge papers.

'You can get dressed now,' Trudy says as soon as he's finished.

I feel slightly nervous as I pull my jeans and a top out of my holdall. I'm looking forward to getting out of here, but I'm going to have to face the music with both Cassie and James now.

***

It's almost lunchtime when James pulls up outside the flat in Chelsea.

'Are you sure you're not too tired?' he asks for the umpteenth time.

'I'm fine, honestly,' I assure him.

We've been making small talk all the way here and he's hardly touched me once. Alex took his own car back to the station, leaving me and James to spend some time together, but I'm beginning to wish he hadn't. The atmosphere's thick with unspoken words. The trouble is we don't have time for the proper heart to heart we need right now. James is still on duty and Cassie's expecting me home at any minute.

'You're back!' Cassie's thrilled to see me, thank goodness, and I'm surprised to see Rob and Ben in the kitchen when I go inside.

'They're skiving,' Cassie says, rolling her eyes as she walks towards me.

'We wanted to make sure you were all right,' Ben calls over.

'Yeah, we were worried about you, Libby. We needed to make sure you were still in one piece,' Rob echoes.

'You're going to be okay,' James assures me, quietly.

'I know.'

'And you're not pregnant,' Cassie says, a little sheepishly, as she throws her arms around me.

'I know that, too.' I frown, suddenly remembering some weird conversations I had last night with the medical staff. 'Who said I was?'

Rob and Ben slowly walk over to us.

'You'd better 'fess up, mate,' Rob says, after giving me a gentle hug.

Ben gives a nervous laugh. 'Well, I didn't actually say she *was* pregnant,' he protests, looking rather uncomfortable.

'You implied it,' Cassie points out.

'Well, what was I supposed to think?' Ben replies, incredulously.

The penny drops.

'This was because of that night in the chemist's?' I query.

He nods.

'But I told you that was for a friend.'

Ben shrugs. 'What else would you have said?'

'You didn't believe me?' I feel hurt as well as offended.

'I'm sorry, Libby. It was just a natural reaction.' He looks quite guilty as he tries to defend himself.

'So, you told everyone I was expecting?' I look around at my friends who all look sheepish—and with good reason.

'We *were* surprised,' Rob interjects.

I shake my head. 'Not as surprised as *me*,' I point out.

'Oh, Libby, I'm so glad you're all right,' Cassie says, putting a hand on my arm. 'We've all been so worried about you.'

'You think I'd have kept something like that from you?' I ask her, shocked at the thought.

'Well, I did think it was *odd*, but I didn't know,' she says with a shrug. 'I was pretty mad at James, to be honest, to think he'd got you pregnant and not even asked you to move in with him—or marry him.'

My mind goes back to the evening when we all played Monopoly together. I'd detected some kind of friction between James and the others but had no idea what they were all thinking. I thought it was because he was doing so well at the game. James had looked quite miserable on occasions, though no one actually said anything to indicate a problem. I'd assumed he wasn't really that keen on Monopoly.

'This is why you were concerned about me drinking that night,' I say to Ben.

He nods.

Now it makes sense.

The happiness I felt about coming home dissipates rapidly as it occurs to me that my so-called friends have all been talking about me behind my back. I feel hurt that they could think I'd get pregnant and not say anything—especially to Cassie, or even James.

'Why didn't you tell me that's what you were thinking?' I ask Cassie. 'How could you keep that from me?' I frown.

She gapes. 'Hang on a minute. I thought *you* were keeping it from *me*,' she says.

'Look, I'd better get back to work,' James says. 'I'll give you a ring later. Maybe we could get together this afternoon and talk things through?' He looks at me questioningly and my heart lurches. I don't want him to leave. He looks gorgeous, as always, and I feel bad that my friends had given him a hard time over something that wasn't even his fault.

'Okay,' I say, following him to the door.

'Take it easy and try not to get upset,' he says, softly.

'I'll try,' I promise.

He kisses me on the top of the head, and I gasp, realising in that instant how far we are from being back to normal. Tears well behind my eyes as I close the door and I wonder for a second if we'll ever get back to the way we were.

'You're not *annoyed* with me, are you?' Cassie asks when I return to the kitchen. 'Because if you are then you're not being fair.'

'Fair?' I reel. 'You've all been saying I was pregnant—you even took it out on James—and you think *I'm* the one who's not being fair?'

'No one said you *were*, exactly,' Ben interjects. 'I just told them that I'd seen you in the chemist's buying a pregnancy test that's all. It was the truth.' He shrugs.

'And we didn't actually take it out on James,' Cassie adds, defensively. 'How could we? He didn't even know until last night that it was a possibility.'

'What? You told him last night with all that shit going on?' I can't believe what I'm hearing. 'As if he didn't have enough to worry about?'

'I told him because we were both worried about *you*,' she replies. 'He'd come round looking for you and I had to explain why you weren't here. We were both out of our minds, afraid something had happened to you. So, I had to tell him about you possibly being pregnant in case you were in some kind of danger. He needed to know.'

'But I wasn't pregnant so there was nothing for him *to* know!' I'm getting more exasperated by the second.

'Well, *we* didn't know that.' Cassie sounds most indignant. 'Perhaps, if you *spoke* to me now and then and actually told me what was going on, I wouldn't say the wrong thing, would I?'

'I didn't tell you because there was nothing to *tell*,' I point out, raising my hands in frustration.

'Yes, but *I* didn't know that, did I?' She gawps at me as if *I'm* the stupid one.

I frown at her, trying to work out what's actually being said here.

'Girls, this is getting us nowhere,' Rob interjects, putting his hands out in a placating manner. 'Why don't we all settle down and have a drink and talk this through logically?'

'Because some of you don't seem to know the meaning of the word *logic*, do you?' I stare at Ben, who frowns at me.

'What's that supposed to mean?'

'I'll put the kettle on,' Rob says, rushing over to the counter.

'It means that if someone says they're buying something for a friend, then the logical conclusion is they're buying something for a *friend*.' I talk slowly, as if he's thick or something, which really pisses him off.

'Duh! And if you'd been buying it for yourself, you'd still have said it was for a *friend*, wouldn't you?' he replies, pulling a face at me and poking his tongue out.

'No, I wouldn't. Because *I'm* not a liar,' I say, throwing my hands in the air.

'Well, how was I to know?' He pulls another face.

'It's a thing called trust. People who call themselves your *friends* are supposed to have it. They're not expected to automatically assume that you're lying to them.' My voice gets louder with each word.

'Chocolate Hobnob, anyone?' Rob offers, passing around the biscuit tin.

I want to say no, as it's clearly just his distraction technique at work, but I'm actually quite partial to a Chocolate Hobnob—and I *am* starving.

I take one from the packet without saying anything and rub my fingers over the knobbly oatiness.

Rob looks relieved. He places the tin in the middle of the dining table and Cassie brings over the tray of drinks.

'Here you go, Libby.' Rob pulls out a chair for me to sit on.

I huff. I know it's the logical thing to do, but it's hard to be a martyr when you're sitting around the table drinking tea and eating Hobnobs.

'Thanks,' I mumble, not really wanting to give him the satisfaction of defusing the situation while I've got the moral high ground. It doesn't happen very often, and I really want to savour the view from up here, but it seems I have to accept that it's going to be very short-lived.

Everyone else piles around the table, and Rob passes round the biscuits again.

'It's good to have you home, Libby,' Rob says, smiling.

I know I should be more gracious, but I can't avoid the snort that emanates from me in response.

'Aren't you glad to be here?' Cassie asks me with an innocent expression.

'I don't know,' I tell her. 'I thought I was coming back to my friends, but it seems I'm just with a group of people who think I'm a liar, for some reason.' Honestly, if my nose got any farther in the air I'd be dusting the ceiling with it right now.

'Well, maybe there's a fine line between lying and just not telling someone the truth,' she replies, curtly.

I narrow my eyes at her, trying to fathom what she's insinuating. *Surely, she's not still trying to make me look like I'm in the wrong?*

'But I did tell the truth,' I point out. 'That pregnancy test was for Fran. You can ask her yourself if you don't believe me.' *I secretly hope she doesn't take me up on that offer, as poor Fran would be mortified.*

'Maybe I will,' Cassie says, airily. Now I know she's just read my mind as she doesn't even know Fran. She's just trying to worry me.

'Or maybe I'll just be the bigger person and believe you anyway, despite your not being entirely honest with me.' Cassie leans over and pointedly takes a biscuit from the tin.

I fume at her, my mind reeling.

'When have I not been honest?' I demand, my voice rising a little more than I intended.

She clears her throat and we all look at her, awaiting her big announcement. When it comes, I just want to curl up and die.

'When you didn't tell me that James had asked you to move in with him all those weeks ago,' she replies, pursing her lips.

She takes a bite from her Hobnob, which snaps perfectly between her teeth, beautifully accentuating her point.

I stare into my teacup, not wanting to meet anyone's eye. It's amazing how quickly you can slide from the moral high ground down to the depths of despair. *Damn!*

'I didn't want to hurt your feelings,' I reply, trying to climb out of the hole I've just got myself into.

'Too late for that,' she says, echoing my reply from last night.

'I was going to tell you when the time was right,' I protest. 'But you seemed so concerned about me that I didn't want to worry you any more than you were already.'

'I was worried because I thought you were pregnant and that James wasn't supporting you,' she says, her jaw clenched.

I gape at her. 'Why on earth would you think that? Of course, James would support me if that was the case. We love each other.'

'Because, as far as we knew, he hadn't even asked you to move in with him. In our eyes—because we hadn't been told anything different—it looked as though he wasn't having much to do with you and was certainly not making any firm plans for your future together.' She leans forward to talk to me, conveying her message as clear as crystal.

'She's got a point, Libby,' Rob says, making me feel even worse. *Thanks, Rob.*

'So, it's *my* fault?' I ask, sarcastically.

'Yep,' Cassie says, before taking another bite of her Hobnob.

I glare at her. I hadn't expected that reaction.

I take a long sip of my tea, giving myself a little thinking time. It's not long enough. I've got no idea what to say after I've swallowed. I reach over and help myself to another biscuit, conscious of Cassie watching me.

I stick my nose in the air and take a bite with as much aplomb as I can muster. Unfortunately, the oaty mass immediately crumbles and bits of Hobnob plop straight into my tea, splashing over the sides. *Why me?*

There's a loud snort and I look up to see Cassie's face turn bright red as she tries not to laugh. Her lovely face is contorted in all directions as she attempts to hide her mirth, but in the end, she just bursts out laughing. Rob and Ben join in, too, and, much to my own astonishment I begin to giggle. Soon, we're all roaring with laughter, and I'm wondering what on earth we were all getting so het up about in the first place.

Tears stream down my bestie's face as she gets up and comes over to give me a huge hug. We're still giggling as I stand up and throw my arms around her.

'I'm so sorry,' she says, smiling.

'Me, too,' I admit, squeezing her even tighter.

'Oh, God. That was so funny though,' she says when we finally recover and pull away from each other.

A vision of my Hobnob taking a nosedive into my tea flits through my mind and soon we're both laughing even more. The boys come over and give me a hug too, and we all apologise to each other.

'You don't have to tell me anything,' Cassie says, softly when we eventually calm down and Rob puts the kettle on for a fresh brew. 'Honestly, I'm sorry for making you feel bad. You're entitled to have your secrets.'

'It's not exactly a secret,' I tell her. 'As I told you, James asked me to move in with him when we were on the beach in Broadstairs and I didn't know what to say. I mean, I want to live with him, but at the same time I didn't want to spoil what we've got here.'

'The lease is up on Rob's flat at the end of the month. He didn't know whether to renew it or move in here.'

'You should have said something,' I say, aghast, as Rob returns with fresh drinks for us all.

Rob looks over at Cassie.

'We were discussing whether it was an option for all three of us to live here,' she says, looking frightfully uncomfortable.

'And?'

'She didn't want to spoil what you already had, either,' Rob says with a grimace. 'You two have such a special relationship she didn't want to ruin it by adding me to the mix.'

'On the other hand, I really want to be with Rob,' Cassie admits, looking sheepish.

'You were in the same situation as me.' I can't imagine why it took me so long to realise it. It all makes sense now I think about it. I just wish I'd thought about it much sooner and saved all this heartache.

She nods.

'So, have any of you made any decisions?' Ben asks, reaching over for the biscuit tin.

I can see how torn Cassie is. I know the feeling well.

'I need to speak to James,' I say, in a small voice. 'I'm not really sure where the ground lies with him. He might not want me to move in with after all that's happened.'

'You haven't done anything wrong.' Ben looks surprised.

'Actually, I have,' I admit. 'I promised him in future I'd keep him informed of anything that happened and I'm afraid I didn't exactly keep him in the loop with all this business with Drew Fisher or the woman I caught shoplifting. Things might have been much easier if I'd just spoken to him in the first place.'

'There seems to be a trend running here,' Rob says, shaking his head. 'I thought women loved talking. How come you never seem to speak up when it actually matters?'

Cassie gives him a playful swat. 'Watch it. You're treading on very thin ice there, lover boy,' she warns him with a grin.

'Yeah, you do realise you're actually inviting them to talk, don't you, bro?' Ben raises his eyebrows. 'Which means you and I won't get a word in for the rest of the day.'

I can't help giggling. It's so good to see everyone back to normal. I just hope the situation with James is resolved as easily...

I'm disappointed to get a call from James a while later to say that he's been held up at work, but he offers to take me for a drink when he finishes, provided I'm not too tired. I had hoped to spend some quality time with him and explain everything properly so we could get our relationship back on track.

Fortunately, when he comes to fetch me, he's actually in a better mood than I expected.

'I thought we'd just go somewhere local,' he says. 'I need to go in again in the morning for a few hours to finish off some work.'

'Oh, okay.' I grab my coat and bag and follow him out to his car.

We go to a lovely little place James knows near the river. It's not as crowded as I'd expect for a Friday night, and we get a table in a quiet corner.

'That Fisher-guy's even more dangerous than we thought,' James says as we settle down with our drinks. 'He's got form.'

'Oh.' My heart pounds. I knew I had a lucky escape, but it looks like the whole thing was even more perilous than I'd imagined.

'I can't believe you let yourself get into such a mess. Libby, you could have been killed or something. Do you realise that?'

I do now.

'He never threatened to kill me,' I point out, though I can't stop my hands trembling a little at the thought.

'So, the first time you came across him was in the shop when he was getting Samantha to shoplift for him?'

I sigh. We went through all this at the hospital, with both him and Alex making copious notes, not to mention repeating the same questions over and over. 'Yes. But I didn't actually *see* her shoplifting.'

'But as near as? And you suspected that's what's she was doing?' He takes a sip of his drink.

'Like I told you, I had no evidence of it. If I'd reported her and she hadn't taken anything I'd have looked like a right idiot.'

'But instead you've let yourself get into all this danger,' he says, raising his eyebrows.

'Yes, but I didn't know that at the time, did I?' I wave my hands in the air in exasperation. 'All I knew was that it looked like the guy was getting her to take something and then he threatened me not to say anything.'

'And it didn't occur to you to tell me?' I can't read his expression.

'James, I didn't know there was anything to tell,' I explain. At the time, I had no proof that she'd done anything wrong and he could've just been an idiot who liked throwing his weight around. How was I to know that it would escalate the way it did? All I was trying to do was my job.'

'And I was trying to do mine,' he points out. 'Which would have been much easier if you'd come clean about the incident and put us onto Fisher in the first place.'

I sit back in my chair, staring at him incredulously. 'Oh, I'm so sorry I didn't help you with your job,' I say sarcastically. 'Of course, I should have known the most important thing was to report every little incident to you.'

'Yes, it is.' He sounds curt.

'You know damn well that if I'd come to you with half a story and a suspicion you would've thought I was just wasting your time and making stuff up,' I tell him. 'Just like at The Chalfont when I tried to tell you my theory about the thefts.'

'That was different,' he says, wearily. 'And it was a long time ago.'

'How was it different?'

'I didn't really know you then.'

'That shouldn't make any difference. Any member of the public telling you something about a crime should be taken seriously, surely? That's your job, isn't it?'

'Don't you start telling me what my damn job is,' he says, gritting his teeth angrily.

I huff before taking a sip of my drink. This isn't going as well as I'd hoped at all.

'All I'm saying is that you should have told me anyway,' he says in a quiet voice. 'You never know where these things might lead.'

'Probably, to you not believing me and telling me to stop wasting police time,' I snap.

'Or to us catching that bastard before he had time to terrorise you as well as other women, and then hold a knife to your throat.' His voice is still quiet, and I know he won't want our conversation to be overheard, but I just want to shout at him. It's so frustrating!

'Well that's easily said with hindsight, isn't it?' I say, sarcastically.

He sighs, sitting back in his chair.

There are a few moments of silence between us before he speaks again.

'Is that the only reason you didn't tell me? Because you were afraid I wouldn't believe you?' he asks, softly.

My mind races. When he talks like that, I want to be all quiet and calm, too, but it's not that easy when I'm all riled up and ready to have a row with him. But I don't want to row. I want us to make up, I really do. I want things to go back to how they were before he accused me of kissing that scumbag—before he even *thought* about it. And we certainly won't get there by going round and round in circles and yelling at each other in public.

'At first, I thought that the woman, Sam, was shoplifting and I should report her,' I explain, calmly. 'Then the guy threatened me if I said anything.'

'Did he frighten you?'

'Well, I was a bit shaken,' I confess. 'But I hadn't actually seen Sam take the item and leave the store with it, so I had no proof that anyone had done anything wrong. There was no point in telling you half a story, was there?' I shrug.

'But a man threatened you in a shop,' James points out, leaning forwards.

'Yes, but I wouldn't have been able to tell you what he looked like, or who he was. How would that help?' I say, leaning forwards, too.

'We knew that scum was out there somewhere. If you'd told me what had happened, I could have added two and two and checked the security cameras of the shop. We could have reported a positive sighting.'

I sigh. When he puts it like that it does make sense to have told him.

'But I didn't know it was him you were looking for,' I protest. 'You never tell me stuff like that.'

'That's because it's my job. I'm not allowed to tell you that sort of information. And besides, we didn't know what the guy looked like. All we had was a first name and his reputation.'

I frown. 'How come?'

James shakes his head. 'We're playing with the big boys now, love,' he says, ruefully. 'He's not the kind of everyday petty criminal that we get files distributed about in the daily round robin. We knew he existed, and we suspected he'd turned up on our patch, but that was about all we had.'

My stomach heaves. James has a really dangerous job, and I don't give him enough credit for that. It also must seem impossible at times when he doesn't get all the evidence he needs to arrest someone. I suddenly feel really guilty for keeping such a vital piece of information from him—not that I did so intentionally. I mean, how could I have known it would be important?

'I'm sorry. I should have said something.'

'No, I'm sorry,' he says, placing a hand over mine.

I stare at him.

'You were right. When we were at The Chalfont, I didn't think you were right with your suspicions.'

'I wasn't,' I say, with a self-deprecating smile.

'You were right about a lot of it,' he says, nodding. 'And I should have listened to you. I made assumptions because I thought you were bringing your personal feelings into it and I was wrong. I can understand why that would make you feel you can't tell me when something like this happens. I need you to trust me and that's my fault. I'm going to earn that trust, Libby, and that's a promise.' He looks so serious I want to cry.

'I *do* trust you,' I tell him. 'Honestly, if I'd thought it was that important, I'd have told you as soon as he threatened me. I just didn't take it seriously enough that's all.'

He smiles weakly. 'In future, I want you to tell me everything. Not just because it could be important to the case I'm working on, but because it's important to you and it's part of your life. I rarely hear about what goes on in your world, Libby, and that's my own fault. Well… that and the fact we haven't had as much time together as I'd like.'

I feel a bit taken aback, to be honest. James has rarely asked me about my day—or at least, in a way that makes me think he really wants to hear all about it. But he's right. Maybe, if we spent more time together, we'd be able to have conversations about what's going on in our separate lives. It would be nice.

'So, what you mean is if I moved in with you, we'd have that time?' I ask, cagily.

He smiles. 'I'm not pressurising you in any way, Libby,' he insists. 'When you're ready and you want to it'll be great, but not until then. You've had so much going on lately, what with Davinia Urquhart and now this scumbag, I quite understand if you want to take more time to think about it.'

I stare at him. He seems so contrite I just want to hug him. I settle for squeezing his hand.

'When I asked you in Broadstairs, I think I was possibly jumping the gun a bit,' he goes on. 'We'd just been through all that business with you nearly getting killed and I wanted you to be with me all the time so I could keep an eye on you. Protect you. Of course, it's not possible twenty-four hours a day, but I thought it would be good to spend every minute together that we possibly could.' He clears his throat and I notice his eyes looking a little watery. *Is he tearing up?*

A huge lump clogs the back of my throat as I realise just how worried he was about me. I mean, I knew he was worried, of course, but not *this* much.

'I could have lost you,' he says, softly.

'I'm sorry.' I can hardly speak.

He smiles, rubbing my hand with his thumb. 'It wasn't your fault.'

'No, but I suppose I've been a bit selfish in all this,' I admit. 'I just didn't realise how much it had affected you or anyone else. I was just glad to be okay again. It didn't occur to me that you might not be able to bounce back quite that quickly. It must have been terrifying for you.' Tears fill my eyes as I imagine how I would have felt had it been him who was in that situation instead of me. Not only would I not have been much use to him, but I would've crumbled under the strain of it, I'm sure.

'When you're in the thick of it you have to just think about number one,' he says, kindly. 'If you spent your time thinking about everyone else you wouldn't be able to act instinctively, and that's what often gets you out of trouble.'

'Yeah, but afterwards I should've thought about you more,' I say, a tear rolling down my cheek. I sniff. 'I was relieved, and I just thought you would be, too. I'd put all that fear behind me but it's not that easy for you. You've had to sit back and watch it all happen, while I've actually had something to do, to think about—like getting out of it.'

'You work well on your instincts,' he says smiling.

'But I should have realised how important it was to you that I moved in straight away, to keep you from worrying about me. I was too busy thinking about...'

'Cassie,' he finishes for me. 'And you were right to. She's been a good friend to you and you're a loyal friend to her. She deserved your concern—after all, she'd gone through all that shit worrying about you, too. It was selfish of me to want you to move in with me straight away. Cassie needed you there and you needed some semblance of normality. You did the right thing. I'm sorry for putting pressure on you to move out.'

I gaze into his handsome face through my tears. He looks so sincere and sorrowful. My stomach roils. I hope he doesn't think he shouldn't have asked me to move in at all—is that what he's saying? Doesn't he want me to live with him now? Oh, God, have I really blown it?

'It's getting late,' he says, cutting into my thoughts. 'Let's get you home.'

'Will I see you tomorrow?' I ask, my voice a little croaky. 'After you finish work?' I hold my breath, waiting for his reply.

'If you want to,' he says. 'But now you need to get some rest. You've been through a lot and you need time to recuperate. I probably shouldn't have brought you out tonight. It was too soon after what happened.'

I stand up and he helps me put on my coat. Even as he takes my hand and leads me out of the pub, I can't help feeling a sort of finality about the whole evening. We climb into his car and he drives me back in virtual silence. I wipe my face and blow my nose.

'Are you okay?' he asks as he pulls up outside the flat.

'I think so.' I'm not sure, but I can't tell him that.

He gets out of the car and comes around to open my door and help me out. He's such a gentleman.

After locking the car, he takes me up to the flat, pausing on the doorstep just outside.

'You look tired,' he says. 'I shouldn't have kept you out so late.'

'I'm fine,' I assure him. 'Honestly.'

'Well, get a good night's sleep,' he says. 'And don't worry that scum's behind bars and will be staying that way for a long time. We've got most of his accomplices, too, so you've got nothing to fret about there.'

I nod. 'Thanks.' I don't want to mention that Fisher and his pals are the least of my worries right now.

James sounds like he's tying up all the loose ends before he leaves me. I'm afraid this is his way of saying goodbye. That lump is burning the back of my throat again, and I know I'll just dissolve in a heap of tears the minute his back's turned.

'Well, goodnight,' he says with a weak smile.

I lean in, hoping for a kiss when suddenly the door opens in front of us.

'I thought I heard voices.' Cassie stops abruptly. 'Oh, sorry, was I interrupting something? I'll just...'

'No, it's fine,' James assures her, stopping her closing the door again.

He leans over and kisses the top of my head.

'Goodbye,' he says to both of us and leaves. Just. Like. That.

My body wilts as I fall into Cassie's arms.

'Oh, hon. What's happened?' She holds me tight as she closes the door behind us.

'I-I think he's g-going to…to f-finish with me.' I was right about that deluge of tears. I don't think they'll ever stop falling down my face.

19

I've no idea what time I stopped crying and fell asleep last night, it's all a complete blur. My throat's sore and my nose feels tender from having wiped and blown it so much. My eyes sting, too, but all that pales in relation to the pain in my heart.

'You're awake,' Cassie comes in with a cup of tea and a reassuring smile. 'Do you feel any better today?'

'No.' I know it's not the answer she was hoping for, but I have to be honest. I feel like shit. I've ruined everything.

'Drink this,' she says, as I squidge myself into a sitting position. 'Tea makes everything seem better.'

I take the cup from her, although I'm not convinced.

'I think you should wait and see what James has to say later,' she continues, perching on the bed next to me. 'He didn't look like he was about to break up with you when he left.'

I gape at her. 'He said goodbye.'

'He was going home.'

'But it wasn't a goodnight, it was goodbye.'

'And he'd just kissed you.'

'On the head.'

'It's still a kiss.'

'It's not the same.'

She sighs. 'Libby, I think you need to talk this through properly with him. You said yourself that you think he's *going* to break up with you. Not that he *had*.'

'It was pretty clear to me,' I say, sulkily, my mind going back to last night's conversation. 'He was apologising for stuff. James doesn't do that normally.'

'Only because he doesn't usually do anything that needs an apology.'

'But this was for stuff that happened ages ago. When we were working at The Chalfont. Why would he bring all that up if he wasn't about to dump me? He's tying up all his loose ends so he can make it quick and painless today. For him anyway.' I wail.

'When we worked at the hotel, he didn't believe your theories were right about the thefts, did he? But you actually had some really good points that helped him pinpoint the thief in the end. From what you told me last night, he was only apologising because the way he treated you then, affected how you felt about telling him what was going on with that Fisher prick. If he'd been a

270

bit more open to your ideas from the start, you might have felt easier about explaining when he first threatened you. That's all.'

It sounds quite plausible when she says it, but it didn't feel that way in my head.

'So, why didn't he kiss me properly when he left? James always gives great kisses.'

She leans forwards as I sip my tea—which isn't doing it's magic, by the way.

'Maybe he felt as unsure about the situation as you did,' she says, calmly. 'It sounds like you both had a bit of a heart to heart and left each other with lots to think about. He was probably still mulling things over.'

I shake my head. 'I'm not so sure,' I confess. 'I don't even think he's all that keen to see me today. I just think he's made his mind up and wants to finish everything between us.'

'James isn't like that. He's as straight up as they come,' she says, decisively. 'He's used to making decisions and standing by them. If he'd decided that it was over between you, he would have said so last night.'

I take a deep breath, willing the tea to do its work.

'I think maybe you're just feeling a bit over-sensitive, which is hardly surprising after everything that's happened lately. Get yourself ready and go and see him,' Cassie suggests.

'But what if he really does want to break up with me? He'll tell me today. Maybe, if I pretend I'm busy he'll have more time to re-think.' The idea's growing on me the more I ponder it. He can't dump me if he doesn't see me, can he? All right, I know he could always text or phone but it's not his style. For something as important as that, I'm sure James would want to tell me to my face. I hope. Well, I hope *not*, actually—I don't want him to tell me at all. Oh, God, this is all such a mess!

***

I have to admit I feel a bit better once I've showered, dressed and put on my make-up. My hair actually behaves itself, and I wear it in a half-up, half-down style. I'm wearing Armani jeans—used, but VGC from eBay—that make my bum look really good, and a pretty jumper.

My head cleared a little while I was in the shower and I remembered a few things that made me think a little more hopefully. Didn't James say 'in the future I want you to tell me about what's happening in your world' or words to that effect? He must really like me if he's that interested in my life—I don't think anyone's ever said that to me before. I usually feel like I'm boring people when I talk about work or my friends—apart from Cassie, of course. And surely that means he's thinking about us going forward? That we have a future together? Unless he just means that he wants to be friends, of course. That might make sense. Sort of. Well, *I'm* not being his friend. That would be far too difficult. Oh, God, I don't even want to think about it.

I pick up my empty cup and head for the kitchen. I hear voices before I get there and realise Rob's here.

'I can't wait until we can do this all the time,' he says.

'I know. I really miss you when you're not here,' Cassie replies, wistfully. 'I love waking up with you next to me.'

'I love it too, babe. Hopefully, it won't be for much longer, though.' Rob sounds quite optimistic.

'I'm not sure how things stand with Libby and James right now,' Cassie says. 'What if they really are splitting up?'

Rob tuts. 'I've already put my notice in at my place. I'll have to start looking for somewhere else if that's the case.'

'I'm sure it'll be okay for you to still move in here,' Cassie tells him, though she doesn't sound convinced.

'I don't know. Let's just see how things go today, shall we?'

Cassie sighs.

A big lump forms in my stomach. If James dumps me, I might end up with nowhere to go myself. I know it would be awkward if Rob moved in here. I like him, don't get me wrong, but I'd still feel like a gooseberry. And it's only fair that Cassie should have her boyfriend living with her instead of her friend if that's what she wants—it's her flat, after all. I think I might have to start looking for somewhere else to live—and I certainly won't be able to afford to stay in Chelsea!

I hear movement so I head into the kitchen, pretending I haven't been eavesdropping round the corner for the last few minutes.

'Morning, Rob,' I say, as brightly as I can manage.

'Hey Libby. You look well. Going somewhere nice?' He smiles. I wonder if it's me he's pleased for or himself—after all, if James and I work it out then Rob doesn't need to worry about moving in here. I quickly admonish myself for being so judgemental.

'Thanks,' I say. 'I'm not sure. I'm seeing James shortly, but I don't know what he's got planned.' *I just hope it's not dumping me!*

'Well, I think you deserve to be taken somewhere really nice,' he says.

'Ooh, and does that apply to me, too?' Cassie asks, coming over and nuzzling into his side.

'I'll take you wherever you like, darling, you know that.' He kisses the top of her head. It's just a simple gesture but it makes my mind reel. It looks so sweet, and I wonder if I've misjudged James' intentions when he did it to me last night. Did he just mean it to be a cute kiss? After all, I'd only just come out of hospital, so he was hardly going to ravish me on the spot, was he? *Unfortunately.*

I wash my mug and glance up at the time. It's almost twelve. I wonder how long James will be kept at the station today. It's not fair him having to work on a Saturday, but I suppose it's part of the job with him being a sergeant. More responsibility. And, knowing James, he probably volunteered to go in to get the work finished. He's dedicated like that.

It occurs to me that the work might be something to do with Fisher, being as he was talking about him last night. It's a bit worrying to think that he's even more dangerous than the police thought, but I'm glad I didn't know that at the time.

My phone pings, and I quickly whip it out of my back pocket.

Hey Libby. Hope you're okay today. Do you still want to meet up? I'm about to finish work now xx

My heart leaps. It's James and he's put kisses on his text. Like normal. Does that mean we're okay? Or, at least that we're going to be? I quickly text back.

Hey. That would be lovely. Shall I meet you at yours? xx

Even if we go out, I know he'll want to go back and get washed and changed first. On the other hand, if he *is* going to kick me to the kerb, I'd rather he did it in private.

Great! I'll be there in about half an hour xx

I let out a huge sigh. He sounds like he's happy that he's going to see me. Maybe I've been worrying over nothing?

'Was that James?' Cassie asks, walking up behind me and making me jump.

'Yep. I'm going over to his place.'

She smiles and gives me a hug. 'Good. You look lovely—you'll knock his socks off.'

'I don't think it's his socks she's hoping for,' Rob says cheekily, as he comes back into the kitchen. He winks at me and grins.

'I'm sure I don't know what you mean,' I say, in my best innocent voice.

Rob snorts. 'Yeah, right.'

I shake my head, stick my nose in the air and leave the room, giggling.

***

The trouble with train journeys is there's too much time to think. Firstly, when you're walking to the Tube station. Then you invariably have to wait a short while for the next train to arrive. Then there's the journey itself and the walk at the other end.

And the trouble with thinking is it can take you in all sorts of directions you might not otherwise have considered.

On this particular journey I started off thinking how hunky James is and how I can't wait to see him. I feel really good in my outfit and hope he's impressed, too. He often makes nice comments about my clothes.

But then I remembered how things had been between us since all that trouble with Drew Fisher. How he thought I'd been kissing the scumbag in the alley, and that the reason I didn't want to move in with him was because I'd found someone else.

And what about the whole pregnancy thing? James actually thought I was pregnant and didn't even tell me—how unfair's that? Especially when I didn't even know myself.

So, was he glad that I wasn't pregnant or not? Would he have wanted to start a family this soon? I mean, I know that ideally we'd wait—we *will* wait—but what if, by some fluke, I had already been carrying his child? Was he happy at the prospect or not?

James often plays his cards very close to his chest, and I know sometimes his job is top secret, but *I'm* not top secret, am I? And neither's our baby—if I had one, of course—which I don't. Not yet, anyway. But *he* didn't know that, did he? And neither did I. So why, when he heard that it was a possibility, didn't it occur to him to talk to me about it? Now I've got no idea how he thinks, and I can't possibly ask him. If I did, he'd think I was disappointed at not being pregnant and that might put him right off me. After all, it's not what we've planned and I'm sure neither of us is ready yet, are we? But even so, he could have at least *acknowledged* it.

None of that was mentioned last night because he'd been too interested in how things had gone with Fisher. In other words, his job. Which was all we'd spoken about at the hospital, too, especially as Alex was there.

I feel quite wound up by the time I arrive at Fulham. I've just spent all night worrying about James dumping me, and actually, I can't help thinking that he should be the one worrying about *me* dumping *him*.

Another thought crosses my mind as I walk up to his building, what if he realises I could have grounds to dump him and he's just planning to get in there first? It's what blokes do, isn't it? To save face? Oh, no, now I feel sick all over again. I shake off my negative thoughts as much as I can as I walk towards the front door and hold my head as high as I can. Here we go...

20

Although James' flat is quite small compared to the one I share with Cassie in Chelsea, it's perfectly neat and big enough—at least, now that Suzanne and her random knick-knacks have moved out. Shelves are no longer cluttered with strange ornaments, and every surface is clear instead of having 'things' placed on them. Even the smell is back to normal—James' Hugo Boss aftershave instead of some sickly stuff that Suzanne wears.

'Coffee or wine?' James offers.

'Coffee, please.' The atmosphere between is still strained and I want a clear head if we're going to have a serious talk.

'Sit down,' he says, gesturing towards the sofa, before disappearing into the kitchen.

I can't help imagining him sleeping on here as I plonk myself down. It's much firmer than the ones Cassie and I have, and I can't really see myself lounging around on here in my pyjamas, somehow. I grimace at the thought. I'm not sure I'd ever be truly comfortable living here—but then again, I'm not certain that's still an option after recent events. My stomach churns at the thought. It was all going so smoothly.

James is just so efficient and ordered that nothing is out of place; it's no wonder he's in such a good job. I wonder what it would have been like had I moved in here. I'm not *messy* as such, I'm just not that tidy. Certainly not as much of a neat freak as James is. Then again, few people are. Except maybe Monica in *Friends*. The thought makes my mouth twitch for a brief moment.

Something catches my eye and I get up to investigate. A pile of papers has been left on a shelf by the TV. A closer look reveals a picture of a block of flats and the heading: Baine, Warner and Simpkiss emblazoned across the top. They're property details from an estate agent.

'Here you go,' James suddenly reappears with two mugs of coffee.

I feel sick, but force a weak smile, hoping he doesn't think I was snooping.

'Thanks.'

I go over and sit on the sofa as he places the drinks on two cork coasters on the coffee table.

I'm relieved when he sits next to me but not so much when he says 'Libby, we need to talk properly.'

The devil in me wants to quip back 'you mean, I have to use my mouth this time instead of my feet?' but

I refrain from joking. He doesn't look like he's in the mood for my humour. Or any humour, actually.

'Okay,' I say quietly.

I'm disappointed he doesn't hold my hand—at least that would soften the blow—but instead he scrubs his hand over his face, staring at his coffee.

My brain resembles the holding stack at Heathrow Airport, with all these questions lined up in logical order, ready to slide down the runway and out of my mouth. Some are like a massive Airbus 380, whipping up loads of turbulence in its wake—like 'how could he have possibly thought I'd be pregnant without telling him?'—while others are more like the Boeing 737, lighter, with less impact, but still important—like, 'how did he find me in Westminster?' Although I'm aware that even the innocuous B737 could turn into an A380, depending on his answer. For example, if he says 'I knew you were in Westminster because you were picked up on the street's CCTV' then it remains a calm B737. If, on the other hand, he says 'I'd been following you ever since you left the flat in Chelsea,' then it morphs into this tumultuous A380 and will probably be followed by a lot more Airbuses—or one of those jumbo ones they're still perfecting—in a quick-fire routine. You just never know. That's what makes this all so nerve-wracking.

'I know you didn't want to hurt Cassie's feelings by telling her you were moving out to be with me, but did it never occur to you that maybe you'd be doing her a favour?' he asks.

I snap my head up. 'You mean, do her a favour by moving out?' My voice is quite curt.

'Only because she wanted to move Rob in,' he says, calmly. 'I hinted at the situation when we were in Broadstairs, if you remember?'

I swallow hard, trying to let common sense and memory replace hurt and anger. He did mention something about them being in love and wanting to be together, I seem to remember, now that I think really hard. In my defence, it was a while ago.

'So, you knew what they were planning?' I ask him, accusingly.

'No. I merely saw the situation for what it was and ascertained it was a possibility. They're obviously in love. It's a natural progression in a relationship.'

That bloody word again!

'Some people would say getting married is the natural thing to do,' I bite back at him. I watch his face for a look of remorse but there isn't one. I was hoping he'd cotton on that maybe I wanted him to propose to me, not just ask me to move in. I'm not sure it's what I want right now, though. It feels like I'm poking a stick at a sleeping dragon, waiting for a reaction.

'I don't think either of them are ready for that sort of commitment just yet,' he says, thoughtfully. 'Are you?'

I consider the question. I didn't expect him to put it quite like that.

'Am I ready to get married?' I clarify.

He nods, standing up.

I huff. It's hard to have a meaningful conversation with a moving target. I want to see the whites of his eyes for a reaction, but he's gone to fetch something from a drawer in the corner unit.

'I don't know,' I mumble. I'm not saying anything committal to the back of his head.

He returns to the sofa carrying what looks like a folded piece of paper.

'So, you wouldn't have wanted me to propose to you, then?' he enquires, sitting next to me again.

I shrug.

'Libby, did you want us to get married?' he asks, facing me head-on.

I swallow hard, my face heating up.

'I told you, I don't know,' I reply obstinately. 'Not that it matters now, anyway, does it.'

'Why?'

'Because you *didn't* propose, did you? So, it's irrelevant.'

'But is that what you wanted? For us to get married? In the near future?' He looks incredulous, which only makes me feel stupid.

I shrug again.

'Is that what this was about?' he asks, unfolding the paper in his hand.

I gape at them. It's the brochure from the Falcon's Wing Hotel.

'Where did you get that?' I ask, my mouth going dry.

'Cassie found it in a handbag she'd lent you,' he says, slowly. 'Apparently, there was also a wedding pack from the same hotel lying on the counter at your place. She was worried about you because she thought you'd been acting a little... odd... lately. She'd already heard Ben's theory about you being pregnant but didn't want to betray you by mentioning it to me. However, it did occur to her that if you were pregnant you might have wanted to get married. She asked me if I had any intention of asking you.'

'And was she disappointed when you told her nothing was further from your mind?' I ask, raising my eyebrows to show him that it doesn't bother me.

He takes a deep breath, and I guess it's to buy him a little thinking time.

'Probably,' he relents. 'But she showed me this to suggest that maybe it was on *your* mind.'

'And what did you think?' I ask, cagily.

'Well, I was surprised,' he says, pouting a little. 'We'd never discussed marriage. I had no idea you might have been thinking along those lines.'

'Well, *you* certainly weren't,' I snap at him.

He huffs. 'Libby, look how hard it's been for you to decide whether or not to move in with me,' he says, frowning. 'How could I expect you to make a decision about marrying me—a lifetime commitment—right now?'

I stare at him. Suddenly, a stream of Airbus 380s disappear into the Bermuda Triangle in my mind. I feel deflated. But he's absolutely right. No wonder he hasn't proposed to me if I can't make my mind up about just moving in with him!

'That was Fran's,' I explain after a lengthy silence. 'Some guy—the one who knew Drew Fisher—was trying to trick her into paying for a wedding there.'

He frowns. 'Really?'

'It's a long story,' I say, suddenly remembering the state poor Fran was in at the time.

'I'm not going anywhere,' he says, picking up his coffee cup.

I stare at him in surprise. 'You mean, you want to hear about it?' I'm not used to him actually having the time or the inclination to listen to stuff like this—not that I'd have expected it to interest him, anyway.

'I'm fascinated,' he admits. 'It sounds like your friends are just like you for getting into weird situations.' A smile twitches his lips as he sits back, making himself comfortable.

I'm not sure if he's laughing at me or not, but he's right. I'd always thought it was just *me* who got into these scrapes. I go on to explain all about Fran and Tyler—mentioning my first encounter with Drew Fisher along the way—and how Beulah and I went back to the hotel afterwards and exposed Daniel to his boss. I also tell him about Tyler trying to convince Fran that she was pregnant in order to coerce her to pay for the wedding quickly. And my encounter with Ben when I went to fetch her a pregnancy test to put her mind at rest.

'Wow!' I've never seen James look so dumbfounded. I think he's impressed. *It doesn't happen very often, which is why I don't actually recognise it.*

'Fran was so relieved when Tyler dumped her,' I tell him, remembering how pleased she was. 'I don't think she's heard from him since.'

'You did a good job, there,' he says, nodding.

'That's how I ended up with the wedding brochure.'

'I told Cassie there would be a reasonable explanation,' he says, pursing his lips. 'Though I hadn't bargained on anything like that.'

'I'm not ready to get married yet,' I admit, as the thought strikes me. 'And I'm not ready to have a baby, either.'

'All in good time, eh?' he says with a warm smile.

I nod. 'Maybe.'

He leans in for a kiss when an A380 suddenly swoops towards the runway.

'So, what made you think I was snogging that scumbag, Fisher?'

The mood turns instantly, and James sits back again, taking a deep breath.

'I'm sorry about that,' he says, quietly. 'I was wrong.'

I suddenly regret bringing it up. I didn't need to. I know he didn't really mean to insult me, and I believed his text when he said he was sorry.

'It's okay,' I say, hoping to get back to the part where he's about to kiss me again.

He sits forward, picking up his cup. 'No, you had a right to ask,' he says. 'At the time, I was afraid that you'd changed your mind about me. I thought you didn't really want to move in with me and that brought up a lot of doubts about our future together.'

'But I told you it was just because of Cassie,' I remind him, frowning.

'Yeah, but then she'd come up with this wedding brochure and I got to wondering if I'd read you all wrong. Maybe you didn't want to commit to moving in because you were waiting for some bigger commitment from me. That would have made sense, to a degree.

'And she'd questioned whether we'd talked about starting a family or anything—just in general. Of course, now I know where that idea came from, but at the time I thought maybe you'd been talking to her about wanting a baby or something. She seemed quite protective of you, which I thought was because she didn't think I was treating you right.'

'I thought it was all because of what happened with Davinia,' I admit. 'Cassie was fussing like a mother hen sometimes and I couldn't figure out why she was still acting that way weeks after I'd got back to normal. I thought the whole incident must have affected her worse than I'd imagined.'

'Ben and his big mouth have a lot to answer for,' James says, shaking his head.

'You can say that again.'

He grins. 'I'd rather forget about it, to be honest.'

'Me, too.'

'My worst nightmare was that you'd changed your mind about me,' he admits. 'So, when I saw that CCTV tape with you and that Fisher-guy...'

'I get that. The first thing I thought when I saw it was that it looked like we were kissing.' I admit, reluctantly. The thought makes me shudder. 'I've got much better taste than that, though,' I assure him.

James smiles. 'I'm glad to hear it.'

I lean forwards slightly, trying to entice him to lean in for a kiss. Then another A380 hits the runway.

'Is that why you decided to move away?' I ask, suddenly remembering the estate agent documents on his shelf. 'Did you think I didn't want you, so you'd move somewhere else?'

A lead weight hits the pit of my stomach as I ask the question—not least because I think I've just passed up another golden opportunity for a kiss.

He frowns. 'What?'

Now it's my turn to stand up. I go over to the TV and pick up the papers on the shelf next to it.

'I couldn't help noticing these.' I hold them up to show him, guilt enveloping me. I had no right to nosey around his flat like that.

To my surprise, he smiles, beckoning me over. 'Oh, you saw those, did you?'

'I wasn't prying or anything,' I tell him quickly. 'They just caught my eye.'

I sit next to him again, the papers on my lap. 'Were you just going to leave?'

A lump forms in my throat at the thought. I guess it would have been partly my fault if he had. After all, I hadn't given him a proper answer about when I was planning to move in, and he knew I must have been having doubts—though not for the reasons he was imagining.

He frowns again. 'Hardly. Did you check them out?'

'Of course not.' *I don't know what sort of nosey parker he takes me for, I really don't.* 'I told you, I just sort of... noticed them.'

'From all the way over here,' he teases. 'Take a look.'

I almost don't want to, now that he's invited me to. I dread to think how far away he was planning to move.

'Go on,' he urges, clearly sensing my reluctance.

I take a deep breath before glancing down at the first brochure.

'It's Chelsea,' I say with a frown. I turn to the next. 'Kensington?'

I stare at him, suddenly lost for words.

He nods.

I check the rest. There's even one in Belgravia, though it's miniscule and horrendously expensive.

'I thought maybe you didn't want to live in Fulham,' he explains. 'So, I took a look at a few places nearer to where you are now. You'd be closer to Cassie, but I'm afraid we might have to downsize a little.' He looks disappointed.

'But we're not a million miles from her here, are we?' I say, frowning.

'No, but wouldn't you prefer somewhere new? Somewhere that's ours, rather than this place?'

I know how fond he is of his flat, and I really couldn't see him living anywhere else now. Besides, it's handy for his work.

'I like it here,' I say, pursing my lips. 'It's your home.'

'But Chelsea's your home,' he points out.

'It's only up the road a bit. And it's even more expensive than here. You won't want to spend out any more on a property than you have to, and besides, Fulham's great.'

He looks taken aback. 'Libby, I want you to be happy,' he says, softly. 'And if you don't want to live here, we can always—'

'I love it here,' I interrupt. 'Okay, maybe we *could* get a comfier sofa,' I prod the firm seat with a grimace.

He frowns. 'Absolutely. You haven't tried sleeping on it. It's like a bed of nails.'

'That's settled, then.' I smile at him, surprised at how thrilled he looks, all of a sudden. I really didn't think the idea of furniture shopping would excite him so much. I can't say I blame him. Just the mention of IKEA can instantly brighten *my* day.

'You really want to move in here?' He looks astonished

Oh. It wasn't the thought of shopping that had cheered him up.

'Yes, of course. Now that I know I won't be leaving Cassie in the lurch, I can't wait to move in with you…if you still want me.'

He leans in and finally I get the warm, lingering kiss I've been hoping for. His lips are soft against mine and his breath is hot. He takes me in his arms, pulling me closer to him.

'What do *you* think?' he murmurs sensually.

What I think can't be repeated in polite company, so I just groan but say nothing.

21

You wouldn't think that moving your things from one flat to another would be that difficult but wait until you try it!

It's Saturday morning, a couple of weeks later, and I'm totally organised. Or, at least, I think I am. The expression on Cassie's face when she looks around my room's giving me grave doubts.

'What?' I know she's thinking something worrying but she's not saying what. 'I've got all my things packed.' I gaze at the gazillion boxes and bags I've stashed all my clothes and shoes in, along with all my other things. To be honest, there were quite a few more 'other things' than I expected, but they're all really important so they have to come with me.

'You have seen the size of James' car, haven't you?' Cassie looks warily at some of the huge boxes I acquired from the office. They were folded when I collected them but once I'd opened them out and taped them together, I realised that they were much bigger than

I'd imagined. Still, I managed to fill them all the same—surprisingly easily in fact.

I frown, remembering his beloved Ford Focus. Come to think of it, it is a bit on the small side, compared to all my stuff.

'I've folded my seats down but I'm not sure even mine will accommodate the size of those boxes,' Cassie explains.

'Oh.' To be honest, I hadn't thought of that. The boxes were a nightmare to get onto the Tube, even folded up, but I hadn't considered getting any further than that. 'I'd need to get loads of smaller boxes to fit all that stuff in.'

'What time's James coming over?' Cassie asks, just as a sound on the intercom alerts us of his arrival.

My stomach was churning enough at the thought of moving—though I'm much happier about it now than I was before—but I dread to think of James' reaction. It's too late to worry, though, as Cassie's already gone through to let him in. I just stare at the boxes all neatly stacked up around the room. I was quite proud at how many I'd managed to squeeze into my not-so-little bedroom, actually, but now I'm wondering if I'd done such a wonderful job after all.

'Jesus Christ!' James stands in the doorway, dressed in those tight jeans I love and a smart polo shirt.

He looks gorgeous, even with his mouth dropping down to the floor.

'Have you got a roof rack?' I ask, as casually as I can manage. It was a brainwave that suddenly occurred to me in a moment of panic. I get some good ideas when my head's whirling and I just hope this is one of them.

'No.'

Oh, it wasn't.

'Nor do I have a Luton,' he adds, his face deadpan.

'Hmm.' It's a shame. One of those would solve all our problems—and imagine how much shopping we could do with one. 'Perhaps you could part exchange the Focus for one...' I was only thinking aloud but the look on his face tells me it's a bad idea.

'Or perhaps you could downsize your things?' he asks, his jaw tight.

I gape at him. *Is he mad?*

'I have,' I inform him, my voice a little shriller than I intended. 'And I've given Cassie back loads of stuff I'd borrowed from her.'

'She has,' Cassie concurs, from behind him. She's such a supportive friend. She gives James a sympathetic look. 'How about a cuppa while we decide the best course of action?' She also has the best ideas.

'I think it'll take a bit more than a mug of Tetley's to figure this one out,' James grumbles as she leaves us.

He takes a step into the room—which is about all there's room for at the moment. I'm sitting on the bed, my island in a sea of boxes.

'Libby, are you *sure* this is all the stuff you need?' He rubs a hand through his hair.

My heart leaps with joy as I gaze at him. He *does* understand me!

'Well, there are a *few* more things I could do with...'

'*What*?'

'What?' I study his expression, suddenly fearing I've misunderstood the question.

'*More*? How could you possibly need more than this lot?' He waves a hand at my possessions, and it occurs to me with more than a drop of disappointment that I was wrong—he doesn't understand me at all.

'Well...'

'Tea's ready,' Cassie calls through from the kitchen. She's like the seventh cavalry, arriving in the nick of time.

'Ooh, let's get it while it's hot,' I say. 'I'm sure it'll help us work this out.'

James stares at me in stunned silence, so I quickly hop off the bed, clamber over a few boxes, and reach him.

'We haven't actually said hello yet,' I point out, as we leave the bedroom and all the chaos behind us. I give him a peck on his cheek.

He takes my lips in a warm kiss, but I can tell he's not as relaxed as I'd hoped.

'Hello,' he says, still clearly scarred by the sight of my belongings. It's not as though he's never seen my stuff before—just maybe not all in one place. I'm hoping once it's spread out in his flat, he might not be so worried.

'Here you go. It's supposed to be good for shock,' Cassie says with a smirk, handing him a mug.

We all sit around the dining table, cradling our cups of tea.

'Rob and Ben said they'd be over to help load up,' Cassie says, brightly.

'Oh, great. That's really good of them,' I say. 'Isn't it, James?'

James turns to face me with glazed eyes. 'How many vans are they bringing?'

I hear the note of sarcasm in his tone, even if Cassie doesn't.

'Well, they haven't actually got *vehicles,* they're just offering some muscle,' Cassie says slowly. She eyes James a little warily.

'We were just discussing, before you arrived, whether some of the boxes might be a bit too big to fit through the doors of the cars.' I'm trying to sound diplomatic, but James is just gawping at me. He does that a lot.

'*Really?*' He sounds incredulous now. And sarcastic.

'We can always get smaller boxes to put it all in,' Cassie says quickly. 'In fact, I'll give Rob a call and ask him to pick some up on his way over.' She gets up and leaves the table to call her boyfriend.

'James, is everything all right?' I ask him, nervously. He looks downright shell-shocked, to tell the truth, and hasn't really spoken since he got here. Well, not properly, anyway.

He frowns at me. He does that a lot, too. 'Libby, you have *seen* the size of my place, haven't you?' he asks.

'Of course.'

'It's quite a bit smaller than here.' He waves his hand to indicate the flat.

'I know.' I don't like the sound of this, but at least he's talking to me now.

'Where do you think all that stuff's going to go?' He raises his eyebrows.

'We can sort all that out when we get there,' I say, trying to sound optimistic.

'That brings me back to the first problem,' he says. 'How the heck are we going to get it all over there? I was hoping to have it all moved over and sorted out today so we could relax tomorrow. At this rate it'll take us all week just to get it to Fulham.'

I get that horrid sinking feeling in my stomach.

'You do still want me to move in, don't you?' I ask in a quiet voice.

His eyes widen. 'Of course, I do.'

I sigh with relief.

'It's just all your stuff that's worrying me.'

I think that sigh was a bit premature.

'It's only clothes and shoes and things,' I protest. 'Like any normal girl has.'

He gives me a look that suggests he's contemplating whether I am a normal girl. I look away, consoling myself in the biscuit tin.

'All sorted. The boys are fetching some smaller boxes on their way over. Then we can transfer the stuff and get it loaded.' Cassie smiles as she returns to the table, but her face falls when she catches sight of me and James. 'What do you think?'

'I think it'll take a miracle to get it all done today,' James says, turning to face her.

'Well, in that case, shall we start loading the stuff we *can* fit into our cars?' she asks, sensibly. 'We can drive over what we can and leave Libby here to put the other stuff into the smaller boxes when the boys arrive. They shouldn't be too long.'

James nods.

I'm a bit disappointed that we're leaving the table quite so soon, to be honest, so I grab another chocolate Hobnob from the biscuit tin before following them back into my room.

'If we put the boxes in first, we should be able to squeeze the bags into the gaps,' James says.

I gape at him. *Squeeze?* I've got some treasured possessions in those bags. The next minute, I'm gaping at him for a totally different reason. He's started reaching over and lifting down some of the boxes, his biceps bulging under the short sleeves of his polo shirt. Phew! I love seeing those muscles.

He looks back, catching me checking him out, and shakes his head. 'Perhaps you could start taking some of the smaller boxes into the living room?' he suggests. 'That'll make more room to move in here and keep them handier for putting in the car once we've got these ones in.'

'I was just thinking that,' I say, turning my eyes from him.

'Oh, so *that's* what that expression was all about,' Cassie pipes up with a giggle.

Humph. I thought she was supposed to be my friend!

I say nothing, but quickly start stacking the smaller boxes and take them into the front room. I also grab some of the bags and put them in a separate pile by the window.

It's not long before there's a buzz and I answer the intercom to let the boys come up.

'We weren't sure how many of these you needed,' Ben says, bringing in a huge armful of empty grocery boxes.

'More than that, I'd imagine,' James says, as he carries through a heavy box.

'That's what we thought, so we've brought these as well,' Rob says, following Ben with even more boxes.

James nods. 'That's more like it. You wouldn't believe how much stuff this girl's got.'

I balk. 'I am *here* you know,' I point out, glaring at them.

The guys all chuckle.

Cassie brings through some boxes and places them on the living room floor before going over and giving Rob a big hug.

'Thanks so much for this,' she says, after a kiss. 'Libby's packed her stuff but some of the boxes are a bit too big to fit into the cars.'

'A *bit* too big?' James sounds incredulous.

'I did my best,' I point out.

'Yes, she did a good job,' Cassie adds, in my defence. 'It was just a shame the boxes were the wrong size that's all.' She smiles at me. 'Nothing that can't be easily rectified.'

I suddenly feel much better. Cassie always has my back and I love her for it. I'll miss having her around when I move out, but I suppose I'll just have to learn to fight my own corner.

'We'll give you a hand to get these down to the cars,' Ben offers, lifting one of the heavier boxes.

'You girls stick to the lighter stuff,' Rob says, giving Cassie a warning look.

She gives him a playful salute. 'Yes, sir.'

He nods with a satisfied grin, before picking up another box and following Ben out the door.

'We can take these,' Cassie says, pointing to a pile of smaller boxes, which contain shoes and bags.

Whether it's because I've got a lot of stuff, or just because the cars are so small, I'm not sure—though I'll go with the latter, I think—but it doesn't take long before James declares that we can't get any more in and the rest will have to wait for the next trip.

'You girls stay here and transfer all that stuff into the smaller boxes while we take this lot over,' he suggests.

I'm about to accuse him of being sexist, when I realise that it does actually make more sense. The guys are much more capable of lifting everything out of the cars quickly and taking it into the flat, while I'd rather have Cassie help me with my belongings.

Cassie hands her car keys to Rob with a stern warning about not getting it damaged, and he just laughs. I can see it does nothing to instil her confidence. We say goodbye and I follow her back up to the flat.

'It shouldn't take long to swap this stuff over,' she says, brightly.

I nod. I can't even remember what's in most of the boxes, to be honest, so I haven't a clue whether it's already packaged inside or not. Most of my books went into the smaller boxes to make them easier to carry and my most expensive clothes went in suitcases. I'm guessing it's probably shoes and toiletries... and make-up... and hair accessories... and...

'How about a drink while we do it?' I suggest. 'It's thirsty work moving all that lot.'

'Great idea.' She grabs a couple of bottles of Pinot Grigio from the fridge and some glasses and we get stuck in.

'It's going to be odd not being here,' I say, looking around the room.

'Now, don't you start. I know it's all different, but that doesn't mean it won't still be fun. And you know you can come over any time—you're not moving to the end of the earth.'

'I know.' We've had this conversation so many times lately, and it always ends the same. I have to agree it's a good move. I want to be with James. I love him more than anything and moving in with him is the next logical step in our relationship. It also makes sense with his working patterns as we'll get to see much more of each other this way.

'When's Rob moving in?'

'Not for a while yet. Maybe a week or two,' Cassie says with a smile. 'He had to give notice where he is, and he wants to book a couple of days' holiday at work so we can get settled in properly. He's a bit of a neat freak, so he'd hate living with his stuff still packaged up for long. He wants it all sorted as soon as he can.'

'That's a good idea,' I say, cheerfully. 'James and I both go back to work on Monday, and I'm sure the place will look like a pig-sty by then. It'll play havoc with his OCD but it's the best we could do.'

We both giggle.

'Poor James,' Cassie says, shaking her head. 'I don't know how he'll cope.'

'I keep having to remind him it was all his idea,' I reply, after another swig of my wine. 'He's brought all this on himself, remember?'

We burst out laughing.

It doesn't take long to empty the huge boxes into the smaller ones. It takes even less time to empty the two bottles of Pinot Grigio, but luckily Cassie has plenty more so it's not a problem.

'Are you sure you don't want to take any more of my bags?' Cassie offers, as we fold up the larger boxes.

'I've still got loads,' I tell her, 'despite all the ones I gave you back. Besides, James will go mad if I take any more over to his place. Look how he's been about it so far.' I pout.

Cassie nods. 'It's only because his place is a bit smaller. And don't forget, he's only just recovered from Suzanne cluttering his place up with all her crap—not that you'd do that, of course.' She adds that last bit really quickly.

'I hope he doesn't think I'm too messy,' I say, frowning as I look at the boxes of my things. 'At least I've got *useful* stuff, not ornaments and random stuff like she had—well, not much, anyway. I've no idea where she picks up things like that. Or why.'

'Remember, she did have that huge house in Richmond to fill,' Cassie says, topping up our glasses for the umpteenth time. 'She could afford to have all sorts of bits and pieces in a house like that without it looking cramped.'

'I wonder if James will want to move to a big house like that again,' I muse. 'Perhaps if we had a family or something, I mean.'

'Would *you* want to?' she asks, standing and swaying a little. I grab her leg to steady her. Instead, I pull on it a bit too hard and she hurtles forwards, flopping unceremoniously onto the bed.

'Oh, no!' I yell, jumping up, but she's already rolling about on the soft mattress, laughing her head off. Thank goodness.

'I was trying to help,' I explain, joining her on the bed.

'You did help,' she says, a little slurred. 'I might have fallen on all your boxes of stuff if you hadn't held my leg.'

I suddenly feel much better. 'Oh, good.'

I lie on the bed next to her and we both giggle. I'm not sure what we're finding so funny, but we just can't seem to stop.

We're still there when the guys get back.

'Glad to see you're working as hard as us,' Rob says, suddenly appearing in the bedroom doorway.

I blink. It appears that there are two of him.

'We've done all our work,' Cassie informs him, trying—and failing—to sit up. She waves her hand around the room. 'As you can see.' She looks up at him and frowns. 'And *I* can see you've brought your twin brother with you.'

I'm glad it wasn't just me!

'We worked really, really hard,' I add, as more people fill the room. I look at them all, trying to focus. 'Oh, are we having a party?'

'I think you've already had one by the look of it,' James says, walking towards me. 'How about some coffee?'

'I'm on it, 'Ben says, leaving the room.

'It only takes *one* of him to put the kettle on,' I remark.

James picks up the bottle by the bed.

I frown, seeing about six bottles in his hand. 'Crikey, we didn't have that many, did we?'

Rob holds up what appears to be another three— or is it just two? Nope, it looks like four now. If he'd stop moving them about, I could see them a lot more clearly.

'We didn't drink *all* of them,' I protest.

'You drank enough,' James says, shaking his head.

I shake my head, too. Bad move. It hurts. 'Ow.'

'Cassie don't move your head,' I warn my bestie. 'Someone's done something to our brains. They've loosened them and now they rattle every time you move.'

'Oh, no!' Cassie groans beside me.

'See?' I reply, wishing she'd listened to me in the first place.

'I'm going to be sick,' she blurts out.

'Not in here, you're not. My stuff!' I practically scream—which does nothing to help the pain in my head—imagining my lovely clothes and shoes being covered in vomit. It wouldn't be the first time for some of them, to be honest, but it's still not pleasant.

'Come on.' Rob towers over me, reaches across, and lifts her effortlessly into his arms. 'Let's find the bathroom, shall we?'

'You're not about to puke as well, are you?' James asks me as two of him lean over me. I breathe in the gorgeous scent of Hugo Boss, and sigh.

'Nope.' I almost sing to them. 'But if you guys want to lift me up and whisk me away somewhere nice then I'm all yours.' I wave my hands in the air just to accentuate my words. I love you so much, James Harper.'

He chuckles. 'I love you, too,' he says, planting a kiss on my cheek.

I gasp. 'But there's only *one* of me,' I tell him, narrowing my eyes. 'Have you been drinking, Sergeant?'

22

I wake up next morning wishing I hadn't. My head's pounding and my mouth feels dry and disgusting. I'm in a strange bed in a strange place. Though it all looks vaguely familiar now that my eyes are adjusting a little.

'Morning, gorgeous.' James' voice is a little too loud for my poor head, and I've got a feeling he knows it.

He grins at me, placing a cup of coffee and a packet of paracetamol on the bedside locker.

'Thought you might need these,' he says, a little more quietly.

'Thanks,' I mumble, sitting up.

Looking around the room, I now recognise it as James' bedroom. Of course, I was moving in with him. I frown, trying to piece together the fragments of yesterday. I reach for the coffee, hoping it might help. The smell takes my breath away—it's black and strong, almost like tar.

'You shouldn't drink if you can't handle the consequences,' he says with an irritatingly knowing look.

Honestly, if he wasn't so handsome, I could go right off him this minute.

'I only had...' My mind whirls as I try to remember how much I actually drank last night. I remember seeing James hold up several empty wine bottles, but I'm sure I didn't have *that* much.

'You had more than enough,' James says, in his sensible, policeman's voice.

I say nothing but take a sip of coffee.

'Urgh!'

'It'll do you good,' he assures me. 'Now drink up because you've got work to do.'

'What?' Work? I'm sure it's the weekend. He wouldn't have let me sleep in otherwise, and besides, he'd be working himself. Then reality hits. Oh, he means unpacking. Damn!

I drink the foul-tasting coffee as quickly as I can. I'm not sure it does me any good, to be honest, but the paracetamol certainly help.

It's great to shower in James' bathroom, and I notice my toiletries have already been put in here ready for me. I smile at the thought. It's going to be great living here with him—not that it wasn't fun with Cassie, of course, it's just... different.

I pull on a pair of jeans and a T-shirt, tie my hair up in a messy bun, and then go to find James, feeling much better.

Unfortunately, the feeling doesn't last long. As soon as I walk into the living room my heart just about stops beating. Boxes are stacked floor to ceiling, taking up every inch of the room. I squeeze between boxes and over bags to get into the kitchen and find it also packed with my belongings.

'Luckily, I can just about get to the kettle,' James calls from somewhere amid the cardboard jungle. 'Do you fancy another cuppa before you start with this lot?'

I could really do with something much stronger, but the pain in my head reminds me what happened last time I tried that.

'Yes, please,' I say, my stomach churning. I wonder where he is. I can hear his voice but that's all I've got to go on.

He suddenly appears from behind a stack of boxes.

My heart sinks. He warned me there wouldn't be that much room here, but I couldn't just throw my stuff out, could I? I'm beginning to think that maybe I shouldn't have packed quite so much of Cassie's stuff, but she insisted I could borrow her things and it's not like she's just in the next room anymore, is it?

I stare at James, wanting to cry. How did I ever think I could just move my stuff in here? It was always going to be a challenge, I knew that, but this is clearly impossible.

He comes over to me, his arms outstretched, smiling. I feel his warmth as he gives me a big hug.

'It's okay,' he says, 'We'll sort something out.'

'I'll have to get rid of some of it,' I whimper, terrified at the thought. There's nothing here that I can happily part with. It's all important stuff. To me, anyway.

'Let's have a cup of tea and draw up a plan of action,' he says, before kissing the top of my head. I love it when he does that, I've decided.

'Where?' I ask, in despair. Every inch of carpet is covered with boxes, and the table and every counter's piled high with bags containing even more of my belongings.

'The bedroom,' he says, decisively.

I'm really glad he left that room clutter-free. It's our little sanctuary in a world of chaos.

We take our drinks and go and sit on the bed.

'I've emptied out that wardrobe for your clothes,' he says, gesturing towards a double-sized wardrobe near the window. 'And you've got that chest of drawers.'

I nod, gratefully.

'Oh, and there's space under the bed.'

'Really?' It looks like a divan without any drawers.

'You just lift it up and it's empty under the mattress,' he says, getting up. 'Look, I'll show you.'

I didn't really need the demonstration, but as soon as I see him flexing those biceps to lift the top half of the bed, I'm more than thankful for it. He's absolutely right about the space underneath, too, it's vast.

'Think you could make use of it?' he asks with a cheeky grin.

'Hmm, I think I could manage that,' I reply, nodding.

'Come and show me what you want bringing in first,' James says, leaving the bed up while we head for the living room.

It's amazing how quickly the furniture gets filled and I'm disappointed to see so many boxes still waiting to be unpacked once I've run out of space.

'We'll get another bookcase in here,' James says, nodding to some wall space in the living room. 'And perhaps I could put up some more shelves in the bedroom.'

'I have got quite a lot of books,' I say with a sigh, wondering how we'll ever get everything in place. Maybe I should invest in a Kindle, which would free up so much more space. There's just something about the feel of a book in your hands, though.

He smiles. James has been an absolute diamond today. He hasn't mentioned me and Cassie getting drunk last night and not being able to help with the last of the move, or the fact that I've brought so much stuff with me. I think he must realise how important it all is—after all, who doesn't need clothes, shoes, and books? Oh, and make-up, hair things, jewellery and toiletries, of course. And photographs and a few souvenirs from different places. And the odd little 'thing' that doesn't really fall into any particular category but is essential anyway.

When we've crammed everything into every nook and cranny we can find, it's time to reward ourselves with a late lunch. James fills a couple of fresh baguettes with some chicken and salad and we finally get to sit at his little table by the window in the living room. Okay, so I've had to put a few things on the floor around us, in order to clear some space for our plates, but it's good to feel some semblance of normality again.

He looks around the room, while munching on his food.

I take a sip of tea, waiting for him to say something about the number of boxes we've still to find homes for. The trouble is I don't think we'll ever find somewhere to put all of it. It's just not going to work.

'I was thinking,' he says, when he's finished eating for a minute. 'I mean, I know it seems a shame when you've only just moved in and everything...'

I stare at him in stunned silence. I know exactly what's coming.

'That I should move back out again?' I say if for him, a blanket of misery suddenly cloaking me.

He grins. 'No, not exactly.'

Relief immediately sweeps over me. 'Oh.'

'That maybe *we* should move out,' he clarifies. 'Maybe not straight away, but certainly in the near future. Some of those places I found at the estate agents looked quite promising, you know? Not too expensive, and with much more space than we've got here.'

I frown at him. 'Do you want to move, though? I thought you loved this place?'

'It was quite adequate for my needs when I was on my own,' he says with a nod. 'But I think we've outgrown it a bit, don't you?'

'You mean *I've* outgrown it *for* you?' I feel deflated. It's good of him to consider moving to a bigger place but this is his home and it's not fair for him to have to move just because of me.

'Wouldn't you like to move?' he asks, surprised. 'I thought it might be nice to have somewhere that we've chosen together. This is definitely a bachelor pad, and I have to admit I'd rather not regard myself as a bachelor anymore. We could have somewhere that's *ours*, rather than my old place.'

I gawp at him. 'You're serious, aren't you?'

He chuckles. 'Deadly.'

'And you'd really like to move? Not just because of me, I mean. And all my stuff.' I look around at the overcrowded room that looked so neat just a few days ago.

'Libby, I want you to be happy,' he says, taking my hands across the table. 'And I don't think you'll ever feel at home if some of your things have to stay in boxes because we simply don't have enough room for them.'

'What about you?' I ask, enjoying his warm thumb stroking the back of my hand.

'I think I'd be happier somewhere else, too.'

'I love you, James Harper,' I tell him with a smile.

'Well that's good, because I love you back, Libby Lawrence.' He leans over and takes my lips in a sensual kiss that makes me feel all gooey. It's good to feel like this again. Back to normal.

***

We spend the next few weeks looking at properties in the local area, trying to keep close to James' work. He sometimes has to put in some long shifts, and it would be cruel to add more travelling time onto an already long day.

318

Cassie kindly offered to store some of my books and summer clothes at her place, as she and Rob would only be using my old room for storage and the occasional guest, anyway. She's an absolute Godsend, and it gives me even more excuses to pop over and see her more often—not that I need any.

It's so lovely to be able to sleep with James every night and wake up with him in the mornings—though his cheerfulness at 4 a.m. takes some getting used to. I'm compensated for the early start to the day by a lovely, home-cooked meal when I get home in the evenings, though, so it's all good.

When James works late, I take the opportunity to spend some time with Cassie, which is great. Rob gets a night out with his mates, and we get to gossip for hours on end, just like old times.

'What are your plans for tonight?' Fran asks me one Friday afternoon. We've nearly finished for the week and everyone's just tying up loose ends and clearing things away.

'James is on the late shift, so I'll be on my own,' I say, with a sigh. 'Cassie's going out with Rob, so I won't be stopping off at Chelsea on the way home. I might take a look around the shops to kill some time and then I'm off home. Probably snuggle up with a good book.' I'm not too keen being on my own in the flat. I know James has told me to regard it as mine as well as his, but I still feel like a bit of an intruder when he's not there with me.

'Come out with us,' Beulah pipes up. 'We're just going for a drink, but you're more than welcome to join us. It'll be fun.'

'Yes,' Fran says, rushing over to my desk. 'Go on, Libby, say you'll come. It doesn't have to be a late one; we just thought it would be a chance to catch up properly.'

'Talk about us lot, you mean,' Tammy teases from the large table where she's gathering some paperwork. 'Watch out girls, our ears'll be burning tonight.' She turns to everyone else, shaking her head.

'As if!' Fran gives her a look of mock horror.

'I think we can find much more interesting things to discuss,' Beulah says with a cheeky grin.

'More interesting than *us*?' Eva joins in, feigning a look of hurt, as she tidies some hair products into a cupboard.

'Wash your mouths out.' Brie chuckles.

'Hey, maybe we should *all* go,' Kiki calls over from one of the side-counters while pinning labels to some clothes.

'Oh, no!' Eva cries. 'Anything but that! Remember what happened the last time those three got together?'

Brie puts her hand to her mouth. 'Oh, yes, you're right. I think we'd best keep away from them in future. All that trouble might just be contagious.' She giggles, giving me a wink to let me know she's only joking.

'It wasn't *my* fault,' I tell her, raising my eyebrows.

'I still think we're better off out of it,' Brie says.

'Cowards,' Beulah calls over from the big table, where she's tidying up.

Everyone bursts out laughing—even Izzy cracks a smile.

'We're meeting at the Dog and Bell about half seven,' Fran says.

'Great, I'd love to tag along.' I smile, glad to have such good friends.

'That's the place to avoid tonight then, girls,' Brie adds, giggling.

I'm sure I don't know what she means.

23

It's not the same getting ready to go out without Cassie around—or her wardrobe. I pull on a pair of skinny jeans and a creamy-beige cashmere jumper I bought in the Miss Selfridge sale. I team it with a pair of Stuart Weitzman suede ankle boots, in gorgeous natural beige. They're the 'Juniper' style with three-inch stiletto heels. Luckily, I'm taking an Uber tonight, so I won't have to walk far. They look great, though. and make my legs look long and slim, especially in these jeans. They would have cost £470 but I got them for £270 on eBay—never worn, they just had a black mark on the toe of the left one, which Cassie managed to get out with a special sponge she uses. I'm taking Cassie's Chloe Marcie Mini shoulder bag in nut brown. She's also got it in black, as well as the Marcie, which is the same bag just a bigger version. It's curved in a sort of saddle-shape and I lengthen the strap to wear it across my body for a slightly more casual look.

My hair's in a messy bun, and I apply a final sweep of lip gloss before grabbing my coat. My phone pings to tell me the driver's nearly here and I take a deep breath before braving the cold, night air.

It doesn't take long to get to The Dog and Bell, and I'm surprised at the rowdy atmosphere before I even get inside. Fran and Beulah are already sitting at a table near the window, and I head over.

'I got you a white wine,' Fran says, nodding at a glass on the table.

'To start with, anyway,' Beulah adds with a giggle.

'Thanks.' I take off my coat and put it on the back of my chair. 'This is busy,' I comment, looking around.

'Yeah, I didn't expect it to be quite this bad already,' Fran says with a grimace. 'We can go somewhere else later if you want.'

'If we can still walk in a straight line by then.' Beulah grins, then takes another swig of her drink. I'm guessing she's not on wine, as hers looks suspiciously like a gin and tonic to me.

I'm glad we're away from the bar, as I don't think we'd be able to hear each other talk over there. At least it's a bit quieter near the window, even if it *is* a bit cold with the bare glass.

'Are you all moved in, now?' Beulah asks. She's wearing jeans and a thick jumper, too, and looks really pretty. Her light brown, shoulder-length hair's in a sort of half-up, half-down style with a pretty, sparkly clip keeping it in place. She's wearing a little more make-up tonight, too, and looks great.

'Just about. It's really odd being there when James is at work, but I suppose I'll get used to it. I was so glad to be coming out tonight, to be honest.'

'I'm sure it has its advantages,' Beulah replies with a raised eyebrow.

I nod. 'I can't deny that,' I say with a smile.

'You lucky thing. He's gorgeous,' Fran says, tucking a loose curl behind her ear.

I just smile at her. It's nice to see the girls away from work and in casual clothes. We all dress smartly for the office, but even Fran's wearing trousers tonight with a really pretty embroidered top. which looks great, but she must be freezing.

'How on earth did you get such a hunk?' Beulah asks, her eyes twinkling.

'I met him in my last job,' I tell them. 'He came to investigate a theft at the hotel I was working at.'

'Aw, that's really romantic,' Fran says, smiling.

I don't like to admit that it was the total opposite when we first met. I thought James was a really grumpy customer—albeit a very handsome one.

'Have you found anyone else, yet?' I ask, swiftly changing the subject.

She sighs. 'No. I went out with a guy the other night, but it didn't amount to anything. He was quite boring, to be honest—and had bad breath.'

Beulah frowns. 'Then why go out with him in the first place?'

'We were in here and he was too far away from me to smell him,' Fran says with a tut. 'And it was too noisy to talk properly, so I thought he just wasn't saying much to save me having to lean in to hear him.'

Beulah shakes her head. 'I don't know how you pick them,' she grumbles.

'What about you? Have you got anyone?' I ask her.

'Actually, there is someone I've got my eye on,' Beulah replies with a grin. 'He often pops in here, as a matter of fact.'

Fran opens her eyes wide. 'So that's why you chose this place.'

'It *might* have had something to do with it,' Beulah replies with a giggle.

'I thought it was a bit farther for you to come,' Fran says. 'I'm just down the road and even *I* don't come in here that often, just because it can get so rowdy.'

'So, what's he like?' I ask, looking around the room.

'He's not here,' Beulah says. 'It's a bit early for him. He's a really nice guy; big bushy beard and built like a brick shithouse.'

'Sounds delightful,' I say, shaking my head.

'Oh, don't let that fool you,' Beulah says. 'He's the nicest guy you could meet, honestly. Seems really kind and considerate, you know? And he's really fit. *I* think so anyway.'

'It's not that biker-guy, is it?' Fran queries, leaning closer. 'Geoff something-or-other?'

'Yeah, that's him. D'you know him?' Beulah looks surprised.

I am too, to be honest. Fran doesn't look the type to go around with hairy bikers.

'He lives in the flats near me,' Fran says, after another sip of her drink. 'I often hear his bike going up and down the road. He's not one of those idiots that rev up all the time, though. In fact, he wheels it down the street when he gets back really late. He's really considerate. I know a lot of people wouldn't even think about the noise, no matter what time of night it was.'

'Have you been spying on him?' Beulah frowns.

Fran shakes her head. 'No, the old lady who lives beneath me told me. She was really impressed. He transports blood for the hospitals, apparently.'

Beulah sits up even straighter in her seat. '*Really*?'

It seems Fran's elderly neighbour isn't the only one to be impressed by the guy.

'Well, it's certainly a worthy job,' I say, before taking another sip of my wine.

Beulah actually blushes. It doesn't happen often. In fact, I think it's the first time I've ever seen her redden up.

'I'll get the next round,' she says and quickly jumps to her feet.

Fran and I giggle as Beulah pushes her way through the crowd.

'Looks like she really likes him,' I say with a smile.

'Good. It's been ages since she had a proper boyfriend,' Fran replies, a little wistfully, as she gazes out the window.

'And what about you?' I ask, softly. 'How are you getting on now that that idiot's out of your hair?'

Fran's eyes widen. 'Well, I thought he was,' she says, pointing. 'Look.'

Beulah arrives with a tray of drinks and peers through the glass to where Fran's indicating. 'Oh, you're joking!'

'Look the other way; he might not have seen us,' I say, quickly turning my back to the window.

'I think it's a bit too late for that,' Beulah says, before taking a large gulp of her drink. 'They're coming in.'

'Who's that with him?' Fran asks, her voice a little croaky.

I chance a peek out the window and immediately wish I hadn't. 'Damn. It's that guy from the hotel—Dan, the imposter.'

'Sup up, ladies,' Beulah says and then downs the rest of her gin and tonic in one big mouthful.

I try to do the same with my drink. It's not until I swallow that I realise it's much stronger than the one I had before. Vodka, if I'm not mistaken.

'Ooh.' I shudder as it goes down.

Beulah grins. 'You might thank me for that one in a minute. Here they come.'

'Is there another way out?' I ask.

'Nope. We're going to have to ride this one out,' Beulah says, cracking her knuckles.

'At least it's a public place,' I tell Fran. 'They can hardly start anything in here.'

'I hope you're right,' Beulah says, doubtfully.

'Don't look at them,' I mutter, as the two guys come through the door, heading straight for us. 'Keep your cool.'

'Well, well, what a surprise,' Tyler sneers as soon as they arrive. 'Mind if we join you, *ladies*?'

'Yes,' Beulah says, bluntly.

'Actually, we're having a girls' night out,' I say, airily. 'Sorry. Maybe another time.'

'Like never,' Beulah adds.

Tyler and Dan immediately pull up a couple of stools as though we hadn't spoken. Tyler sits between me and Beulah and Dan between Beulah and Fran.

'What part of that didn't you understand?' Beulah says, forcefully. 'We're talking and you're interrupting.'

'Funny that,' Dan says, 'being as you girls interrupted my whole career.'

'Yeah, he lost his job thanks to you,' Tyler scorns.

'That's nothing to do with us,' I say, trying to put on my best innocent expression. It's been well-practiced.

'Yeah, we only went and looked at the hotel like you arranged,' Beulah says. 'I thought you did quite a good job, actually, showing us around and explaining everything. It was a lovely venue. Perfect for a wedding. A small one that is. It's just a pity I don't know of a Billy-no-mates who's getting married.'

I raise my eyebrows, amazed at how she can keep a straight face.

'You know full well,' Tyler says, narrowing his eyes. 'You did something to make him lose his job, we know you did.'

'What?' I've got my innocent face on again. 'You were with us the whole time, Tyler, and you know it.' I turn to Dan. 'So, how did you come to lose your job? As the manager that must've been something pretty serious.'

Dan swallows hard. 'You know full well what happened,' he snarls.

'How would I know? One minute we're planning Fran and Tyler's wedding and the next he breaks up with her,' I say, wishing I hadn't drunk my vodka quite so quickly as my head starts swimming.

'We didn't realise you two were such good mates,' Beulah adds. 'It sounded like you were just acquaintances from the way you were talking. Do you know each other well, then?'

The guys exchange an uncertain look.

'You'll pay for this,' Tyler growls.

'I'm going to be sick,' Fran interjects, standing up. I'm guessing her drink was something a bit stronger than white wine, too.

I grab her arm. She's a horrid shade of green. 'Come on,' I say, looking round for the loos.

'Take her outside, it's quicker,' Beulah says, jumping to her feet.

I leave Beulah to grab our things, and lead Fran through the crowd to the door. It's amazing how quickly people move out of the way when they see a woman beginning to retch as she walks towards them.

The fresh air hits me as soon as I step outside, and for a second, I think I'm about to join Fran in the barf chorus.

'Eww, that's gross!' A woman in a mini skirt with goose-pimples all up her legs was having a smoke outside and shrieks when she catches sight of Fran spewing up in the bushes outside the door.

'I hope you're planning to clean that up.' a gruff voice shouts from inside, and I notice a large man I presume to be the manager coming towards us. Out of the corner of my eye, I also see Tyler and Dan following him.

'Run!' I yell, as Beulah joins us, and we race down the street as fast as our heels will let us.

Poor Fran's still heaving as she runs, and Beulah's carrying our coats as well as her own. There's hardly anyone about, and the guys are rapidly gaining on us. My stomach heaves like Vesuvius about to erupt.

Suddenly, my heel gets stuck in a pothole and my legs buckle beneath me as I head for the ground.

'Argh!' The pain in my ankle's excruciating as I crumple in a heap.

Beulah starts running back towards me.

'Go—get Fran out of here,' I yell. 'And call the police!'

Beulah frowns uncertainly as she looks down at me, and then behind to where I can hear the guys gaining on us.

'Run—get help!' I urge her.

She nods and speeds away, joining Fran as they quickly head down the street. A big, red bus passes me, and I see Beulah put her hand out for it to stop as she and Fran near the bus shelter.

'You bitch!' Tyler yells at me as I crouch huddled on the ground, clutching my ankle.

'I'll get them!' Dan shouts as he comes up behind Tyler.

I instinctively put out my good leg and trip Dan up, seconds before the bus takes off. He hurtles to the ground, screaming and using expletives I haven't even heard before. When he rears his head there's blood running down it, and his nose looks all bashed in.

'You've broken my fucking nose!' he yells—or, at least, that's what I *think* he's saying.

'You'll pay for this, bitch!' Tyler grabs my arms, but I punch out at him and manage to hit him on the chin. It's more by good luck than judgement, as I was just flailing upwards, not daring to try to stand.

'Right, you've done it this time,' he yells again once he's recovered from the shock.

'I don't think so!' I shout back, adrenaline pushing down the fear. I put my hands on the ground and force myself to stand up. The pain in my ankle is too much, and I quickly fall again.

'Useless cow!' Tyler hisses, towering over me.

I know I can't escape the two guys, but I have to do something. I pull the boot off my good foot and jab the heel into Tyler's leg.

I won't repeat the language that pours from his foul mouth as he crumples, eyes bulging, to the pavement. His jeans take on a darker hue and I can only guess how badly he's bleeding underneath them.

'You want the same?' I immediately turn back to Dan, who hastily takes a step back.

'Wise move,' I tell him.

I hear cars and bikes zooming past us and can only pray that someone will stop and help me. I'm not sure how long I can keep two men at bay with a stiletto heel, even if it is a Stuart Weitzman. Being on the ground makes me feel like a sitting duck, and I'm only glad that Dan's in too much pain with his face to retaliate.

'You won't get away with this,' Tyler yells, 'we'll fucking make sure of it!'

'Dan doesn't seem so sure,' I bite back at him.

'You just wait.' He yells back, still clutching his leg.

'I think that constitutes a threat in anyone's language,' a booming voice says, making me jump.

A guy holding a motorcycle helmet, dressed in leathers towers over us, completely obliterating the light from the streetlamp. I gasp. Dan takes another step backwards.

'Not so fast, sonny!' The guy reaches out a large, gloved hand and grabs the front of Dan's jacket, hauling him off the ground. He holds him at arm's length, clearly unwilling to get blood all over himself.

Dan jibbers away, but no one can understand what he's trying to say. I've got an idea it was some kind of protest about me, but it'd never hold up in a court of law.

'Good grief.' James' voice grabs my attention, and as motorbike-guy takes a step out of the way, I can see him coming towards me, shaking his head.

'You again.' Alex suddenly appears, rolling his eyes at Tyler. 'I might've known.' He hauls Tyler's arms behind his back, dragging him to his feet.

'Aah, my leg,' Tyler yells, leaning to one side.

'That's the least of your worries, kid,' Alex tells him as he clasps the handcuffs on him.

'What the hell happened to you?' James bends down to help me up, concern etched into his gorgeous face.

'My heel broke.' Suddenly, big, fat tears start pouring down my face.

'Running in heels, eh?' James says softly, lifting me effortlessly into his arms. It's my favourite place to be and I immediately wrap my arms around his neck, nuzzling into him. His scent comforts me. 'I'm sure it can be mended,' he says.

A siren wails nearby, but at the moment all I can focus on is the gorgeous man who's holding me. He's so gentle, as though I'm made from china—I mean the porcelain, not the country. That would make me Chinese, and I'm definitely not that—although I'm very partial to a chicken chow mein.

A couple of paramedics soon arrive and one of them takes Dan from the hands of the biker-guy.

'I think she needs looking at, too,' the other one says to James.

I feel him nod.

'Libby, are you okay?' Beulah suddenly appears and I look up to see a taxi speeding away.

'Where's Fran?' I ask her, stunned, 'is she okay?'

She certainly didn't look it the last time I saw her.

'I took her home,' Beulah explains, calmly. 'That's when I saw Geoff near her flat. I'd already rung the police, but when I told Geoff what happened he insisted on coming after you. I've left Fran with a sick bucket and a gallon of water. She's actually feeling a bit better now, so I came to see how you were.'

'Ow!' The paramedic was prodding my ankle while I was listening to Beulah.

'It could be broken,' he says. 'Hopefully, it's just a bad sprain. Don't take her boot off yet. It'll just keep swelling when we do. Let's get her to the hospital.'

I gawp at him. *It's a Stuart Weitzman, for goodness' sake! I don't want it getting stretched all out of shape. Doesn't this guy know anything about designer boots?*

'Perhaps, I could just unfasten it?' I suggest, hoping to limit the damage.

'No.' The guy's quite adamant.

'Let's just leave it, shall we?' James frowns at me.

Alex has already put Tyler into his car. 'I'll head back to the station,' he tells James.

'Great. I'll follow the ambulance with this one.' He gestures to me. 'Probably best to separate the invalids.'

Relief washes over me. I didn't fancy getting into the back of that ambulance with Dan. He'd only make horrid, nasally comments all the way there, blaming me for his face. *As if it's my fault.*

'Keep that leg elevated as best you can,' the paramedic says.

James nods, then carries me over to his car. He straps me in the back at an angle with my injured leg on the seat next to me, and a couple of cushions under my ankle. The ambulance heads off, closely followed by Alex, whom I notice has another officer with him, sitting in the back of his car with Tyler.

'What about Beulah?' I say, suddenly remembering my friend.

'I think she's okay,' James says with a smile.

I look over and see her chatting happily with Geoff.

'Good luck, Libby, let me know how you get on,' she says, briefly turning her attention away from him to give me a wave.

'You too,' I reply with a knowing smile. 'And thanks, both of you.'

Geoff looks back and waves too, before James whizzes us off to the hospital.

'So much for you having a quiet drink with the girls.' James says with a sigh, and I'm sure I can see his eyes rolling through the back of his head.

'It wasn't my fault,' I protest.

For some reason, I get the impression he doesn't quite believe me.

'You're lucky,' the doctor announces, after hours of waiting around for X-ray results and being prodded like a marshmallow. 'It's only a bad sprain. You could've done yourself a lot more damage.'

He's quite old, with more hair coming out of his ears and nose than he's got on his head. He wears bottle bottom glasses, which he peers over to look down his nose at me. I can tell he doesn't like me as soon as he walks into the cubicle.

I refrain from rolling my eyes and telling him I'll have to try harder next time.

James clears his throat and I'd swear he's just read my mind.

'Thank you, Doctor,' James says, prompting me as though I'm a child.

'Yes, th-thank you,' I stutter reluctantly.

I think I'll reserve my opinion on how lucky I am until I've examined my boot a bit more closely. My ankle's swollen like a balloon and I'm sure my lovely Stuart Weitzman will have done the same. My beautiful boots have been relegated to a tacky 'Patient Property' carrier bag, courtesy of the NHS, which is tucked away on the trolley behind me so I can't even inspect the damage yet. And I've still to find out whether the heel can be mended.

'I don't know why you young girls think you can just run about in those ridiculously high heels,' the doctor goes on, shaking his head at me. 'Surely you must realise the damage they can do. You could have been crippled for life. Is that what you want?'

I narrow my eyes at him. *Does he really expect me to say 'yes, it's exactly what I was hoping for'?*

'It wasn't really her fault, Doctor,' James interjects, firmly. 'Miss Lawrence was fleeing from a couple of assailants. She had no choice. They could have been armed. For all we know, they might have intended to do much worse than cripple her.'

I love it when James sticks up for me.

The doctor clearly doesn't, though. He looks taken aback—presumably people don't stand up to him too often. His mouth gapes open, making him look even more gormless than before, and he clenches his jaw. He's fuming.

'Yes, well. Just be careful,' the doctor snaps, irritably.

Ooh, I'm glad he reminded me. I was planning on being really careless in the future!

'Does that mean I can go home now?' I ask, with a yawn. It's been a long night.

He nods. 'You'll want to take some painkillers. And keep your weight off that ankle for the next few days. Hopefully, the swelling will go down in time.'

Hopefully? I snap my head up. *What the hell does he mean, 'hopefully'? Is he saying there's a risk it might not? That I might end up with one foot three sizes bigger than the other for the rest of my life? I'll have a cankle? How on earth will I get clothes—let alone shoes or boots—on with that? It would be impossible. I wouldn't be able to go out in public. I'd be like The Elephant Man, shunned by everyone and forced to become a hermit— although, actually, I think that might be a crab, not an elephant.*

James clears his throat, pulling me back to the present.

'Thank you, Doctor,' he says.

The guy looks at me expectantly, reminding me that I'm supposed to say something. *I can think of a few things I'd like to say to him, but I really don't want to annoy James, so I bite my tongue.*

'Oh, yes, thank you,' I reply, pasting on my best fake smile. I refrain from asking about my cankle. I think I might wait and see what happens first.

He grunts and leaves the room.

I glance down at my ankle and realise it's not half as huge as I'd imagined. Things might not be quite so bad, after all. And I'm so chuffed that James is on my side.

'Thanks so much for that,' I tell him once we're alone again. 'I can't believe he was trying to blame *me* for what happened.' I'm used to getting the blame for things, but this time it definitely wasn't my fault. Even James said so.

'You're always running in heels,' he says with a wistful look.

'What do you mean?' I frown at him, surprised by his comment. I hardly run at all since I left the newsroom for the fashion department. Except in emergencies, of course. Which, actually, do seem to crop up quite often at the moment, now that I think about it. Not that's it my fault, or anything.

'Libby, I think you're always running,' he says, scraping a hand through his thick, dark hair. 'From me, from situations, from—I don't know—everything.' He perches on the bed, facing me. His expression is sad, almost, thoughtful.

A lump catches in my throat. 'I'm not.'

He smiles. 'I don't mean it in a bad way, I just worry about you. You bottle things up and try to work them out your own way instead of talking about them.'

'To you?' I clarify.

'Yes.'

'But I've told you, I'm not keeping anything from you, James.'

I'm a bit concerned as to where this conversation's heading.

'This wasn't my fault,' I point out. 'I couldn't have known that creep was going to come after us again, could I? And at least, I told you all about that business with the hotel and Tyler trying to get Fran to pay for the wedding. You said I'd done a good thing getting him and Dan exposed like that.'

He nods. 'You did. I'm very proud of you.'

My face heats up. I don't get that many compliments and they always mean so much— especially coming from him.

'And to be honest, he's actually *Fran's* ex. He's nothing to do with me,' I add. 'I was only helping her out at the time. Same with Beulah. To be perfectly honest, we thought it was all done and dusted once the police got involved. They were the ones who were supposed to have dealt with both of those guys.'

'I know.' He nods, giving me a reassuring smile. 'And we did. They were both cautioned but there wasn't much else we could do. They hadn't actually swindled anyone out of any money, thanks to you two. Though I believe Dan lost his job because of it and rightly so.'

'Then... what's the problem?' I hardly dare ask.

He purses his lips, thoughtfully.

'I just get the impression that you're always running away from something,' he says, softly.

'You mean you?' I ask, warily.

He nods slowly. 'Maybe.'

'Is this because you thought I didn't want to move in with you?' I ask, my heart pounding. I'd hoped all that was behind us. We've been over it that many times.

'Partly.'

'But you know that was only because...'

'I know.' He puts a pacifying hand up to stop me. 'I understand all that. I just wonder if you're scared to tell me things that's all.' He glances at his watch. 'Look, it's late. I'm probably just being a bit...'

'James, I love you,' I say, my face suddenly burning. 'I want to be with you all the time. I know occasionally I might seem to be a bit distant, like I'm in a world of my own, but that's just me. Sometimes, I need to work things out for myself that's all. I'm not shutting you out, I promise.' Tears sting the edges of my eyes.

He nods, smiling. 'Thank you,' he says, leaning forward. 'I love you, too. And I don't mean to block you out of my world, either, it's just my job.'

'I know,' I assure him, before reaching over for a loving kiss.

His warm arms envelop me and I'm lost in a hazy world of emotions for a minute.

'I'm glad our worlds collide every now and then, though,' he says, when he finally releases my mouth.

'Me, too.'

I can't help feeling a little concerned that James thinks I'm a bit aloof at times. I'm not trying to make things difficult or to shut him out in any way. I just don't like to burden him with everything that's going on in my life the whole time. I have to admit, sometimes it is a bit chaotic and I don't think he needs it on top of everything that he has to put up with—and I don't just mean with his job!

He gives me a quizzical look.

'What are you thinking?' he asks, narrowing his eyes a little.

I smile, glad that he can't *always* read my mind. That would be horrendous—for both of us.

'It's just that you think I'm always running,' I reply, stroking his arm.

'And you don't?' He raises his eyebrows, his dark eyes boring into mine.

I shrug. 'I'm not saying that,' I reply. 'You might be right.'

He looks surprised. 'Now I'm worried,' he teases.

'But I just think you're a bit pessimistic,' I go on, ignoring his quip. 'You see, it all depends on how you look at it.'

He looks bemused—and not for the first time. 'Well, I'd love to hear how you view the situation, Libby.'

I sigh. 'I might be running but I'm not heading *away* from you—I'm actually running *towards* you.'

He chuckles and pulls me in tighter. 'Well, I honestly can't get you close enough, love. So, you'll have to promise me that you'll keep on running.'

He takes my lips in a searing kiss that I feel right through my body. His hands caress my back and his fingers run through my hair. His breath is hot and his strong torso presses against me.

'I do,' I promise.

'Hmm… that's got a lovely ring to it,' he murmurs against my lips, 'I like the sound of that.'

I gasp. *Does he mean…?*

THE END

May I Ask a Favour?

I hope you enjoyed the latest instalment of The Liberty Lawrence Series. If so, I'd love it if you would leave a review at any (or all) of the following sites:

Amazon.com https://www.amazon.com
Amazon UK https://www.amazon.co.uk
BookBub https://bookbub.com
Goodreads https://www.goodreads.com
Or anywhere else you like

Reviews are extremely important for authors as they help get the word out about their books, and hopefully, gain more readers. They are also essential for some advertising platforms. I really would appreciate your help.

Many thanks
Bea x

Trademark Acknowledgement

The following trademarked items appear in *Running in Heels*. The author acknowledges the trademarked status and trademark owners of the following wordmarks mentioned in this work of fiction:

Alexander McQueen – Kering S.A.

Anna October – Anna October

Anna Quan – ANNA QUAN

Armani - Giorgio Armani S.P.A.

Chloe - Chloe S.A.S.

Chocolate Hobnob – McVitie's Ltd

E-bay - eBay Inc

Ford Focus – Ford Motor Company

Friends – Bright/Kauffman/Crane Productions

Harvey Nicholls – Dickson Concepts

J'adore – Christian Dior Couture

Jaegar – Edinburgh Woollen Mill

Jimmy Choos – Jimmy Choo Ltd

John Lewis – John Lewis Partnership plc

Kindle – Amazon

Louboutins – Christian Louboutin Ltd

Louis Vuitton – LVMH

Malene Birger – Malene Birger A/S

Marc Jacobs – LVMH

Marks and Spencer – Marks & Spencer Group plc

Monopoly – Hasbro Inc

Miss Selfridge – Arcadia Group Ltd

New Look – New Look plc, Brait SA

Next – Next plc

Oasis – Aurora Fashions

Santonis – Santoni Osteria

Saint Laurent – Kering S.A.

Starbucks – Starbucks Corporation

Stuart Weitzman – Coach/Tapestry

Swarovski – The Swarovski Group

Tetley's – Tata Global Beverages

The Elephant Man - Brooksfilms

The Golden Girls tv prog – Disney Enterprises Inc

Uber – Uber ATG

Ugg Boots – Deckers Outdoor Corporation

Valentino Garavani – V VALENTINO GARAVANI

Celebs Mentioned

Jamie Dornan

Brad Pitt

The Hemsworth Brothers

Channing Tatum

Lindsey Kelk

Sophie Kinsella

Paige Toon

Keris Stainton

Colleen Coleman

About the Author

<u>BEA STEVENS</u>

Author of Chick Lit, lover of chocolate (and doesn't think it's pure coincidence that the two sound similar!) Has a penchant for shoes, bags, clothes (the usual necessities), and socialising with friends, family and anyone else who gets dragged along.

Hopes you enjoy her books, get her humour, don't object to her use of British spellings and keep in touch

Please feel free to sign up to her newsletter at:

http://eepurl.com/dnl9bv

And/or follow her on:

https://www.facebook.com/AuthorBeaStevens/

https://twitter.com/beastevensbooks

https://www.instagram.com/authorbeastevens/

https://www.bookbub.com/authors/bea-stevens

https://www.goodreads.com/author/show/17444011.Bea Stevens

And check out her website at https://www.beastevens.com/

Also by Bea Stevens

BEST FOOT FORWARD
(The Liberty Lawrence Series Book 1)
http://mybook.to/BestFootForward

STEPPING IT UP
(The Liberty Lawrence Series Book 2)
http://mybook.to/SteppingItUp

IF THE SHOE FITS
(The Liberty Lawrence Series Book 3)
http://mybook.to/IfTheShoeFits

LOOK OUT FOR BOOK 5 IN

THE LIBERTY LAWRENCE SERIES